W9-BWZ-494

HEADHUNTER

HEADHUNTER

A Steve Flynn Thriller

Nick Oldham

This first world edition published 2017
in Great Britain and the USA by
SEVERN HOUSE PUBLISHERS LTD of
19 Cedar Road, Sutton, Surrey, England, SM2 5DA.
Trade paperback edition first published
in Great Britain and the USA 2017 by
SEVERN HOUSE PUBLISHERS LTD

British Library Cataloguing in Publication Data
A CIP catalogue record for this title is available from the British Library.

ISBN-13: 978-0-7278-8729-0 (cased)
ISBN-13: 978-1-84751-846-0 (trade paper)
ISBN-13: 978-1-78010-906-0 (e-book)

All Severn House titles are printed on acid-free paper.

Severn House Publishers support the Forest Stewardship Council™ [FSC™],
the leading international forest certification organisation.
All our titles that are printed on FSC certified paper carry the FSC logo.

Typeset by Palimpsest Book Production Ltd.,
Falkirk, Stirlingshire, Scotland.
Printed and bound in Great Britain by
TJ International, Padstow, Cornwall.

To Philip, Jessica and James – all amazing young adults on the starting blocks of some very big journeys. I wish you all the best for your futures.

ONE

The man had to die and Steve Flynn had to be his killer.
Flynn broke the man's neck with ease, and although
he knew he had instantly killed him, just for good measure
– and to avoid any error – he kept his forearm jammed tight
across the man's neck to crush the windpipe and shut off all
blood flow to the brain.

Almost intimately, nose-to-nose with the man, Flynn watched
his eyes first glaze over and turn milky in death and then, as
Flynn continued to squeeze and keep up the pressure, he saw
them almost bulge out of their sockets and then haemorrhage
red as what blood remained in his head was forced into the
orbs.

Only when he was completely certain the man was dead did
Flynn release his neck-hold and allow his head to flop. Then he
let the lifeless body slither out of his grip and thump down hard
on to the metal floor pan of the police van. Flynn did not gently
lower him down and the back of his head smacked against the
metal edge of the bench seat while his body twisted unnaturally
on to the floor.

To have eased him down, to have given him that final piece
of dignity, would have been too much like an act of kindness or
contrition on Flynn's part. It was much more than this man,
whose name was Brian Tasker, deserved and certainly more than
he had afforded any of his victims.

Flynn's usually craggily handsome face was twisted, sweaty
and ugly with pain and effort. The sinews in his neck were taut
like strands of plaited steel cable.

He dragged the back of his hand across his mouth, wiping
away the spittle, then glanced down at his outer right thigh and
his bloodstained jeans. A wave of nausea rolled up from his lower
gut and almost engulfed him, but he fought it to remain focused
and concentrating.

The leg had been very basically dressed by a paramedic earlier, and Flynn knew that, in an ideal world, what he now needed was hospital treatment for the gunshot wound.

But Flynn was operating in a far-from-ideal world and a hospital admission would have to wait its turn.

Bracing himself to ignore the agony from his leg and also the throbbing of a burst eardrum, he slid along the bench seat to the back door of the van and pushed it open.

He knew his time was limited.

Although the act of killing Brian Tasker had seemed to take place in slow motion over many minutes, like a woozy nightmare the reality was that from entering the police van – parked up close to the door leading into the custody office at Blackpool police station – to killing Tasker and then leaving the van was perhaps less than sixty seconds.

Flynn had to move quickly, though, to escape, to seek further justice, maybe revenge.

He dropped out of the van, jarring his injured leg which almost crumpled under him; then, clinging to the side of the van to keep himself upright, smearing the Lancashire Constabulary logo with his blood, he edged like an upright crab to the driver's door and checked to see if the key had been left in the ignition.

It was a vain hope, but occasionally vain hopes pay off.

The key was in.

Flynn tore the door open and, using the frame, hoisted himself on to the driver's seat, then had to physically lift his right leg in and position it with his hands before slamming the door and twisting the key.

The van started. Gripping the steering wheel tight, he forced his right foot down on the accelerator pedal, depressed the clutch and crunched into first. The van jerked as the sharp bite of the clutch caught him by surprise and he stalled the engine with a judder. He fired it up again, released the clutch a little more carefully and, as the van began to move, Flynn glanced into the door mirror to see the two uniformed cops who'd been crewing the van emerge from the back door of the station.

They halted in momentary shock at seeing the van moving.

Then they gave chase and screamed for Flynn to stop, although at that point they thought it was their prisoner who had somehow managed to get out of the van and steal it to escape.

Flynn gunned on down the shiny concrete surface of the police garage, the tyres squealing. He aimed for the accordion-like exit door which, if he recalled and hoped correctly, opened automatically on the approach of vehicles leaving the station.

He was right.

The door began to fold open, but far too slowly for Flynn.

He had to slam on the brakes, virtually standing on them, hissing with pain from the leg wound which felt like shards of hot glass being shot into his body. The van screeched to a halt. From behind, he heard and felt Brian Tasker's body roll, then thud against the reinforced panel dividing the front cab from the rear section of the van.

The door continued to slide open with agonizing slowness.

He glanced into the side mirror.

The two cops were almost alongside him.

Flynn's face creased as he jammed his right foot down again on the accelerator, the door opening just wide enough for the van to scrape out, snapping off the nearside door mirror as he shot through just as the quickest of the cops banged his fists on the side panel and screamed at Flynn to stop. The cop spun away from the van as Flynn ignored the request and left him standing.

Once more, he heard and felt Tasker's body rolling around in the back and, glancing in the door mirror again, Flynn realized he had left both the back door and inner cage door of the van wide open.

He gave a shrug and powered the van along the short stretch that was Richardson Street, then swung right into Chapel Street and, with no particular plan in mind, raced towards the seafront.

Before reaching the traffic lights opposite Central Pier, Flynn flicked on the switch for the blue lights and two-tone horns and swerved through the lights, which were on red, and sped north on the promenade, again hearing and feeling the roll of Tasker's dead body in the back like a heavy duvet clunking about in a spin dryer as he careened through the teatime traffic.

His eyes flickered to the door mirror once more and he caught sight of Tasker's arms as his body rolled out of the still-open door and on to the tarmac of the promenade.

Flynn punched the air as the car behind anchored on, tried to swerve but was unable to avoid Tasker's body, mounting it and crushing it under the front wheels.

Flynn grunted, but not unhappily, as he raced on, recklessly negotiating traffic then swinging across the tram tracks on his left, narrowly missing an oncoming tram and driving on to the car-free promenade itself. He weaved around a few pedestrians and, as he came close to the entrance to North Pier, he re-crossed the tram tracks, back on to the road again, still heading north as the road cut inland at the Metropole building. Then he went a tight right on to Springfield Street, which was narrow and made even snugger by cars parked on both sides. The gap between them was just wide enough to allow one vehicle to pass at a time.

Another car was heading towards him.

Flynn braked hard, as did the driver of the other car, who tried to tuck his vehicle into a space between two parked cars in order to allow the police van to squeeze through, as it was obviously on the way to a dire emergency.

Flynn silenced the two-tones as he negotiated the constricted gap and made it through by snapping the wing mirror off a car parked on his nearside. He gave the open-mouthed driver of the car that had allowed him through a quick wave of thanks, then put his foot down again, swung left and entered the warren of terraced streets behind the promenade, until he finally met his match and his luck ran out when he swerved though a junction, skimmed the side of another oncoming van and, because he was travelling far too fast, flipped the police van over on to its side. It spun once, embedded itself in a parked car and Flynn, not wearing a seat belt, was pitched across the width of the cab, crashing awkwardly against the passenger window.

He hauled himself out, clambering through the driver's-door window and tumbled on to the road, much to the dismay of the driver of the van he had just collided with.

'You OK, mate?' the man asked. He had rushed back to the police van to try and assist. He juddered to an uncertain halt when he saw Flynn's feral appearance, blood-soaked jeans and wild face. Realization dawned. 'You're no fuckin' cop. You fuckin' nicked this, didn't you?' the man demanded.

The man was not small, but chubby and unfit. That did not

prevent him from approaching Flynn while at the same time reaching for his mobile phone. This was too good a photo opportunity to miss.

Flynn, slightly dazed from the accident, stood there momentarily, gasping and swaying. His wide shoulders were hunched and his big shape resembled that of an exhausted mountain gorilla.

The man's phone flashed. Photo taken.

Flynn winced. The flash actually hurt his eyes.

Then he came back to life and made a threatening gesture towards the van man, who recoiled in terror.

Flynn turned and, as quickly as he could but with both hands clasping his bloodied leg, he fled the scene and plunged into the gathering darkness of an alleyway.

Behind him, van man tapped out a treble-nine on his phone after posting Flynn's photograph on social media.

Flynn pushed himself as far as he could before the agony overwhelmed him and brought him down in a dank alley somewhere close to Dickson Road, one of the resort's main thoroughfares, running parallel to the promenade on North Shore. He staggered, tried to keep upright by clinging to a reeking, overflowing wheelie bin, but eventually submitted to the inevitable and sank on to his backside on cold cobbles. He leaned against the bin, his brain a seething whirlpool of rage, pain and confusion about the way forwards.

He exhaled unsteadily, his heart ramming mercilessly against his chest until the beating subsided and he calmed himself down, tried to think of a way through while both his hands cradled his throbbing leg.

The first thing was quick medical treatment. That was the priority.

He could hardly present himself at the A&E department at Blackpool Victoria Hospital because the first thing they would do was call the cops, as they tended to do when a wild man with a gunshot wound clattered through the doors.

He knew he had to get treatment of some sort, though. The question was how to achieve it under the radar.

Once, many years before, Flynn had been a cop here in Blackpool and had known the resort and its inhabitants well, particularly the less-savoury denizens of this particular jungle. That had been over a dozen years ago. He had known backstreet abortionists (they still existed) and struck-off doctors (often back-street abortionists) who he could have approached, but not now, not at that moment. They were all past history.

He was alone without a plan, a phone or money or access to transport. Nor did he have his passport, which he knew he would need soon.

He gritted his teeth as he fought off another wave of pain-induced nausea.

Maybe he could self-medicate.

He looked down at his bloody jeans, swallowing hard.

The paramedic who had dressed the wound had told him the bullet had gone all the way through the flesh of the muscle of his outer right thigh, in and out, although Flynn had not been taking too much notice of the diagnosis at that time. Other things had been on his mind, such as murder.

He eased his arse off the ground and slid his jeans down to his knees. The dressing applied by the paramedic was saturated in blood. Flynn slowly eased the padding away from his flesh and exposed the wound. He had been shot purely to debilitate him, a bullet put in him just to keep him from moving. It had worked.

He slid his right forefinger into the gaping hole, trying to work out if it was possible to treat it without having to go to hospital. He hoped that if it was simply a hole, with no bone or artery damage, just tissue, maybe it could be done. A wave of giddiness hit him, making him feel like he had his head in a bucket and the *Doctor Who* theme tune was being blasted around it.

He extracted his finger, with blood, up to the middle joint.

'Shit, shit, shit,' he gasped.

He reapplied the now useless, blood-soaked dressing and pulled his jeans back up. Glancing down the alley towards Dickson Road, he saw the lights of a shop on the opposite side of the road. Almost as if he were seeing a mirage, he shook his head and refocused – but it was still there, for real. Flynn's oasis. He whispered, 'Thank you, Lord.'

Using the wheelie bin to haul himself back to his feet, he hobbled towards the end of the alley and stopped by the wall, keeping in shadow from where he surveyed the shop and the immediate surroundings.

Suddenly, from his right, a police car with flashing blue lights appeared over the slight rise in the road and hurtled down Dickson Road from the direction of the town centre. Flynn flattened himself against the wall, a metre into the alley, and watched the car whizz by, recognizing the Ford Galaxy as an ARV – an Armed Response Vehicle – with two cops on board, a man and a woman. Flynn knew they were out looking for him and soon the whole resort would be flooded with cops searching for a murderer.

He gave it a minute to disappear, then took a steadying breath and limped quickly across to the shop, a pharmacy.

It was not a big shop, just a corner store, one of a small, local chain.

Flynn entered.

There was one customer at the counter being served by a middle-aged lady. Behind the white-coated shop assistant was an eye-level dividing wall, beyond which was the prescription preparation area where all the drugs were kept and dispensed. Working in there, head down tipping out some pills into a container, was another woman in a white coat who Flynn assumed was the pharmacist. None of the three even glanced in his direction.

He selected a basket from the stack by the door then went to the shelves, found plasters, dressings, bandages and antiseptic cream which he scraped into the basket, all the while keeping an eye on what was happening at the counter. The customer was served and went out. Flynn edged behind her as she exited and, as soon as the door was shut, he flipped over the 'closed' sign to face outwards, ran up the top bolt and went to the counter.

The woman behind had turned to speak to the pharmacist, and when she looked back at Flynn her face sagged in horror.

He slammed the basket on the countertop.

'I want the best pain relief you've got,' he rasped hoarsely. His eyeballs rolled as he fought with the agony shooting up inside him.

'That'd be Co-codamol,' she squeaked.

'Nah. Stronger than that,' he insisted.

'You'd need a prescription.'

Flynn leaned ominously towards her, not wanting to frighten her but doing so anyway. 'I don't have a fucking prescription,' he growled, unimpressed with himself for making a woman cower away from him but unable to rein back the wounded beast that he was. 'So you'd better just give me the pills or I'm gonna get angry and help myself.'

He attempted a smile. It seemed to terrify the shop assistant to an even higher level.

As he spoke, he had watched the woman's eyes taking him in and her expression become increasingly horrified at his dishevelled, bloodied presence.

The pharmacist came out from behind the dividing wall, looking curiously at Flynn with her eyes fixed on him. She asked, 'What's going on, Margaret?'

'This man wants painkillers,' the shop assistant said.

'Strong ones,' Flynn added. A sudden rush of agony from his leg almost made him collapse. He grabbed the countertop.

The pharmacist, a no-nonsense-looking woman in her forties, stepped through the gap at the end of the counter and said, 'You need a doctor, probably a hospital judging by the look of you.' She pointed at the blood on Flynn's leg and also saw the ragged hole in the denim. 'Has someone stabbed you?'

Flynn shook his head. He was starting to sweat very heavily now; his body seemed as hot as a furnace.

'Shot me,' he corrected her.

'In that case you definitely need to get to hospital.' She turned away from him. He realized she was going for a phone.

'No,' he said, barged past her and stood in her way. 'Gimme the junk I need and I'll be out of your way,' he pleaded.

'I can't do that,' she said firmly, scared but unafraid at the same time.

Flynn's face must have turned monstrous at that point, making her recoil.

Then he added, 'Please. I'm desperate.'

He knew he wasn't being himself, particularly in respect of intimidating women.

'I'm sorry,' she said. Her nostrils flared warily as she eyed him. 'You need hospital treatment.'

'I've just killed a man,' he uttered.

Behind him, the shop assistant – Margaret – inhaled with a dramatic squeak.

Flynn's eyes took in the pharmacist's face, working over her features, looking for any sign that she would willingly – kind of – help him. 'Just show me where the painkillers are and I'll go . . . When I'm better, I'll come back and pay, honestly.'

In return, she weighed him up. He saw her make a decision. 'This way.'

She eased herself past him and led him through to the area at the back of the shop where the shelves were packed with pharmaceutical products.

'Morphine would be good,' he suggested.

'Why, are you an addict?'

'Do I look like one?'

She gave him a look that said, *Yes*.

'No, I just know it'd be good.'

'We don't have any in stock.'

'Shit. Methadone, then.'

'Locked away for the night, needs two keys and my partner has the other.'

'Shit.' Flynn knew it was a lie and, as much as he would have liked to throttle her, he stopped himself from putting his hands around her throat.

He watched her take a few boxes of tablets from a high shelf and drop them into a small plastic bag. She then went back to the counter, put the rest of Flynn's earlier selection into the bag and handed it to him.

'Thank you,' he said meekly.

'As soon as you walk out of that door, I'll be calling the police,' she told him, holding his gaze unwaveringly.

'I get that.'

'Now fuck off.'

'I'm going.'

Flynn pivoted around with his newly acquired bag of goodies clutched to his chest and stumbled out from behind the counter into the public area of the shop at the same moment as the front door was rammed open and two armed cops, one male, one female, kitted out like *Star Wars* troopers, entered in a well-rehearsed move, one going left and low, the other right and high.

No weapons were drawn but the palms of their hands rested significantly on the stocks of the Glock pistols in the holsters at their waists. The fastening loops on both guns had been unclasped.

Flynn stopped. He swayed.

The female cop took the lead.

She raised her left hand in a police-stop gesture, her right staying on the Glock.

'You stop right there, matey,' she shouted. 'Drop that stuff, put your hands up and get down on your knees.'

'No, can't do that,' Flynn replied stubbornly.

'If you don't, I'll either Taser you or shoot you,' she said, unsurprised by his refusal to cooperate.

Flynn shook his head. His mind was reeling and struggling now. 'I need to get out of here,' he said. 'I'll put you . . . I'll put you down if you try to stop me.'

'No, Mr Flynn, I'll put *you* down . . . Now drop the gear, hands up and get down on to your knees, then on to all fours, then on to your belly and we'll remain good friends, OK? I'll get you to hospital and get you treatment, OK?' she concluded lightly.

'OK,' Flynn said. But his brain was playing tricks with him, telling him he could do this, barge his way out, deck both cops before they got anywhere near drawing their guns. It was probably something he could have done under normal circumstances.

He gripped the bag containing his drugs tightly to his chest like a rugby ball, lowered his head and began to charge.

He got maybe two-and-a-half strides before the female cop, acting so quickly, so decisively, drew her Taser from the holster at the small of her back, aimed and discharged it at Flynn.

The electrodes connected with his shoulder and upper chest.

50,000 volts zapped through him, instantly closing his body down and flooring him. He landed face down on top of his shopping, bursting the bag, jerking every limb, then hissing and moaning as the charge subsided and every bone, sinew and muscle stopped working, everything except his vital organs.

He looked up at the female officer standing astride over him.

'You should've done what I said,' she reprimanded him.

TWO

The dining table was impeccably laid out.

The cutlery was gold-plated and all the crockery and glasses rimmed with gold. The candelabrum – the magnificent centrepiece to the table – was solid gold with sprays of tiny diamonds and the tablecloth made of the finest Vietnamese silk inlaid with gold thread.

Viktor Bashkim surveyed it all with satisfaction.

He loved gold.

He had strived for it all his life, ever since he had ripped the chunky gold necklace from the teenager who'd harboured aspirations to become his rival on the streets of Tirana in Albania almost seventy years before; a young man Viktor Bashkim had stabbed forty-four times for this temerity and left to bleed out into a stinking gutter.

Viktor had stood towering and victorious over the dying boy before fleeing the scene, holding up the heavy chain against the moonlight and instantly realizing he wanted more.

Only then had he fled as a battered cop car turned into the alley with its blue light making a scraping noise as it rotated lazily.

Viktor smiled at the cherished memory of that tableau in his brain.

His first kill. His first caress of gold, almost in the same moment.

That night was also when he'd had his first full sexual experience. The testosterone produced by the killing had fuelled his young body with lust and he'd forced himself on to his then girlfriend in a frenzy.

A very good night.

Viktor touched the chain still hanging around his now-scrawny, eighty-four-year-old neck. He had worn it every day since so he would never forget his origins.

His ultimate intention had been to gift the chain to his eldest son, Aleksander, but that wish was not to be any more.

Viktor blinked sadly, his eyes milky with age, cleared his mind and looked down the table again, then nodded with appreciation as it brought some pleasure to his old eyes.

'This is good, Mikel,' he said to the head waiter.

'Thank you, sir.'

'And the meal?'

'On schedule, sir.'

Viktor nodded. The waiter bowed and reversed away.

Viktor walked slowly past the table, allowing the tips of his arthritically gnarled fingers to brush against the tablecloth, then he stepped out of the banqueting suite and main saloon on to the equally expansive upper rear deck of his fifty-metre-long luxury motor yacht named *Halcyon*, constructed by a Turkish boat builder seven years before, now presently berthed in the port of Zante Town, capital of the Greek island of Zante or Zakynthos.

He inhaled the sweet aroma of the early evening air and looked forward with anticipation to the nine-course meze that would be served for his special guests, yet to arrive. It was another hour before they were due.

He leaned on the rail and looked across the twelve-mile stretch of the Ionian Sea towards mainland Greece. That country's rugged silhouette was clear, made even more so when Viktor slotted his thickly lensed glasses on to his nose and was able to see the rocky coastline with even more clarity.

Yet despite the magnificent view, the setting, the position of the boat in the pretty harbour and the flowery scent of the evening, Viktor sighed heavily. His old heart was still pounding as healthily as a man thirty years his junior, but it felt like lead in his chest thanks to his terrible loss.

His jaw rotated in fury.

At least the wheels of retribution were in motion.

It had taken a few months to come about, but it was here and he was waiting impatiently for news.

Now his jaw set grimly and his bony fingers gripped the rail as he looked down to the deck below on which the big Jacuzzi bubbled away around the bikini-clad body of his remaining grandson's latest female companion, a heavily chested twenty-something with long black hair and Slavic features who was quite happy to take Niko's money and lifestyle and tolerate the screwing.

Viktor watched as Niko himself then emerged from the lower cabin, attired only in his black and silver Speedo swimming trunks, displaying his generous goods to great effect. He glanced up at Viktor and gave the old man a grin before clambering into the Jacuzzi alongside his lady friend, who was already pouring champagne into two slim fluted glasses. Niko settled alongside her, took a glass and raised it to Viktor before swallowing the expensive contents in one. Viktor saw the woman's right hand slither under the surface of the water, through the bubbles like some kind of aquatic snake, and her fingers encircled Niko's engorged privates.

Repulsed, Viktor turned away and re-entered the saloon, making his way through to the bridge where the boat's skipper sat at the complex dashboard, messing with the GPS system.

He stood quickly on Viktor's entrance, but the old man gestured for him to stay seated.

'Have we heard anything more yet?'

The skipper shook his head. 'Not since . . .'

'Do we need to be concerned?' Viktor asked. His voice was harsh with age but still strong and commanding. Despite his background and its many temptations, he had steered clear of the excesses which had made him a fortune big enough to spend thirty-five million euros on this super yacht. He had never been a great fan of alcohol, never taken a drug other than on prescription, never smoked and never paid for sex. These were all goods and services he was happy to provide for others and reap the profits, but they were not for him.

'Let me see again,' Viktor said.

'Sure, boss.'

Viktor turned and crossed to a large-screen TV fitted to the back wall of the bridge which came to life.

He watched the images with cold but satisfied detachment masking an inner delight as the young woman on the screen, naked and tied to a chair, had her head yanked back and was then expertly decapitated by a masked man with a finely honed panga, an African machete, with four perfectly aimed, slashing cuts, working through the spraying blood, gristle and bone until the head came free. The severed head – the once-beautiful female features now distorted and almost unrecognizable – was then jiggled in front of the Go-Pro camera lens which was relaying the footage and recording the brutal execution of an innocent.

'What was the bitch's name?' Viktor asked as the footage paused.

'Santiago, Maria Santiago,' the skipper said.

'Spanish bitch,' Viktor said. He ran the back of his hand across his old, dry lips. 'Spanish cop bitch.'

Steve Flynn's eyes flickered open and slowly focused on the white tiled ceiling above him. It took a few moments before his brain lost its fuzz, some semblance of clarity returned and he remembered where he was.

His recollection was confirmed by two things.

First, the two intravenous drips feeding into him via the cannula inserted into the vein on the back of his left hand and the electrodes stuck on his upper chest, wired to the monitor just behind and to one side of the bed, which was displaying his vital signs.

The handcuff ratcheted around his right wrist and, securing him to the framework of the metal bed, also assisted his memory.

He was in a hospital bed but he was a patient going nowhere because he was also a prisoner.

He raised his head slightly and squinted down the length and breadth of his six-foot-three-inch body. An arc of incredible pain akin to forked lightning lanced through the centre of his cranium, ear to ear, with the movement also reminding him of his burst eardrum.

He had no bedcovers on and was wearing a grubby off-white hospital gown, blood-stained around the lower hem just below his groin, beyond which he could see the surgical dressing around his right thigh, through which blood blossomed like cumulous clouds. A drain ran out from underneath the dressing, half-filling a clear plastic bottle attached to the side of the bed with liquid, the colour of which reminded Flynn of a frog smoothie. This was another reminder of why he was here in a side ward at Blackpool Victoria Hospital.

A further reminder – these were all piling up as his mind began to function properly – was still the vivid sound of Brian

Tasker's neck as he had broken it. He could hear it, satisfyingly, reverberating around his brain, even among the blur and slight confusion he was experiencing as his thought processes were retuning.

The sound of that neck breaking, Flynn knew, was one that would stay with him for the rest of his life.

A trapped groan came from his throat as a fresh jolt of pain seared up his right leg and told him that whatever painkillers had been administered were now wearing thin.

Painkillers? he thought. What *was* it about . . . painkillers? He winced as that memory also came back to him: a pharmacist, two frightened women . . . cops crashing through the door, a Taser deployed and poleaxing him. His own search for pain relief to self-administer coming to an embarrassing finale on the floor of a chemist's shop.

Flynn caught some movement in the periphery of his vision. He angled his head slightly to look.

The uniformed cop by the door had her back to Flynn. He could tell the officer was female and she was engrossed in composing a text on her mobile phone, her head hunched low, hands up in front of her chest as she thumbed the phone's keypad. Flynn heard the flapping of wings, the sound indicating that a text had gone up into the ether.

Flynn frowned when he saw the Glock pistol in the holster on her right hip, plus all the other cop accoutrements: ballistic vest, rigid handcuffs, CS gas canister, the Taser, an ASP – the extendable baton – and the personal radio.

She was armed and guarding him.

Flynn had been correct: he might have been a patient but was also definitely a prisoner and not going anywhere.

He opened his mouth to speak, to attract her attention, but his lips, teeth and tongue seemed to be superglued together. He tried to make some saliva but the anaesthetic had completely dried him out. At least he assumed it was the anaesthetic. Instead of speaking he made a muted buzzing noise, loud enough for her to hear and make her turn.

Flynn gave her a lopsided smile, just as much as his bonded lips would allow. He guessed it wasn't a pretty sight.

'You're awake, then?' she said, businesslike, slipping her phone into her trouser pocket. She was pretty, but with her hair scraped back into a tight, practical bun and only the merest dab of make-up, she was all no-crap, purely professional – and she did not smile back.

She was the officer who had Tasered Flynn in the pharmacy.

He nodded and attempted to expand the smile all the way across his lips, maybe to try and melt her heart, but all it did was become a grimace and she just scowled hard at him.

The phone in her pocket buzzed as a text landed.

She ignored it, kept her eyes on Flynn and spoke into the microphone clipped to her shoulder tab, which was connected to the personal radio on her utility belt.

'Alpha-Romeo Eight to Superintendent Dean, receiving?'

'Go ahead, Molly,' came the clear reply.

'Prisoner's back in the land of the living, sir.' She kept her eyes on Flynn as she transmitted this snippet.

'Roger, thanks for that.' Flynn recognized Rik Dean's voice. 'I'll be with you ASAP . . . Be careful with him,' he concluded with a warning.

'Will do, sir.'

She took her thumb off the transmit button and continued to study Flynn, clearly uninspired by what she was seeing. She stepped across and found the call button on the wall to summon a nurse. She held her thumb over it.

'I'm told I have to be wary of you,' she said to Flynn, her eyes half-lidded in a challenge. 'So all I'm saying to you is this, Mr Flynn – don't try anything or I'll shoot you in the other leg, CS gas you, Taser you again then beat your wounds with my baton while the snot and tears gush out of your eyes from the CS. Understand?'

Flynn's crooked attempt at a smile dematerialized with each word she spoke.

He nodded compliantly, believing her.

By then he had induced some saliva into his dry mouth and had produced enough to get his lips open and whisper, 'I'm desperate for a pee, though.'

A sly grin came to her face. 'No problem – pee away.'

'Eh?'

She pointed towards his lower stomach. 'In case you hadn't noticed . . .'

Flynn raised his head to look. She was correct; he hadn't noticed. He had seen the drain from underneath the dressing of his leg wound but had not seen or felt the catheter tube sneaking out from the other side under the hospital gown. It had been inserted into his bladder via his penis, draining his urine into a bottle affixed to the other side of the bed.

'Feel free,' she said, 'to pee.'

He thought she had a very cruel expression on her face which, despite the circumstances, he now realized was far more than pretty. She was actually quite stunning.

After a nurse had primped up his pillows, made him comfortable, emptied his piss and puss bags and organized a small meal for him of scrambled eggs on toast, which she diced up for him like he was three and gave him a plastic spoon to eat it with (as the police had informed the hospital that real cutlery should not be given to him because he might use it as a weapon), which he had then gobbled down, and then administered more intravenous painkillers and saline into him via the drip, creating a soporific effect, Flynn had dozed off into a troubled sleep peppered with flecking blood and the undead.

He woke an hour later, still feeling groggy and sore.

The armed policewoman – Molly Cartwright – was still watching over him, sitting by the door, busy with her mobile phone but facing him this time.

She had earlier given him some detail about the period of time from their first encounter when she had Tasered him – 'You went down like a baby,' she'd sneered at him, and the fact he had passed out, been taken to A&E at Blackpool Victoria for treatment, was admitted, underwent surgery on his leg and was where he was now. It filled in a few gaps for him because the time between the Tasering and waking up post-surgery was a period of blackness, interspersed with vivid, wild images, none of which made sense.

The period of time from breaking Brian Tasker's neck up to the Taser zapping him was quite clear in his mind, though.

Molly glanced up at him from the screen of her phone as Flynn moved and made a dry clacking sound with his mouth, which had gone dry again. He eased himself into a more comfortable sitting position, not easy with one arm manacled to the bed and the other an input for drugs.

The over-bed tray had been wheeled to the side and he was unable to reach the jug of weak orange juice on it.

'Need a drink,' he croaked weakly. 'Could you do the honours?'

She closed her eyes impatiently for a moment, then slid the phone into her cargo trouser pocket and stood up. Flynn watched her face, curious to confirm if he had been correct as to how beautiful she was; yes, he had been right, but now he also saw that her eyes were red raw from crying and she avoided making direct eye contact with him.

With sloth-like reluctance, she half-filled the plastic tumbler for him, then manoeuvred the tray across his knees so the drink was now in reaching distance of his free hand.

'Are you all right?' Flynn enquired, picking up the juice and taking a long swig of it. Even though it was tepid, it tasted good and sweet.

This time she did look at him. He saw that her previous facade of hard features was now not quite so granite like.

Annoyed with herself, or so it appeared to Flynn, she rubbed her eyes ferociously with her knuckles and said, 'No o'your business.'

'OK,' Flynn said philosophically. 'When's Mr Dean coming to see me? I mean, what time is it now? Midnight?'

'One a.m. And when's he coming? When he's free. You've given him a lot of things to sort out, not least his own injuries. He's been in casualty.'

'Casualty?'

'Yeah, y'know, A and E – the place you go when someone assaults you, breaks your cheekbone and knocks you unconscious.'

'Oh, *that* casualty,' Flynn muttered. 'I'd almost forgotten about that.'

'You literally punched his lights out, didn't you?'

'Suppose I did.' Flynn sighed. Headbutted, actually, but he didn't correct her. It had hurt his own head doing so. 'I had my reasons.'

'I know,' Molly said. She looked at him, he thought, with some compassion in her sea-blue eyes. 'But you're like a bull in a china shop. I am sorry about your girlfriend . . . I have heard,' she finished quietly.

A dreadful image spliced into Flynn's mind's eye: a severed head being juggled around by the hair, like a football in a net bag.

'Yeah.' Flynn's voice was muted by the memory. He blinked as his own eyes became moist before he forced himself to expunge the vision.

'Look!' Molly said. Flynn turned his head slowly, the anguish clear. She was pointing at her own teary eyes. 'Nowhere near what you've been through,' she said quietly. She swallowed. Flynn saw her throat rise and fall as she gave an apologetic shrug. 'I just dumped my bloke, that's what these are about. Caught the bastard cheating on me – and other stuff. Now he's been sending me pathetic texts and I've been sending pathetic ones back.' Her mouth tightened. 'I don't know why, but I thought he was for keeps.'

'I'm sorry,' Flynn said sincerely. He too had been dumped in the not-too-distant past by a woman he'd been convinced he would spend the rest of his life with. It wasn't to be because she needed more than he could offer: the life of a sportfishing boat skipper on a sun-baked island, always scrabbling for cash, clearly did not do it for her, but that was all he had. Then fate brought someone else into his life – a dark, beautiful, incredible woman now cruelly, brutally taken from him by men of evil.

The flash of that ghastly image again: the severed, bloody head, one eye open, the other closed, mouth distorted, the sawn-through neck.

Flynn said, 'Want me to pay him a visit when I get out of this?'

'What? No!' Molly blew out her cheeks and made a horrified face at the prospect of Flynn beating up her ex. 'No, it's fine . . . I've seen what you do when you get angry, and anyway, I'm not convinced you'll be out of this situation any time soon . . . And *anyway*, why am I even talking to you? You're a murderer and you smashed up a police van.'

'Because I have an honest face?' Flynn ventured.

She regarded him stonily, shook her head and backed away.

Out of the blue, Flynn asked, 'Who's the biggest drug dealer in town these days?'

'What?' Molly's face screwed up, confused by the change of tack.

'Who's the biggest, baddest, richest drug dealer in town?' Flynn asked again.

Before she could reply, the door opened and Rik Dean, the Detective Superintendent in joint charge of Lancashire Constabulary's Force Major Investigation Team (FMIT) stepped in. Flynn fleetingly spotted another armed cop, presumably the policewoman's firearms partner, standing in the corridor beyond the door.

Rik Dean dismissed Molly with a curt jerk of the head. She frowned – not at the superintendent as that could have been seen as insubordination – and left, then Rik dragged the plastic chair Molly had been sat on over to the side of the bed and eased himself painfully down next to Flynn, who was sardonically eyeing the senior detective's face.

The left side was badly swollen, puffed up, bruised red and purple around the eye socket. His bottom lip was cut inside and out, the visible wounds glued back together, but it still flopped big and puffy like a burst inner tube.

Rik leaned forwards, rested his elbows on his knees, interlocked his fingers and turned his head slowly and with a certain degree of malevolence to glare at Flynn through one good eye and one closed up to a sticky slit.

Flynn sniffed. 'That looks sore.'

Rik nodded in agreement. 'Sure fucking is, Steve. You head-butted me very, very hard and just the once, for Christ's sake – so how did I get all this?' he demanded. 'One hell of an impact.'

'Mm,' Flynn said, 'it didn't quite land as intended.'

'I've had to have my frickin' skull X-rayed. Not fractured, luckily, but my cheekbone is splintered like a dry twig, you bastard. I can only see out of one eye and even then I'm seeing double.' Rik's voice sounded slightly disconnected. Flynn guessed his mouth was numbed up by painkillers and synching his voice to his lip movements wasn't easy.

Flynn said, 'I had to put you down. It was the only chance I'd get . . . to cause a diversion, to get people falling over themselves like the Keystone Kops, just long enough . . .'

'Just long enough for you to get into the back of an unattended police van and kill the occupant – a prisoner in police custody.'

'Let's face it, Rik,' Flynn said, 'you were a tad reluctant to let me get in with him, so I had to think outside the box. Once he was in a cell it would've been much more difficult for me.'

'To kill him?' Rik interrupted, his rubbery, distended bottom lip flapping. Normally Rik Dean was a pretty handsome guy, but now he looked in bad shape following his encounter with Flynn's forehead. 'Jeez,' he continued, the 'z' sounding like 'thh' as his injuries made him lisp. 'The word "reluctant" seems to imply I was in two minds: should I let him get in with a prisoner or should I not? I wasn't in two minds, and now we know why. Christ, and then you even nicked the section van with him in the back, dead, until, of course, he rolled out into the path of the car behind – the body is one hell of a mess – and the driver is now having a shed collapse. Then you crash the van and try to rob a chemist's shop of its junk. What the fuck were you thinking, Steve? We had Tasker, banged up, bang to rights, and now you've completely ballsed it up, particularly for yourself.'

Flynn listened to Rik's lisping rant without apparent emotion, then thought for a few moments before opening his mouth and saying flatly, 'Brian Tasker killed, or had killed, or killed on behalf of others such as the Bashkims, too many people close to me,' although his heartrate monitor could not hide just how quickly his heart had begun to pound. He was seeing the faces of all those dead people, not least the face of Maria Santiago, whose head had been severed from her body and shaken on a video link for Flynn to see, to be taunted and traumatized in the moments before Tasker intended to murder Flynn himself. Just so he knew, prior to his own horrific death, he had lost everything and the final image he would take with him was that of Maria's head.

But Flynn's end was not to be. The armed cops surging into the basement where he was being held captive ensured that.

'Fuck, Steve.' Rik hung and shook his head despondently. 'You're as bad as Tasker now, and the Bashkims. At least we still have two Bashkim guys under lock and key, out of your reach,' Rik said, referring to the two men who had been arrested in the basement, who were steadfastly still refusing to reveal their personal details. Rik exchanged a quick look with Flynn.

'Oh, no, no, no, no – you're not getting anywhere near those two . . . and anyway, they're just enforcers, gofers.'

'Who also killed people we both know, liked and worked with,' Flynn pointed out.

'Maybe so, but Brian Tasker and those two should now be in the justice system on the first step of a journey lasting the rest of their lives, rotting in jail.'

'He was already in prison,' Flynn reminded him about Tasker. 'He escaped, then came after the people who sent him there in the first place.' Flynn pondered a moment. 'He should've been in jail for life then, and to be fair I used to believe in that sort of justice, Rik.' Flynn's mouth turned down at the corners. 'But not now – not for people like Tasker or the Bashkims. They don't deserve to be fed and watered on the taxpayer.'

'And now, instead, that'll be you inside, Steve. I'll have to charge you with murder.'

'I didn't have a choice, Rik.'

'Everyone has choices.'

Flynn looked meaningfully at Rik Dean, a man he had known for a lot of years. 'This isn't over, not by a long chalk, not even started . . . You know that, don't you?'

THREE

Viktor Bashkim slowly wiped his lips with the Egyptian cotton napkin.

The nine-course meze had been delicious – mini-courses with a basic Albanian theme served over a leisurely two-hour period to him and his four guests, his main partners in crime that he now had to deal with directly since the demise of Aleksander, his son. Following the food, they had all been shown to their individual bedrooms in which their treats awaited: three hand-picked girls, one for each of the sexually voracious men, and another girl for the woman.

Bashkim had bid them all a goodnight, because with one exception they all deserved their presents. The one who didn't would be dealt with in due course but was treated with the same courtesy as the others so as not to arouse suspicion. Bashkim would not see any of them for the remainder of the night as he would be ensconced in his own very palatial cabin where he would sleep alone. Pleasures of the flesh were long behind him, and now that his wife had died he was eager to retire alone, listen to some simple Albanian folk music for a while then, hopefully, sleep.

First he needed a progress check.

He indicated for Mikel, the head waiter, to start to clear away the dishes, then, dropping his napkin on to the table, he made his way to the bridge where the skipper remained at the controls, alert but lounging now.

He shot upright when Viktor entered.

'News?' the old man asked.

'Nothing has come through as of yet.'

Viktor scowled and walked over to the control panel, leaned with both hands on it and stared thoughtfully at Zante harbour.

'We should have something by now.'

'I agree.'

'What is Niko doing?'

'He's . . . er . . . in his room,' the skipper answered delicately.

'Get him.'

Rik Dean left Steve Flynn under no illusions.

Flynn was under arrest and under armed guard, the latter for his own safety and also because he was now considered a dangerous man in his own right. Once a doctor confirmed he was well enough to travel and be in custody, he would be taken to a police station and thrown into a cell. Until his good health could be confirmed he would remain a hospital patient, would not be interviewed formally but would understand he was under caution and not be allowed to contact anyone else. And he would stay handcuffed to the bed.

Flynn bleated that this was a blatant breach of his basic human rights.

Rik counter-argued that he had buggered up that argument by murdering someone and nicking a police van, but promised that once he was banged up he could have all the human rights under the sun.

When Rik had gone, a nauseating tsunami of tiredness threatened to overwhelm Flynn.

He swallowed back a horrible, bile-like taste in his throat, lay back on his pillows and closed his eyes.

He wanted to sleep but the image of Maria's severed head refused to leave his mind's eye. Unable to un-see what he had seen, he began to cry.

'Grandpa, what the fucking hell?' Niko protested wearily as he appeared on the bridge, tightening a silk dressing gown around himself. His thick black hair was tousled but his face was gaunt, showing deeply etched lines from the ravages of cocaine, vodka, sex and little sleep.

'There has been no news,' Viktor stated.

Niko shrugged without care. 'I can't help that,' he whined. 'There was always going to be a delay of some sort, only natural.'

Viktor had been perched on the skipper's chair. He slid off, walked over to his grandson and glowered up into his face. Viktor was much older and physically inferior now, although he'd once been a bull of a man, but his aura still made others cower like beaten dogs.

'Put your cock away, wipe your nose and find out what has happened,' he ordered the younger man. 'Do it now and let me know as soon as possible. I will be in my room.'

More drugs helped Flynn relax – took the pain away but not the mental torture. He managed to sleep for about four very fitful hours until eventually coming awake again, opening his eyes and seeing PC Molly Cartwright still on guard duty over him. She was sitting on the plastic chair by the door, arms folded across her chest with her legs stretched out, crossed at the ankles.

She was staring into space, lost in deep thought and initially unaware of Flynn's awakening until he shifted position slightly and the handcuff clanked on the bed frame. Her face turned towards him. Her eyes were red raw.

Although Flynn's mouth had dried up again, he managed to say, 'A right couple of crybabies, us two, aren't we?'

Molly's lips twisted cynically. 'I've been instructed not to talk to you, or if I do, to record the conversation and remind you you're under caution,' she said frostily.

'I don't actually recall being cautioned in the first place,' Flynn said, 'after you electrocuted me.'

'Whatever.' She shrugged. 'But no conversation, eh? Then our lives'll be much easier.'

'How about filling that juice glass again for me?'

She sighed, rolled her eyes and stood up. She filled the glass on the over-bed tray and manoeuvred it across him. He took it and drank half.

Molly backed off a few steps.

'So we can't talk? Sad, that,' Flynn said.

'Way of the world. You're a murderer.'

Flynn accepted the accusation with a small gesture and laid his head back on the pillows, now deeply indented by his head.

'I don't want to jeopardize the investigation,' she explained.

'I understand. Still sad, though. The two of us going through our own trials and tribulations and no one to blab to . . . Problem shared and all that.'

'I'm not sure you can halve your problem. All I've done is dump a cheating love rat and gambler. Just one of those things, whereas murder isn't . . .' She paused. 'One of those things.'

'But you do want to talk about it?' Flynn offered. 'Promise it won't jeopardize the murder investigation. I'll listen, you talk . . . keep my mind off a certain image that keeps playing through my brain.'

At the mention of which, it came back. His face twitched.

'Are you OK?' Molly asked, seeing the flinch.

He eyed her. 'I'm fine.'

'Look,' she said, relenting, allowing her shoulders to wilt, 'we can talk if you like and I'll just deny we had a conversation – unless you start admitting you killed that Tasker guy, in which case . . . y'know. But don't try anything. I still mean what I said. I'm very happy to shoot you if necessary.'

'I'll bear it in mind.'

From the corridor outside came the sound of raised voices. Flynn and Molly looked towards the door.

Molly stepped away from Flynn and her right hand came

up to the holster on her hip. Her thumb flipped the release
stud over the handle of the Glock as she prepared to draw it
if necessary.

The voices continued: an argument of sorts, though the actual
words were mute and indistinct.

Then came a knock on the door, then a pause, then two sharp
taps.

'It's me, Molly,' a male voice called.

Flynn saw the tension visibly leave her face and body.

'OK, open up,' she called. From the side of her mouth, she
said to Flynn, 'My partner.'

The door opened and the armed cop in the corridor leaned in
the gap with an apologetic look on his face. He opened his mouth
to explain something but was rudely barged out of the way by
another man in his early thirties, who then sidestepped him and
entered the room.

'Alan, what the hell d'you think you're doing?' Molly
demanded of this man. Flynn clocked she had thumbed the
stud on the safety strap back into place over the butt of
the Glock.

'I came to see you. I had to . . . to explain,' the man said
dramatically.

Behind him, Molly's ARV partner gave a helpless shrug. To
him, she said, 'It's OK, Robbo.' Then she held up her right hand,
palm out, into the face of the intruder who, Flynn assumed, was
the aforementioned cheating, gambling love rat in Molly's relationship scenario. Through gritted teeth, she growled, 'You've
no right coming in here. I'm working. This is a serious situation;
you shouldn't be here.'

The man shot Flynn a glare of contempt. 'Guarding a murderer.'

'Yes. I'm off-duty in an hour, so just fuck off, Alan.'

He stood his ground, instantly making Flynn dislike him. 'Not
until we talk,' he demanded. 'Till I explain.'

'Explain shagging around? Explain blowing my money on
your debts? Can't wait for *those* explanations . . . But not here,
Alan. Not now,' Molly hissed at him.

Flynn's next assumption was that Alan was a cop, probably a
detective, otherwise the armed officer in the corridor would surely
not have risked opening the door at all. He was probably familiar

with Molly's break-up and maybe 'Alan' outranked him and he'd used this as a lever to bully his way past.

'But babe . . .' Alan reached out his arms for her. Tears welled in his eyes. 'Babe,' he repeated, blubbering.

Flynn coughed. 'May I make a suggestion?' Both heads swivelled to him. 'Take your fucking private lives elsewhere or I'll summon nursey in on this.' He held up the emergency call button. 'And have you both ejected for jeopardizing the mental health of a patient.'

With pleasure, Flynn saw Alan bristle. 'Who the hell do you think you are, shit-head?'

Flynn sighed, disliking Alan even more, though he kept quiet.

'Come on, out,' Molly said to Alan and shooed him towards the door, then through it, but not before she managed one dagger-laden scowl over her shoulder at Flynn, who returned it with a generous smile. Molly propelled Alan out and had a speedy, low-level conversation with her cop partner, who then stepped into the room and replaced her. The door closed.

Beyond it, Flynn heard two voices in argument. He closed his eyes.

When he next awoke, Molly was back in the room sitting on the chair by the door. Her eyes were open but she was staring moodily into space, her face set grim. Flynn hadn't heard her return and he wasn't sure how long he had been asleep or how long she had been out dealing with the unexpected arrival of her recent ex. It could not have been long.

'Did you get rid of him?'

She stirred out of her reverie. 'What? Yeah, sorry about that.' She yawned long and hard.

'Whatever,' Flynn said. 'None of my business, but never trust a man called Alan. I take it he's a detective? I can tell from the moustache.'

'Detective sergeant, actually, hence how he blagged his way in.'

'I remember that,' Flynn said wistfully. 'Pulling rank.'

'You were a cop?' she asked, slightly taken aback.

'A detective, though I never, ever, had a moustache. I thought you'd know about me.'

'No, never been mentioned ... What, a DI? Here in Lancashire?'

'Yes and no – never reached the dizzy heights of being a DI. I was a DS on drug squad. Left about twelve years ago.'

'You don't look old enough to have been a police pensioner for twelve years.'

'Very kind of you to say, but I left before my time. Under a bit of a cloud.'

'Oh, right.' She regarded him thoughtfully. 'So what's the big story, then? Why are you here? Why have you reached this point?'

'Are we talking now?'

'Suppose so, but only if I can offload on you, too.' She checked her watch. 'I'm off-duty soon,' she told him while wondering why she suddenly felt compelled to talk to Flynn other than it seemed the right thing to do, murderer or not.

'You first,' he urged her.

Flynn only half-listened to a story about a marriage gone wrong, a rotten divorce, then the failure of further relationships until Molly found someone special in Alan – also a divorcee – who she thought she could trust and make a life with . . . until she discovered his predilection for using his rank as a DS to lure unsuspecting but willing and ambitious young female officers into his bed. There was also the spectre of big debts, followed by a loan from Molly (to the tune of £1,000) which she never saw again, gambling and too much time spent in the company of unsavoury characters, although Alan claimed it was a detective's job to hang around with toerags.

Flynn was only partially taking it in because his mind was elsewhere.

He knew he had to be free from custody – and that he had acted rashly and without foresight in taking Brian Tasker's life. But he had been driven by crazy rage and emotion and he was glad he had done it, though on reflection he should have planned it a little better.

There was very little wriggle room for him now.

Once he passed through the doors of the custody office, even if he subsequently got bail, he could probably kiss away at least three very valuable days of his life while sitting in a cell, maybe more. But he knew he would not get bail, at least not straight away after being charged. It was police policy not to grant bail to people charged with murder; any bail would have to be granted by a court, possibly on a remand hearing that could be weeks down the line.

He knew he had to be free sooner than that.

He was in pain from his leg wound and his burst eardrum but now, having had surgery on the leg, just as long as he was relatively careful, he thought he should be able to operate.

Trouble was his window of opportunity – the time between where he was now and a cell door slamming behind him – was closing rapidly.

He watched Molly's mouth moving as she spoke.

Breaking free from her and her partner, Robbo, would entail having to hurt them both, something he did not wish to do, which reduced his options even further.

He concentrated on her words.

'I thought I was really in love with him,' she was saying sadly, drawing things to a conclusion, 'but on reflection I can't have been because I don't want to fight for him.' She screwed up her face. 'You know what I mean?'

'I understand,' Flynn said, liking her voice, liking the way she twitched her nose and hating the thought he might have to cause her harm. Perhaps if he could disarm her, not by his charm but by snatching her Glock and locking her and Robbo in a cupboard – maybe that would work, he speculated. Flynn instinctively knew it would not happen, because something about Molly told him she would not be manoeuvred into any compromising position where the weapon could be wrested from her. She was far too canny for that.

'So what about you, Steve Flynn? What brings you to this juncture?' She looked expectantly at him: his turn.

Flynn wasn't really one to discuss and delve into his thoughts and feelings, but he made an effort, marshalling his thoughts. 'I once arrested a man who was so desperate to remain at liberty he murdered his own family – wife and baby – just to do that, just to cause a diversion.' Molly's mouth popped open. 'Before your time, I think,' he said. 'Anyway, he spent a lot of time in prison blaming me and the rest of the team who had caught him for his family's deaths and his own misfortune. That's how warped and twisted Brian Tasker's mind was. He plotted a prison escape, escaped, then went after the team, linking up with an Albanian crime family to help him, a family I crossed a while ago . . . and they bore a serious grudge against me . . .'

'You crossed an Albanian crime family?' Molly interrupted. 'How the hell did you manage that?'

'Long story.'

A few things began to slot into place for Molly at that point. 'DCI Alford's murder?' she said.

'He was the team leader in the operation against Tasker . . .'

'And his poor family . . . and Jerry Tope?' She gasped. 'Oh, God, he was lovely.'

'Also one of the team.'

'He was found dead in Preston docks . . . it was horrific.'

'Yeah, Tasker's hit list – the team that constituted Operation Ambush.'

'And your girlfriend? How does she fit into all this?'

'Tasker and the Albanians were in cahoots . . . I'm the link that straddles the two. Tasker wanted me dead, the Albanians wanted me dead plus anyone close to me, hence Maria . . . She was murdered and then it was going to be me, but Rik Dean kicked down the door before Tasker could kill me.'

'He put a firearms team together at short notice. I missed the call,' she said with a shrug. 'Happens.'

There was a pause. Flynn rubbed his features with his free hand.

'Now maybe you see where I'm coming from.'

Molly was about to respond when the door opened and Rik Dean stepped in.

Viktor Bashkim listened coldly to Niko, whose voice quavered slightly as he recounted the little chunks of information he had pieced together from a series of increasingly frantic phone calls, many of which had been unanswered or clicked straight to voicemail.

'I tried to call Agron and Besim and Gjon,' he explained to Viktor, who watched his grandson squirm under his sea-grey gaze. 'None of the useless bastards came back to me,' Niko whined.

'And what did that tell you?' Viktor said quietly.

Niko could not look the old man in the eye. 'That things are not going well?' he ventured.

'That things are not going well,' Viktor mimicked him with irony. 'Because?'

'Because they are all usually good in replying, answering phones?'

'Exactly. All three are good men . . . So what have you gleaned?'

Niko swallowed. 'Agron and Besim are in the custody of the police in Blackpool.'

Viktor nodded his head at this news. 'And Gjon?'

'Still at large . . . It's him I spoke to, eventually.'

Viktor waited.

Niko's toes curled in his silk slippers. 'Agron and Besim were with Tasker when armed police burst in and managed to stop Tasker from killing Steve Flynn. All three were arrested. Gjon had been the lookout but hadn't been able to warn them of the approach of the police, who came very quickly.'

'So that is where we're up to? Three arrests?'

Niko hesitated. 'Not quite.'

Rik Dean sat down heavily, wearily. His facial injuries were maturing, looking darker and uglier the more tired he became.

Once again, he dismissed Molly curtly.

Or at least he attempted to until Flynn intervened. 'She can stay as far as I'm concerned.'

'What is this? Some kind of counselling session?' Rik snorted.

'She can stay. I just don't mind, is all.'

Rik shrugged his shoulders, too exhausted to argue the point. He made her stand by the door and took her seat from her, then gathered himself.

Flynn saw the inner wrestling match and said, 'Spit it out.'

'The police in Gran Canaria have been back to me,' he said. 'They've moved pretty quickly on this. They would, I suppose, Maria being one of theirs. Security camera footage at the airport shows her returning to the island from the UK, passing through immigration, flashing her passport then getting into a taxi outside the terminal. The cab looks to have been forced off the road between the airport and Puerto Rico. The driver is dead – shot through the head – and there was no sign of Maria at the scene. A team of officers entered yours and her apartment in Puerto Rico a short while later.'

He stopped talking.

Flynn waited, not making it easy for him.

'They found her body,' Rik said.

Flynn cringed, then nodded, and saw even more reluctance to speak on Rik's part.

'She'd been decapitated.'

So it was all real. The images that Brian Tasker had been torturing Flynn with, beamed via the Internet from the apartment in the Canary Islands, were not a trick or an optical illusion.

'We know that,' Flynn said mutedly.

Rik closed his eyes, pinched the bridge of his nose with his thumb and forefinger.

'What?' Flynn probed, sensing even more to come.

'Like I said, they found her body . . . but . . . but there was no . . .' Rik struggled with the words, then he went for it. 'There was no trace of her head. Whoever did this to her took her head with them.'

Viktor Bashkim looked up at the knock on his cabin door and placed his iPad down. He'd been skimming through the family photographs of his dead son Aleksander and also his dead grandsons, Pavli and Dardan.

'Yes?'

The door opened and Niko sidled in, now wearing jogging pants and a tracksuit top, both items speckled with blood.

'Grandpa, we're ready for you.'

Viktor stood up, taking hold of the pickaxe handle propped up next to his chair.

It was time to dissipate some of his fury.

There was a very long silence.

Flynn stared into space, deeply shocked by what Rik Dean, who had just left, had just told him, beginning to wonder if he himself was going slightly insane.

It was appalling enough that Maria had been executed in such an horrific manner, but then to learn that a trophy had been taken – because that is what Flynn imagined this to be, some sick prize that would end up on a spike somewhere for someone to gloat over, and just maybe that would also have been his own fate if Brian Tasker had managed to kill him and get away with it.

Molly touched his cuffed hand. She said nothing but was sharing some of the horror with him, her imagination running riot.

He brought his eyes back into focus and looked at her.

'I thought you were going off-duty?'

'I am. Soon.'

'In that case, we may never see each other again,' he said. 'I hope you sort your shit out.'

'I will . . . but we will also see each other, I'm certain of it.'

The door opened and her replacement entered the room, a burly male officer with a gun strapped low and cocky on his waist. Flynn knew he would not get along with this guy at all.

On Viktor's instructions, *Halcyon* had quietly slipped her moorings and left Zante harbour twenty minutes earlier, so smoothly that none of his guests on board – who were all either asleep or still indulging in the pleasures of the flesh – noticed until they were roused or interrupted by Niko and ushered to the lower rear deck to find the boat was now anchored about a mile south down the coast, holding steady on a gentle swell.

They were taken on deck, where one of the guests was already waiting for them.

His name was Michel Barkin, a French gangster and one of the Bashkim family's major partners who was responsible for most of the drug- and people-trafficking supply lines used by the family across the length and breadth of Europe. He was a man trusted with huge amounts of money and drugs valued in the millions. His own private yacht almost, but not quite, rivalled Viktor's.

His relationship with Viktor could be traced back many years and together they had built up efficient and flexible routes across the Continent. Unknown to Viktor, however, Barkin had also been putting his own systems into place alongside the joint enterprise and had been slowly, carefully channelling funds, drugs and people into them, progressively skimming Viktor's pot to the tune of about eight million per year.

It was relatively small change for Viktor, who made a hundred times that each year. The older man – Viktor was twenty years Barkin's senior – was philosophical about some losses. They were inevitable and, when identified, Viktor usually took some form of retribution from the offender: a hand chopped off or maybe a crippling bullet in a kneecap, occasionally two slugs in the head. These punishments were mainly for piddling amounts but substantial skimming on an industrial scale, such as Barkin's, had to be dealt with by issuing a message that could not be misinterpreted by anyone thinking of doing the same.

Hence why Michel Barkin was hanging by his feet from a hook on the on-deck crane, his ankles tethered, his wrists bound behind his back, the crown of his head swaying gently, just inches above the polythene sheet laid out to protect the deck.

He was also naked, having been stripped by Niko, who'd had to subdue him first, rendering him unconscious by smashing his nose flat against his face with a powerful punch as he had been unwilling to accompany Viktor's one remaining grandson out on to the deck. He'd had a fairly good idea where this was going.

Blood dripped from his badly injured face, down across his eyes and forehead, pooling on the plastic sheet. He had given up struggling against the fastenings of duct tape.

The other three guests stumbled out, pulling on their night attire, muttering their annoyance at first, the interruption of their night of pleasure, until they were silenced by the sight of Barkin hanging there like a specimen marlin.

Viktor stood to one side of Barkin's body, leaning on the pickaxe handle like a golfer waiting on the first tee. His guests naturally fanned out around the deck, exchanging glances but not like lovers in the night, more like people terrified for their own lives, let alone the fate of the person dangling in front of them.

Viktor Bashkim's temper historically was petrifying, but over the last few years it was rumoured that age had mellowed him.

He waited for the guests to settle.

Barkin gagged for breath as the blood from his nose clogged the back of his throat.

'There are several things at play here tonight, gentlemen and lady,' Viktor began, addressing his guests. His voice was controlled in spite of the fury boiling within him. 'And this is only one of them.'

He jabbed the thick end of the handle into Barkin's gut, making him jerk as if he had been electronically cow-prodded.

'No, no,' Barkin spluttered through his blood and spittle.

Viktor continued. 'Together, us – we – have established one of the most profitable and diverse organizations in Europe, have we not?' His blazing eyes roved across the small audience. They all nodded in agreement. 'And we are all wealthy because of it, are we not?'

Once more the eyes; the urgent nods.

'So there is no need to take what is not yours, is there?' he demanded.

The nods turned to shaking heads.

He prodded Barkin again, who began to struggle violently against his bindings once more and failing. Niko was good at securing people. He had done it many times.

'So if someone steals from me, I feel it here.' He placed a bunched fist over his chest. 'In my broken heart.'

He sighed and then bounced the thick, heavy stick in one hand, slapping it into the palm of the other.

'And because of the loss of my son, Aleksander, and my two grandsons, I also feel that possibly people, you, maybe' – he pointed the wood at the three standing partners, who all cowered slightly – 'believe I am weak and old . . . but this is not so. I am not one to be taken advantage of or to be usurped. Not yet, anyway. Do you all understand that?'

They nodded in unison.

'And as for you . . .' Viktor squatted down on his haunches. His knees popped hollowly. He peered into Barkin's face and tapped it with the tip of the handle. 'You stole from me.'

'No, no, no,' Barkin gasped. 'Never . . . I wouldn't . . . we've been partners.'

'And familiarity and contempt go hand in hand,' Viktor said. 'You have made me look a fool.'

'I didn't, Viktor,' Barkin insisted. His eyes jerked one way then the other, searching for help, sympathy, a means of escape.

'This will be brutal,' Viktor said quietly, rising up again and spinning the pickaxe handle between his hand, finding a firm grip with his bony fingers.

There was one last deep breath, one last roll of the shoulders, one more glance at the stars, a look towards the twinkling lights of Zante, then he braced himself like a batsman and drew back the heavy shaft of wood.

It was a long time since he had beaten a man to death, but he still had the skill and technique and, more importantly, the strength and energy to complete the task. He worked downwards from Barkin's ankles, which broke like crushed walnuts, slowly down his legs, knees, stomach, all the while piling on the agony, stroke by stroke, just enough to keep the victim conscious and howling for mercy or death.

Finally he asked Niko to winch the wire up about a metre so that Barkin's head was shoulder height for Viktor's best swing. Then he went to work on the jaw, teeth, skull, before, exhausted and flecked with blood, Viktor lobbed the handle overboard and shouldered his way between his three remaining, dumbstruck guests without a further word.

The shower was long, hot and revitalizing, washing away all of Barkin's blood splatter from Viktor's lined face. It also served to dissolve more of his anger and calm him down a little. He emerged more relaxed in his cabin with a large bath sheet wrapped around his midriff, rubbing his close-cropped hair with a hand towel.

Niko was sitting in a chair by the writing desk, nursing a large whisky.

'The body?' Viktor asked. He walked stiffly over to a drinks tray on top of a chest of drawers and poured himself a large shot of Sauvelle French vodka from the sleek black bottle, to which he added two chunks of ice, then rolled it around the glass.

'Fish food,' Niko said. He and Mikel, the head waiter, had rolled Barkin's corpse into the polythene sheet he had been hung above, wrapped it tight with coil and tape, weighted it down with barbells and flipped it over the side of the boat.

Viktor nodded and perched on the edge of the bed.

'Family is all I have left, Niko. All this' – he gestured at the plush cabin and the boat – 'is meaningless without family. Something you should remember. Get a real woman, not a whore. Get a son – two sons, a daughter – to bring you joy.'

'Yes, Grandad,' Niko said with no intention of doing so.

Viktor tossed the hand towel on the floor. 'Where are we now?'

'Two things,' Niko said. He had the old man's iPad on his lap. He tapped the screen then rose and came across to Viktor, tapped the screen again and a grainy, hurriedly taken photograph came up on the Twitter feed. 'A witness took this then posted it on social media.'

Frowning, Viktor leaned sideways and squinted at the images on the screen: an upturned police van and a man staring ferociously into the lens, his shoulders hunched over, his right leg soaked in blood.

Steve Flynn.

'He ran away but the cops arrested him a short time later.'

'Where is he now?'

'In hospital under armed guard. Once he's discharged he'll be taken to a police station for questioning.'

'So we know exactly where he is at this moment in time?'

Niko nodded. 'Gjon walked past his room in Blackpool's Victoria Hospital. Saw him through the door, cops either side.'

Viktor absorbed this. 'You said two things.'

'Mr and Mrs Jackson have arrived. Their private jet touched down an hour ago. Mikel picked them up from the airport. They're getting some sleep.'

'Have they brought the prize?'

'Yes, yes, they have.'

FOUR

I t was one of the easiest executions that Mr and Mrs Jackson had ever carried out.

To be fair, most killings were easy, the hard part being

the actual self-will to end someone else's life, either close up and brutal or from a clinical distance. It was that aspect that put real assassins apart from a crowd of wannabes. No matter how sure you were that you could prepare for, then commit murder, and then escape with no conscience to haunt you, many people could not find that last degree of courage to do the deed. It was not something that could be learned; it had to be in you from an early age – the ability to take life and enjoy it.

The majority of killings committed by the Jacksons were close-up and personal – often because they were contracted to make them that way – and were often preceded by a period during which the target (read: victim) was held captive in a state of terror before the final event that was the brutal death.

The relationship between the Jacksons had begun, accidentally, many years before when they had been neighbours, kids together at school, just good buddies.

Neither bore the name Jackson at that time.

Matthew Ainsworth and Elizabeth Barnes. Two northern kids, normal kids – Matt and Lizzie.

Their close connection came about when they were at junior school, through a meeting of minds and just one shared look into each other's eyes when, aged only eight, they realized they were on the same wavelength.

Lizzie had spotted Matt in one corner of the school playground, studying something intently in the grass. Up to that point in their short lives, they had not really spoken to each other, but Lizzie, intrigued by the object of Matt's infatuation, had stopped her furious skipping and wandered over with the rope in her hands.

'What you doing?'

Matt was startled. He flipped guiltily on to his bottom, clamping the palms of his hands together to hide something. 'Nowt.' He squinted up at her pretty face.

'You are, I can see you are,' she teased him. 'It's in your hands. What is it?'

Matt glanced furtively around. No one seemed to be taking any notice of them.

Carefully, he revealed his treasure.

The long, slim body of a daddy-long-legs, minus its legs but with its wings still intact and quivering weakly.

It was alive, and Matt imagined he could hear it screaming.

Lizzie gasped. 'You're torturing it!'

'Yeah.'

He looked into her eyes. They sparkled with glee and in that moment he knew she was just as into it as he was.

He proffered the suffering insect to her in the palm of his left hand. 'Here, pull its wings off.'

She dropped the skipping rope, and with her forefinger and thumb she gently took hold of the fluttering, gossamer wings to stop them flapping.

Then tore them off.

Matt's smile was jerky yet genuine. He had a new friend.

'He screamed, you know?' Matt said.

'I know. I could hear him within me.'

Matt curled his hand tightly around the limbless, wingless, helpless tube that was the body of the unfortunate insect and crushed it, relishing the sensation of ultimate power – to take life.

They were twelve years old when they killed their first human being.

Four years of unexplained animal deaths in their neighbourhood culminated in the horrific murder of a forty-five-year-old man.

But, they often argued between themselves for years after, he actually deserved to die. Clearly, they knew that the killing of another person would happen at some stage in their lives, but it was circumstance that propelled them to commit their first murder.

For once, they had been playing fairly innocently on a marshy patch of ground close to the housing estate on which they lived. It was during an idyllic, baking-hot summer and they were both in shorts and T-shirts wading into the water, catching sticklebacks with fishing nets and plopping them into water-filled jam jars; later they intended to perform autopsies on the fish after first having killed them by a variety of methods from simple suffocation to beheading. Matt had even smuggled two sharp knives out of his mum's kitchen and into his father's shed, which would act as the mortuary.

The marshy pond, known locally as The Swanee – for reasons no one could explain – had two footpaths running either side of it, and as the two kids played in the reeds they noticed a man walking along the path on the opposite side from where they were but paid him little heed – until he appeared a few minutes later on the banking just above where they were splashing around.

They stopped, shaded their eyes from the sun and looked at him.

Matt thought he was dressed like a workman. He had baggy jeans streaked with white paint and a bulky zip-up jacket over a blue denim shirt. He had thick, greasy black hair and was unshaven.

'Hi, kids, what're you up to?' he called affably, but even then Matt sensed the man was not quite right, a danger.

Lizzie also frowned at him. 'Just fishing,' she answered and turned away.

Matt continued to watch him through narrowed eyes.

'Caught anything?' The man's voice was raspy.

'A few sticklebacks.'

'Let me see.'

The two jam jars were balanced on a rock jutting out of the water. The little fish swam around in circles.

'They're here,' Matt said.

'Bring 'em here.'

Matt shook his head and saw a strange look come over the man's face.

'Bring them here,' he said again. 'And both of you, come here and sit down.' He pointed. 'Next to me.'

Matt swallowed and exchanged a worried look with Lizzie, who was standing tensely now. She picked up the jars by the string handles she had fashioned around the necks and waded slowly through the water to the sandy bank. Matt was behind her.

'Put them down here,' the man said, 'and you sit either side of me.' He lowered himself to the ground and patted it. The children cautiously sat either side of him.

'I think we need to go,' Matt said. His voice was thin and afraid.

'No, no, I don't think so,' the man said.

Matt's mouth moved slightly, no words coming out. The man regarded him threateningly.

'Have you ever had the belt?' he asked Lizzie.

'What do you mean?' She swallowed.

'Have you been leathered? With a belt, is what I mean.'

'No.'

'Then had salt put on the wound?'

'No.'

'So that it's excruciatingly painful?' The man smiled and touched the inside of Lizzie's left thigh. She recoiled as if electrocuted, but he grabbed her flesh in his hand and dragged her towards him. 'Well, it's going to happen.'

Matt shot back up to his feet. He had spotted a woman walking along the path on the other side of the marsh. 'That's my mum,' he said convincingly.

'Where?' Suddenly the man was worried.

'There!' Matt said and shouted, cupping his hands around his mouth. 'Mum, mum!' It was too far for even his amplified voice to carry but he continued with his pretence. 'We're going to meet her at the Spar on Thwaites Road.'

He acted then, swooped down past the man and grabbed Lizzie's spindly arm, hauled her to her feet and dragged her along the path, leaving the man scrambling up the sand bank. They thought he would chase them, but when Matt looked around after about fifty metres of running he was nowhere to be seen, having scurried away in the opposite direction.

Gagging for breath, both kids stood doubled over with their hands on their knees, looking at each other, both thinking the same thing.

It was Lizzie who voiced their thoughts.

'We should kill him.'

They easily tracked him down, then took their time.

He lived alone in a grotty terraced house, seemed to have no friends and they had little problem in learning about him. Watching his comings and goings. Seeing him lurking around entrances to infant schools, the town swimming pool and around children's play areas.

They even saw him snatch a young child who managed to wriggle free from his clutches. He scuttled away before the kid's mother saw him.

His name was David Carson and he was going to die, strangled by his own belt, covered in salt.

Matt and Lizzie planned it carefully, neither swaying from their course of action and, when the time came, one night when they watched Carson stumble home drunk, they broke into his house to find him face down, asleep on his disgusting bed. Lizzie knelt on his back; Matt ripped the leather belt off Carson's trousers, slid it round his neck and throttled him. They poured a packet of salt over his head.

He was not missed, being discovered four months later, his body having almost rotted away to nothing. A half-hearted police investigation concluded that local paedophile David Carson had been murdered by a vigilante and no one in uniform came knocking on Matt or Lizzie's front door.

By that time they had killed a second time and were on a roll.

A dozen years later, their undoubted skills were on offer and used by the highest bidders until their progression put them in touch with the Bashkim family, to whom they were exclusively contracted and their latest killing had been simple and great fun.

The target had been easy to apprehend and then murder by hacking off her head in front of the cameras, because as Viktor Bashkim had said, 'This is very personal to me.'

Matt and Lizzie had been pretty exhausted by the time they landed in Zante and were glad to be met and whisked away from the airport by a waiting car and on to Viktor's luxurious motor yacht where they could start to relax and chill out in their own time before having to appear in front of the old man.

When eventually they wandered on to deck they were dressed elegantly, Matt in loose-fitting linen trousers and a shirt, espadrilles on his feet, Lizzie in a fine chiffon dress through which the slim but curvaceous lines of her body could be seen, much to Matt's delight.

A table was set for them on the lower rear deck – the location, unbeknownst to them but which would have given them a thrill, where a man had been beaten to death only hours earlier – and a servant brought them champagne, oysters and lobster which they devoured voraciously, slurping and giggling as they consumed the delicious food.

After eating, they took their drinks to the back of the boat and lounged sophisticatedly against the rail, looking at the pretty port and clinking their fine champagne flutes.

Viktor chose this time to appear.

Nothing was said as Matt lifted a large picnic cool box made of polypropylene on to the dining table, flipped the locking mechanism and raised the lid.

Viktor looked in at Maria Santiago's severed head nestling on a bed of crushed ice, her face staring upwards at him, distorted and bloody, one eye open, the other half closed diagonally, her once-gorgeous mouth twisted and her tongue protruding through her lips.

Viktor looked at the killers.

'Depending on how this goes,' he told them, 'you might have to bring me another head.'

Steve Flynn looked at his face in the mirror affixed to the wall above the washbasin, not really recognizing the battered reflection, nor liking it.

'Get on with it,' a voice behind him said.

Flynn's eyes flickered and focused on the figure of the armed officer who had taken over the watch from Molly Cartwright, who, as Flynn had instinctively predicted, he would not become great friends with.

After Molly's departure, Flynn had slept for a long time thanks to a further input of drugs. A dark sleep, no dreams this time, and he had woken feeling more refreshed than before. Still in pain, still stressed, but physically a touch improved, though still emotionally unstable.

Flynn realized he needed to get moving, to start to stretch his limbs and muscles, to get himself in action again, and being chained to a bed was not the best way to recuperate.

When a nurse came in to check his drip and vitals and make him comfortable, he refused a bed bath and requested a proper shower instead. She didn't have a problem with it – but he was still hooked up to the monitors and drip, although the urinary catheter and tube from his leg wound had been removed, so he would have to somehow shower while still attached to the drip.

The armed cop, by the name of Mike Guthrie, was not happy.

'I'm beginning to reek,' Flynn argued. 'I've not been discharged,

I'm still a patient and I want a shower. Speak to Superintendent Dean. He'll OK it.' Flynn glared at Guthrie, and then smiled sweetly at the nurse and urged her, 'Tell him.'

'He really needs to start moving,' she said on the prompt.

'I'll check,' Guthrie said unenthusiastically.

'Thanks,' Flynn said to the nurse. 'Any chance of a bite to eat, too? I know it's not feeding time . . .'

'I'll see what I can rustle up,' she promised.

Guthrie stood aside for her to leave the room, then straddled the threshold of the open door as he called Rik Dean via his personal radio, which also doubled as a mobile phone as well as having the facility to dial up other officers directly by just inputting their collar numbers.

The other officer stationed in the corridor watched impassively.

Flynn didn't like him much, either.

Flynn listened, up to the point where Guthrie came over, held out the radio and said, 'Mr Dean wants to talk to you.'

Flynn took it and said, 'Hello.'

'Flynn?' Rik Dean said, his voice sounding strained. 'Have your fucking shower, but promise me you won't do anything nuts – like do a runner.'

'I won't. Not capable, as you know, having been seriously wounded.'

'Give the radio back to the officer.'

'One thing,' Flynn said quickly.

'What's that?'

'Going to need clothing. What I had on won't do. All bloody and I guess you'll want it for forensic anyway?'

'There's a zoot suit on its way up to you for when you're discharged.'

'Shit. Thanks a mill.'

Flynn handed the radio back to Guthrie.

Some food came for him – a red-hot microwaved Cornish pasty, which he wolfed down with a mug of tea that tasted like nectar.

After this he looked plaintively at Guthrie, then rattled the hand-cuff around his wrist, clanking it on the bed frame. 'The shower won't come to me.'

Clearly unhappy, the PC released him and the nurse disconnected him from his monitors and drips, saying he should be OK to take a shower because of the cannula in the back of his hand, but would need to be hooked up as soon as he was back in bed. Flynn sat upright, stiffly, on the edge of the bed, carefully allowing his feet to dangle. The nurse covered the dressing over the gunshot with a waterproof bandage, then Flynn slid apprehensively on to his feet, swaying slightly as he got his balance and winced with the pain from the wound which, so far, had not had any pressure on it since the operation.

He sat back down again quickly.

Guthrie grinned at him. 'Bed bath?' he suggested.

'Uh-huh, shower time,' Flynn said and pushed himself determinedly back upright.

The shower room was a little further down the corridor and it was here, with sour-faced Guthrie standing behind him, that Flynn was taking a long, considered look at his reflection, interrupted by the officer's impatient geeing-on.

'Privacy,' Flynn said.

'Not gonna be any of that,' Guthrie snorted. He had apparently taken a dislike to Flynn, as Flynn had to him, so the feelings were mutual. There was no particular reason for it, it simply existed.

'Fine,' Flynn said haughtily. He pulled the fastening of the surgical gown. It split open down the back to reveal his buttocks, then he allowed it to slide to the floor and pool around his ankles. He stepped out of the circle of the material, glanced at Guthrie, gave him a salacious wink as his genitals swung loosely into view – Guthrie rolling his eyes at the gesture – and stepped into the shower cubicle that Guthrie had checked for any possible weapons. There was only a bar of harsh, unscented soap.

At first, the water was freezing cold. Flynn jolted with the icy chill, but gradually it heated up and Flynn lifted his face into the jets and allowed the hot water to mingle with his tears as his thoughts once more turned to Maria Santiago. Then to grief, then rage, then revenge.

Flynn was a man who was unlikely to sit back and wallow because he knew, as he had told Rik Dean, that what he was involved in was far from over. He knew if he did not end it now

– somehow – he would be looking over his shoulder for the rest of his life, because that was how the Bashkims operated.

PC Molly Cartwright struggled to get Steve Flynn off her mind. Although she had only just met him and under very inauspicious circumstances, she had seen something kind and generous in him, together with the fact he was a bit of a bronzed specimen and a scarred alley cat in wolf's clothing.

Not that there was any way she could even contemplate getting involved with him other than professionally, but she was definitely drawn to him, even though he had committed the cold-blooded murder of a man in police custody.

But was it so cold-blooded?

Actually it was hot-blooded, driven by passion and anger, and although Molly would never admit it verbally, Brian Tasker had got exactly what he deserved. Surely any court in the land would see that. Yes, Flynn would have to be convicted of the offence but should be allowed to walk free from court under the circumstances.

Now, if that happened, maybe she could start to think of Flynn in a different way.

All silly conjecture, she chided herself.

First of all, she had her own personal problems to sort out, namely in the guise of DS Alan Hardiker.

Molly admitted to herself she was a poor judge of men. She should sever all connection with Alan and then take a vow of celibacy for about ten years.

On handing over the responsibility to guard Flynn to another armed crew (including Mike Guthrie, whom she loathed), Molly had driven with her partner, Robbo, back to Blackpool nick and booked herself as off-duty. Her own car was parked on the secure police-only section of the multi-storey car park adjacent to the station, accessed by leaving the nick on the first floor, walking across the mezzanine area in front of the magistrates' court and going through a secure gate on to the parking level.

Her car was at the far end of a row, necessitating a fairly long, lonely walk in the poorly-lit concrete edifice to her ancient British racing green Mini Cooper.

She thought nothing of it. She'd done it a zillion times there and back in the ten years she'd been in the cops, based in Blackpool for all that period of time.

It was only when the shape materialized from the darkness behind her car that she suddenly felt vulnerable.

'You scared me,' she told Alan Hardiker coldly as his face came clear of the shadow.

'Sorry, sorry,' he muttered meekly. 'Didn't mean to.'

'Yeah, well, blokes hiding behind cars tend to do that.'

She unlocked the driver's door.

'We need to talk,' he said. His apologetic voice had vanished.

'Alan, you slept with at least two other members of staff and I'm pretty sure you've also been sifting money from my bank account. When my statement comes this week, I'm going to go through it with a fine-tooth comb. You've been using my debit card, haven't you?'

'Just for bits,' he admitted. 'We're a fucking couple, aren't we?'

'No,' she said contemptuously. 'We're not a couple and we're certainly not fucking.' She opened her car door an inch. 'I'm going home, and don't you dare turn up.'

He moved quickly and forced the door shut. His right hand shot up to Molly's neck. He gripped her windpipe with his fingers, spun her around and crashed her hard against the car, pushing his pulsing red face up to hers, spittle flicking from his lips, terrifying her.

'We are a couple,' he hissed. 'We help each other out.'

She struggled to break free but he forced himself right up to her, keeping his fingers locked on her throat. She started to feel weak but then, with a surge of power generated by self-preservation, she manoeuvred her right leg between his and rammed her knee up, driving it hard and accurately.

He bellowed in agony, released the grip and sagged away, covering his groin with both hands as he doubled over. 'Bitch!'

'The old ones are the best. It's over,' she informed him. 'End of.'

She yanked open the door and dropped in. The Mini screeched away on the shiny concrete floor, leaving Hardiker down on one knee, watching the back of the car swerve down into the exit ramp.

'I'll make you pay for that, I so fucking will.'

He stood up slowly, slid his right hand down the front of his trousers and tenderly cradled his throbbing balls.

Flynn stood under the shower, eyes closed, now thinking about his recent past and his unsolicited connection with the Bashkim crime family from Albania, a road down which he had not wanted to travel.

They had initially moved in on his boss, Adam Castle, who had been the co-owner of the sportfishing charter boat that Flynn skippered in Puerto Rico, Gran Canaria. Adam had got into bad business debts but had turned to the wrong people for help – the Bashkims. His attempts to wriggle free had ended in his own brutal murder and Flynn being wrongly accused of it, which was the point at which Flynn met Maria Santiago, one of the detectives on the case. Flynn had found himself drawn deeply into the Bashkim web and had dealt with the situation as only he knew how – meeting force with greater force and ultimately being involved in the deaths of some Bashkim family members, as well as taking the opportunity to raze to the ground some of the Bashkim's seedier operations in the UK. He had also blown up and destroyed millions of dollars en route to the crime family from a Mexican drug cartel.

Naively, perhaps, Flynn had thought this was the end of the game, but as he'd delved into the violent deaths of some of his former cop colleagues who had formed the squad responsible for bringing down a man called Brian Tasker, Flynn had discovered that Tasker had got into league with the Bashkims, and together they had targeted Flynn and murdered Maria Santiago in violent retribution.

Flynn had been forced, via an Internet video link, to witness Maria's horrific death, watch her being decapitated and her head dangling in front of the lens, taunting him in the moments prior to his own death at the hands of Tasker.

He had been saved by the intervention of an armed police team assembled by Rik Dean, who had arrested Tasker and the duo of Bashkim heavies just before Flynn was about to be killed.

Although injured – he had been incapacitated by Tasker, who had shot him in the leg – Flynn had assaulted Rik Dean to cause a diversion which he used to climb into the back of the police van that Tasker was being held in before being brought into custody at Blackpool. And broken his neck.

Flynn did not regret it.

He was slightly sorry for headbutting Rik Dean's lights out, but that was about it. Minor collateral damage, he supposed.

He was definitely not sorry about Tasker, who deserved to die a slow, lingering death rather than the quick one Flynn had gifted him.

Now, somehow, Flynn knew he had to find a way to conclude this horrible mess.

'Oi, hurry up,' PC Guthrie called, interrupting Flynn's shower-time recollections. The officer was still impatient, making Flynn like him even less.

Flynn picked up the bar of soap, rubbed it between his palms to make a lather and applied it to his scalp in lieu of shampoo, carefully massaging his battered skull.

There were certain things he had to do.

Up to that point, his conflict with the Bashkims had been simply in reaction to their actions. He knew a little about them but obviously not enough, and he had to change that somehow. Get to know his enemy, take the fight to them and either destroy them or make them see sense.

He guessed it would come down to option number one.

It had to be intelligence-led. The question was where did he source that intelligence from?

Once upon a time, he could have called on the skills of a certain DC Jerry Tope, his old friend and Lancashire Constabulary intelligence analyst. But Tope had been on Tasker's hit list and that avenue was no longer open to Flynn – to search police databases. He could do his own Internet searches, and indeed had done so, but there was no real depth to those findings. He needed deep intelligence, naming people and places, and he wasn't sure he could achieve that alone.

As he had revealed to Molly Cartwright, he'd once been a detective sergeant in the drug branch, but that was a long time ago. He had a network of contacts and informants which was also dated. No doubt some of the major players still existed, but he guessed he needed to speak to some of the new kids on the block and break their fingers for information.

He let the shower run for a few more seconds, then stepped out naked and smiled genuinely at Guthrie, who looked ready to shoot him.

FIVE

I t took over half an hour for the pain in Alan Hardiker's testicles and lower gut to subside. He had considered following Molly back to her flat but dismissed it as a bad idea. One phone call from her to report his stalking her would be counterproductive. Not that he couldn't have smarmed his way out of any allegation she desired to chuck at him, but it was something he did not need at this moment in time.

Maybe later.

He shuffled back to the police station, trying his best to walk normally. He took the lift up to the dining room, grabbed a mug of coffee and some toast, then sat alone at a table next to one of the floor-to-ceiling windows with a view of Blackpool Tower and took out his little black book.

At other tables, a few uniformed cops were discussing the case surrounding Steve Flynn and Brian Tasker.

Hardiker half-listened to the uninformed chatter.

Instead, with a great degree of trepidation, he opened the moleskin notebook, read it, closed it and shut his eyes.

Like many gambling addicts, he kept a close watch on his outgoings and winnings.

His debt, in other words.

His debt to several unsavoury characters operating in the underworld of Blackpool who did not care one jot he was a cop.

A debt of £19,642.45 overrode that.

Without doubt, unless he began to seriously service the debt then very soon he would be visited one cold, stormy Blackpool night by nasty men brandishing baseball bats and not afraid to use them.

And that debt did not include the ridiculous amount he owed to three payday loan companies whose astronomical interest rates were crippling him mentally, whereas the baseball bats would cripple him medically.

His coffee tasted bitter, his toast like cardboard. He consumed them perfunctorily, then stood up gingerly and walked back to the lift which he had to share with three uniforms still chattering about Flynn, Tasker and the two supposedly Albanian nationals in custody, suspected of murders surrounding the Flynn/Tasker debacle.

It was nothing to do with Hardiker, professionally speaking. He was just a jobbing detective sergeant with few ambitions now, other than to feather his own nest. But as his ears homed in on some parts of the conversation about the Albanian mafia and rumours about their wealth, he became interested. The chatter went on to some rumours that there was a bounty on Flynn's head for the things he had done to a certain Albanian clan called the Bashkims.

The lift doors opened. The uniformed cops stepped out, leaving Hardiker alone. He pressed the button to take him down to the basement level where the custody office was located.

His mind churned, working out the angles, the threats, the benefits, because if what he had overheard was true, maybe there was something in this for him – but he would have to be clever and quick.

The lift jarred to the ground; the doors opened with agonizing slowness. Hardiker stepped out, turned right then left into the narrow corridor leading to the custody office and beyond to the rear exit of the nick.

Just before he reached the gate to the custody office, it swung open and a very stressed-looking Rik Dean came out, deep in conversation with a detective constable who Hardiker knew had been drafted on to the Flynn/Tasker investigation because of his interview skills.

Hardiker stood aside as Rik Dean and the DC shouldered their way past him without acknowledgement, even though Hardiker gave Rik a nod and a 'Boss,' getting just a passing glance from the superintendent.

Hardiker caught the gate before it closed and swivelled into the custody office which was, as ever in the case of the Blackpool custody office sausage machine, heaving with bodies. The holding cage was crammed; four prisoners were queued at the desk with their arresting officers, waiting to be processed.

Good, Hardiker thought, knowing that the best place to hide was in plain sight.

He scanned the prisoner board. Most cells were occupied.

The ones that interested him were the two cells on opposite sides of the complex, as far away from each other as it was possible to be. Each one had the name 'Bashkim' felt-tipped next to it, both with question marks by the names.

Hardiker's eyes flashed around the busy room.

Two custody sergeants were busy at the desk. Two gaolers were in and out of the cells' corridor, keys jangling.

Hardiker collared one, a civilian in a pseudo-cop uniform. His name badge said Gary something-or-other. He had been in the job six months or so and aspired to be a real cop one day.

'One of the Bashkims, the one in cell twenty-two?' Hardiker said, pointing at the board.

'Yes, boss?'

'Can you bring him to the fingerprint room? Superintendent Dean says he needs to be printed, photographed and DNA'd. Given me the job.' Hardiker tutted and rolled his eyes, as though this was beneath him.

'Yeah, OK,' Gary said, a little flustered. He patted his pockets for the cell keys and found them actually dangling from the fob on his belt.

'I'll come with you.'

'You need to put an entry on the custody record.'

'Yeah, yeah.'

Gary dived back through the door into the cell corridor, which was a low, oppressive place with an almost medieval pall to it. It was grubby and smelly in the way in which only a cell corridor can be, reeking of sweat and piss, a pungent odour. Gary led Hardiker to the cell at the far end of the complex.

Bashkim – if that was his name – was a young, sour-faced man, tired looking with a very shiny, swollen left eye.

He was alone in the cell, dressed in a white forensic suit, elasticated slippers and nothing else. All his possessions had been seized for evidential purposes. He scowled at the two men as the door opened, reminding Hardiker of a trapped rodent – back against the wall but still capable of inflicting a nasty bite.

Hardiker beckoned with a crooked finger. 'With me.' The prisoner rose uncertainly. 'Follow me.'

With the prisoner between gaoler and cop, the trio trooped along the corridor and into the Fingerprint/Photographic/DNA suite, grandly titled but just a cramped, grimy room off the main custody office.

Once the prisoner was seated, Hardiker gave Gary the nod to leave, then looked at Bashkim as the door closed behind the gaoler.

'Now then, lad . . . there's very little I can do for you person-ally,' he said without any foreplay, 'but we might still be able to assist each other. How does that sound?'

Molly slept fitfully that morning after leaving Flynn and her contretemps with Hardiker, although the satisfying crunch of her knee up into her ex's balls was quite pleasing.

After about four hours of tossing and turning, she decided enough was enough, got out of bed and went for a run. She lived, following her divorce, in a one-bedroom flat on the first floor of a large house on the seafront in Bispham, just north of Blackpool, next stop Cleveleys. It was a slightly shabby place but in a great position and it belonged entirely to her. It was all she could afford at the time.

Hardiker had half moved in but now she was back to being alone, which suited her for the moment.

It was a great location to run from, along the seafront in either direction, and that day she chose to jog north, a four-mile round trip, ending up back under her shower, still unable to shake off the thought of Steve Flynn until she chided herself as the suds cascaded from her hair. *Apart from anything else, he's, like, twice your age, lass.*

Flynn had been glad to get back into bed from the excursion to the shower, but he did exaggerate his pain for the sake of his captive audience, PC Guthrie, complaining and whining about the handcuff which had gone back on as soon as he was on the bed, saying it was too tight, biting into his wrist, even though it wasn't. As Guthrie wrestled with the ratchet to open it slightly, the officer's Glock was tantalizingly close and Flynn was almost tempted to disarm him and snatch it.

As if Guthrie had read his mind, he gave Flynn a knowing look as he adjusted the cuff, then backed away and said, 'Yeah, right . . . love you to try that.'

'I won't be doing,' Flynn had promised, settling back on to his pillows and closing his eyes.

Hardiker was kept busy throughout the day with the normal workload of a DS, which in Blackpool was enormous. Even so, his mind continually drifted back to his conversation with the prisoner.

If he could find the courage, the compensation could be considerable.

Flynn dozed most of the day. He was visited by the surgeon, who had performed the operation on him and who was pleased the procedure had gone so well. He made Flynn grimace with pain as he prodded and squeezed around the sutures, then declared, 'All good.'

'When do I leave?'

'Because of the nature of the wound, I want to keep you in another day for observation and, if everything is OK this time tomorrow, you can go.'

Flynn thanked him for his handiwork.

He ate between sleep, then, when his eyes flickered open after a longish snooze, his bodyguards had changed and Molly Cartwright had returned. She was sitting on her customary chair by the door, ready for Flynn to wake.

He grinned at her but winced when he moved his wounded leg, which had tightened while he'd been asleep. Even so, it was feeling much better, as was his burst eardrum, now just a slight throb and hum.

Molly looked at him. 'How are you feeling?'

'OK . . . All the better for seeing you,' he said, and could have sworn she blushed. So he added, 'That PC Guthrie isn't my cup of tea.' He paused. 'How's the boyfriend – the lovely Alan with the moustache?'

A wicked grin came to her lips. 'I was forced to take action,' she said. 'I'll leave it at that.'

'Good. He's a shit,' Flynn said.

'You don't know the half of it,' she said, gently rubbing her neck. 'Anyway, you get taken into custody tomorrow.'

'This could be my last night of freedom.' He rattled the hand-cuff. 'If you let me go.'

Hardiker finished his day at 6.30 p.m. almost a nervous wreck, but kept it together until he reached his car in the police car park. When he sat in it, he felt his body turn into a form of jelly, but then it became tense again when he spotted Molly's Mini Cooper in the row opposite, about four cars down, and saw an opportunity.

Other than for vehicles, the car park was deserted, and he knew he had a little chance for some very peevish revenge here.

Slipping out of his seat, he went around to the back of his car and rooted out the tyre jack from his boot. He crept across to Molly's car, crouched down behind it, waited to ensure he was definitely alone, then rose to his full height and, in one fluid moment, smashed the jack into the back window of the Mini. The window did not disintegrate but cracked like a spider's web.

That was enough. Point made.

Hardiker knew enough about glass fragments from broken windows to realize he could put himself in an indefensible forensic position if he smashed the window completely. There would be minute particles of broken glass all over his clothing and in the soles of his shoes which he would not be able to see or brush off but which a scientist could find easily. He had convicted a lot of people that way.

As much as he would have liked to go completely berserk and do all the windows, he left it at that, then ran back to his own car at a crouch.

He had someone to meet.

Flynn was getting impatient. He was a man of action, not reflec-tion, and being shackled to the bed was starting to grate on him. He was achieving nothing in hospital and realized he might even be better off in the custody system, from which he could plan an escape. He knew there would be several chances, although he also knew that the best chance of all would be when he was being transferred between the hospital and the police station. From his own experience as a cop he knew that police officers were a bit slapdash when it came to escorting prisoners, even though it was a bread-and-butter part of their job.

He looked at Molly.

The problem was that an escape from police custody usually included violence and he did not want to hurt her if she ended up with the job of transferring him to the nick, although he didn't have the same dilemma with her partner, Robbo, or preferably PC Guthrie if it happened to be him.

She was still sat on the chair. They had been sitting in silence for a while, just occasionally letting their eyes catch.

'I checked up on you,' she said eventually.

'Really?'

'Rumour is you left under a cloud because, apparently, you helped yourself to a million pounds in cash belonging to a drug dealer.'

'I wish,' Flynn said. He had no great desire to elaborate.

'Then you went on to become the skipper of a sportfishing boat down in the Canary Islands. It all fits. A million quid. The lifestyle.'

He guffawed. 'I worked for someone. It wasn't my boat. I lived hand to mouth, still do. I crashed in other people's flats and villas – still do, more or less . . .'

She regarded him sceptically. 'But you own a boat now,' she accused him.

'Yeah, I do . . . and if your enquiries take you anywhere, you'll find I've been working hard in Ibiza all summer trying to make ends meet by helping a pal who owns a day charter business, taking tourists out on day trips around the island. Not really my preferred option, Molly. I work hard and don't make much money. A sportfishing boat is an expensive mistress.'

'It is a nice life, though?' she inquired dreamily.

'Up to the point where Albanian crime families come sticking their noses in and won't take no for an answer, it can be.' He looked at her and decided on a cheeky punt. 'You know, I could do with finding out more about the Bashkims.' He yawned, trying

to make it sound inconsequential. 'All I've done so far is react
. . . I could do with a strategy.'

Her expression informed him how clearly unimpressed she
was. 'Any chance you could delve into the constabulary's intel
database for me? Was that going to be your next question?' she
probed, mimicking him. 'No, I fucking can't.' She answered her
own question.

'OK . . . however, you could tell me who the biggest drug
dealer is in town, couldn't you?' he asked hopefully. 'That
wouldn't be breaching any confidences, would it?'

'I could, yeah – but I'm not going to, so stop asking.'

With some trepidation, Hardiker relived the tense, bladder-
emptying moments spent earlier that day in the fingerprint room
with the young prisoner. To make it as realistic as possible, just
in case there was some comeback, he did take the lad's fingerprints, a photo and a DNA swab from inside his mouth. Then
he'd sat down opposite, pretending to take his antecedent history
but instead had a very cagey conversation with him.

Hardiker looked him in the eye.

'I hear your family wants to kill Steve Flynn in retribution for
the bad things Flynn has done to them.'

The lad did not flinch. At that moment he only believed he
was being tricked. He said nothing.

'I know you're saying you don't understand much English,
but I know that is a lie.'

'Solicitor,' the prisoner said.

'You don't need one, not with me.'

The lad's eyes remained blank and unreadable.

After a pause, an intake of breath and a swallowing of something that tasted quite appalling, Hardiker whispered, 'I can give
you Steve Flynn.'

Sitting in his car later, the engine ticking over, the heater
keeping his toes warm, Hardiker shuddered at the memory of
those words. The moment when he'd crossed the line. When he'd
thought he was still in control but had, in reality, stepped off a
precipice and was plummeting through space.

He was parked behind an empty industrial unit now on Marton
Moss Side, not far from the actual end of the M55 motorway,

where it fizzled out from three lanes into one and became Yeadon Way, the old railway line, now a main road into Blackpool.

His car was an old, four-door Micra – clear evidence of his financial decline as he'd had to trade in his treasured VW Golf GTi for the Nissan, which reminded him of a mobile biscuit tin. He claimed to his colleagues that he'd ordered a new GTi but there was a four-month waiting list for the spec he wanted and a large cash deposit was required.

He had been instructed to leave all the doors of the car unlocked.

The next moment in which he had almost peed himself in the fingerprint room had been when he'd handed his iPhone to the prisoner and then stood at the door with his back to the window, just in case anyone peered in and wondered what was going on – a prisoner using a mobile phone.

'Shit,' Hardiker breathed, sitting in his car, reminiscing.

He had been watching, keeping an eye on the rear-view mirrors, but the man who yanked open the back offside door and dropped in behind the driver's seat must have approached in a blind spot.

Instantly Hardiker smelled the reek of body odour and strong cigarette smoke.

Then he felt the barrel of an automatic pistol being screwed into his neck, and then the hot, garlic breath of the man leaning forwards and speaking into his ear.

An exhausted Rik Dean appeared in Flynn's hospital room at 6 a.m. the following morning.

Flynn and Molly had spent the night in strained silence following his completely inappropriate requests for information.

He had dozed sporadically but she had remained alert and awake, fuming about what Flynn had asked of her – to search the intel database to unearth as much information as possible about the Bashkims. Actually, she doubted she would have got very deep into it anyway as her access was fairly restricted. She also guessed there wouldn't be much to find as still not much was known about organized gangs from Europe at her level, and most police investigations into them were carried out by specialist squads anyway.

So she had taken a wary step back from Flynn.

In turn, he realized he had offended her.

He went through the night feeling the pain in his leg worsen again as the analgesics wore off, but he put off calling a nurse for some more pain relief, please, until the last possible moment.

The nurse came in just behind Rik.

She checked the patient over, then handed him a couple of very large tablets to swallow with water and began to dismantle the drips and strip the electrodes from his chest.

Rik watched, unsmiling.

'What's happening?' Flynn asked, a little groggy.

'I've spoken to the surgeon and you've been discharged,' Rik told him. 'As of now you are very much in custody and, just so we're clear, you are under arrest on suspicion of murder. You do not have to say anything unless you wish to do so, but it may harm your defence if you do not say anything now which you later rely on in court. Understand?'

Flynn's insides did a tricky somersault.

He said nothing. It wasn't the first time he'd been cautioned, but he didn't like it.

Unless he escaped, this was now the beginning of what was likely to be a long process and his options were starting to disappear. Once in the justice system, as he was sure he would be, because bail is never given by the police to someone on a murder charge, he would more than likely end up on remand, incarcerated until his trial, unless a court allowed him bail, which was pretty unlikely. Flynn also knew that he would be vulnerable in this period, too. People like the Bashkims had a lot of influence and, although Flynn was hard and mean enough to stand the rigours of prison life, he would also have to be on guard every minute of every day, because not even he could survive a blade between the ribs. If a contract was put out for him, inmates would be queuing up to skewer him. He assumed he would be a good payday for any shit-head wannabe desperate to make his mark. So his earlier musing that he might be better off on remand didn't seem such a good idea when properly analysed.

The nurse finished her tasks and left the room.

Rik dropped a square package on the over-bed tray. 'You need to put these on.'

Flynn looked at the package. It was the promised forensic – zoot – suit and slippers. His mouth twisted.

'Just so you know, I've spent a lot of time talking to the Spanish cops and the FBI, who have suddenly shown an interest in events . . .'

'Karl Donaldson?' Flynn asked.

Rik shrugged with a gesture that told Flynn he had no great desire to say too much. Then he sighed. 'Look, let's get you to the nick, get you booked in and then you can start telling me your story . . .'

'You know my fucking story,' Flynn blurted.

'Finished?' Rik said crossly like a primary school teacher. Flynn nodded. 'Good. Let's get it all on tape and paper – I mean everything – and I promise you I'll get the CPS to speak to your brief and put your side of it fully and without too much of a challenge from us.'

'I don't have a brief,' Flynn said.

'Well, you're going to need one. You know we'll provide a duty solicitor for you.'

Flynn nodded. It was one of his rights as a defendant – free legal representation.

'It's a big operation, all this, and I've got to pull it all together,' Rik went on.

Flynn couldn't help but chuckle mirthlessly.

'What's so funny?'

'And the result will be?' he asked, stone-faced. 'I'll tell you. Those two Bashkims you have in custody, if they are Bashkims, will be as far as you'll get. They'll go down for murder and that's where it'll stop, Rik.'

'I . . . I . . .' he stammered. 'It might take time but I vow to dismantle the whole of the Bashkim Empire, at least in the UK, and also bring to justice those who ordered the killings.'

Flynn closed his eyes and sighed irritably. 'Not going to happen. You'll hit a brick wall, but if you do, by some freak of fate, get close to the top of the tree, get ready for a bullet in the back of your head, mate, because that's how they roll.'

'Whatever,' he said uselessly.

'And in the meantime, I'll be sent to prison for life. Now that's real justice.' Flynn leaned forwards earnestly. 'What you need is a headhunter, Rik. Someone who'll give them what they deserve. Someone who'll cut the head off the snake and see the rest of it wither and die.'

'Someone like you?'

'If you insist.'

'Don't be an arse.'

'OK, I won't.' Flynn rattled his handcuffs. 'If you want me to put that zoot suit on, you're going to have to let me go.'

Rik turned to Molly, who had listened silently to the exchange. 'You got the key?'

She crossed the room, digging into her uniform trouser pocket, and stepped in front of Rik, putting herself between the detective and prisoner. Her eyes caught Flynn's as he watched her insert the key and release the cuff firstly on his wrist, then the one around the bed frame. Although the cuff had not been on tight around his wrist, it was a relief to be free. He kneaded his skin gratefully.

'I'll step outside,' she said, backing off with one last glance. Flynn sensed he had a bit of an ally in her but decided not to ask anything more of her. He liked her and did not want to compromise her, and anyway, once he was incarcerated he doubted he would ever see her again. She left the room and her partner, Robbo, stepped in to replace her, although it would not have bothered Flynn for her to see him unclothed.

Neither did it bother him that Rik and the male AFO would see him naked either but, just to wind them up, he made a show of wanting some privacy to get changed into the paper suit and insisted the curtain was drawn around the bed.

He discarded the hospital gown and climbed into the suit, which also came with paper underpants that reminded him of Huggies. The suit was also baggy and unflattering, but he was no fashion icon at the best of times, so wasn't too uptight about his appearance.

'Where's the rest of my gear?' he called from behind the curtain. Before all this had kicked off he had been on his way to Manchester airport to get on a flight to Ibiza to collect his boat from Santa Eulalia. He'd had some hand luggage with a change of clothing in it, and his passport and wallet had been in the hire car he'd been using. 'Passport, money, et cetera,' he said.

'All booked in,' Rik replied.

'I'm going to need some real clothes pretty soon.'

'I'll fix it, no need to worry.'

He drew open the curtain just as Rik leaned out of the door to beckon in the cops who were going to transport him to the police station. Molly re-entered, followed by PC Mike Guthrie and his running partner, whose name Flynn did not know. Guthrie had his rigid handcuffs swinging on his right forefinger and Flynn could see from his expression that he was looking forward to cuffing him.

'Hands out in front,' he told Flynn.

Flynn had one moment of ridiculous seriousness when he considered seeing if he could put them all down, but there were five, four were armed and one was Molly, and there was every possibility of it all going wrong and Molly shooting him in the leg as per her previous promise.

He extended his arms and Guthrie expertly applied the rigid cuffs so his hands were bound in front of him. Guthrie then gripped the rigid bar and gave it a little twist to demonstrate his control over Flynn as the steel cuffs dug into his nerve endings on the inner part of his wrists and sent a jolt of incredible pain up his arms.

He gasped and his whole body submitted.

If Guthrie had continued with the pressure, he could have had Flynn down on his knees, begging for mercy. He was tough but not that tough.

Guthrie almost instantly released the pressure, having proved his point. He was in control. Flynn was his. It was known as pain compliance.

He gave a hard-faced smile and said, 'Are we on the same wavelength?'

'Yes, boss,' Flynn said reluctantly, fighting the urge to call him something he would regret.

He kept hold of the cuffs and turned to Rik, who had watched the little show of power with a half-grin. 'Preston nick?'

'Yes, please.'

Which was news to Flynn. He had expected to be taken to Blackpool, not Preston. He considered asking for the reason, but he understood. Two Bashkims were lodged in Blackpool cells and Rik Dean did not want to risk Flynn going anywhere near them. Taking Flynn to Preston would ensure there would be no possibility whatsoever of him getting his hands on their throats.

SIX

A lot of money had been spent on the frontage of Blackpool Victoria Hospital, giving it an air of slick modernity, although behind the facade of a nice new entrance with coffee shops and a newsagents, the infrastructure was still old and not a little shabby and decrepit.

A new multi-storey car park had been built close-by on the opposite side of the drop-off turning circle outside the main entrance, and Alan Hardiker was sat in his car on the first floor of this new build, looking across the low wall to the big revolving doors.

He had been up all night, ever since his clandestine meeting with a man screwing the barrel of a gun into his neck.

It had been a torrid time and his mind had been in turmoil in one respect, but calm in another.

He had seen Rik Dean arrive at the hospital, park on the ground floor of the multi-storey and scurry over to the entrance. He knew that Dean, like himself, had been up all night but for very different reasons.

A short while after Rik's arrival, a liveried Ford Galaxy had turned up and stopped in the drop-off bay. The two uniformed occupants got out and also went into the hospital. Hardiker recognized them as armed response unit cops, knew both of them well. One was Mike Guthrie who he played five-a-side football with most weeks. Hardiker swallowed a very heavy lump in his throat.

He knew exactly what it was: dread.

He also knew that inside the hospital was Molly Cartwright and Robbo, her ARV partner, and that the plan was to use all four armed officers, in two vehicles, to convey Steve Flynn over to Preston. It had been easy enough for Hardiker, as a DS, to discover all this without really trying, and then pass on the details.

His mind flicked back to the meeting with the man in the deserted industrial park.

Crossing the line.

Easy money.

The information he had passed had netted him £1,000 in very dirty-looking money, crumpled notes probably all tainted with cocaine.

It only made a small dent in his overall debt but at least it was a start, and he had been promised another two grand if the information he gave was genuine and led to Flynn.

He had insisted it would be.

He had also insisted that no cop should be harmed.

The man with the gun had guffawed at this condition as he tossed the wodge of money on to the front seat of Hardiker's car.

The sound of that contemptuous laugh continued to resonate around Hardiker's brain.

So the two sides of the coin: calm and turmoil.

Calm because his debt was at last being serviced; turmoil because four armed cops were about to convey a prisoner the dozen miles or so from Blackpool to Preston and any attempt on that escort was not going to be pretty.

Hardiker fumbled nervously for his mobile phone.

Crossing the line.

The cops kept Flynn waiting while Molly hurried out to her police car, which she had left overnight on the ground floor of the multi-storey, and brought it out to the drop-off at the front of the hospital so there would be no delay in setting off. Flynn could be bundled straight into the Ford Galaxy, put into the back seat alongside Mike Guthrie, and the two vehicles could roll immediately with no need to pause for anything.

Molly walked quickly through the revolving door at the exact moment her personal mobile phone rang.

She kept moving as she checked the screen, which read: Alan xx calling.

She did not answer, thumbed 'end call' and pocketed the device.

*   *   *

From his vantage point, Hardiker saw Molly emerge from the hospital. It was pure coincidence that she exited the building at the moment he called her on his mobile.

She didn't even break her stride as she reached into her pocket, pulled out the phone, saw who was calling, dismissed the call and carried on across towards the car park.

Hardiker ducked back into shadow, watched her entering the ground floor of the car park and go out of sight. He hadn't realized she was parked there; hadn't even thought of looking for a cop car, liveried or otherwise.

He was furious, though, that she had dismissed his call.

'Bitch, I was trying to do you a favour,' he mumbled.

Something in him made him try once more.

'Fucking what?' Molly answered cantankerously as she lowered herself into the unmarked Ford Mondeo, annoyed by his harassment.

'Molly, Molly,' Hardiker cooed cloyingly.

'What? I'm at fucking work. I have a job on – and why are you calling me at this time of day anyway? Why are you fucking calling me at all?'

'I know. I know you're at work, lovey . . . I just . . . just need to see you now. Come on, book off-duty or something . . . say you're ill . . .'

'Yeah, as if I could. I'm about to go on a prisoner escort.'

'I know. Look, I need to see you now . . . just . . .'

'Just what?' She ended the call and started the engine.

Hardiker looked accusingly at his mobile phone screen. He knew he couldn't have directly warned her or told her to be careful as that would have incriminated him.

He heard a car start somewhere below in the car park, heard the squeal of tyres, then saw Molly's Mondeo exit and pull up behind the ARV Galaxy.

She climbed out and stood by the car door, saying something on her radio, waiting for the appearance of the prisoner and his escorts.

'I *did* try,' Hardiker whispered to himself.

* * *

'OK, guys, I'm in position.' Flynn heard Molly's voice on all four personal radios attached to the uniforms of the three firearms officers and the one in Rik Dean's hand.

Guthrie looked Flynn in the eye and mischievously tweaked the rigid bar on the handcuffs just to reiterate his dominance. They all waited for Rik Dean's nod, and then they were on their way.

Flynn wasn't certain what floor of the hospital they were on, but they led him out into the main ward corridor, then out on to a landing to wait for the lift, which they bundled him into, although Rik did not join them. It dropped a couple of floors, clattering to a halt, and the doors opened on to a corridor leading to the hospital exit.

Guthrie kept a firm hold of the cuffs.

The other two guys flanked him like wingmen. Flynn could just about see them out of the corner of his eyes. All three looked to be handy fellows, and he thought that if he kicked off they could probably have flattened him.

They passed a few people in the corridor who couldn't keep their eyes off a prisoner in his forensic suit being led out between sour-faced cops. In the past, he had done the same to many prisoners and not really cared about how they felt as individuals, and he assumed the same applied to the guys escorting him. He was just a package to be delivered, nothing more.

They reached a set of stairs with an escalator to one side and once more they took the easy option, the moving stairs down to the foyer. Guthrie had to be one step in front to keep a grip of the cuffs and had to contort slightly awkwardly to do so. The other two were on the step behind Flynn.

This was another position in which he could have been awkward.

It wouldn't have taken much to push Guthrie down and break his grip on the cuffs, then turn to gut punch one of PCs behind him and barge him into the other one, and he did seriously consider this until he spotted Molly standing on the other side of the revolving doors, and knew she would shoot him without compunction.

So, in a happy line like four oversized dwarfs, they trucked off the escalator without incident and walked towards Molly, who had opened one of the side doors so there was no need to leave through the revolving one.

Flynn saw the two cop cars by the kerb.

It was good to step out into the fresh air of a newly forming day. Flynn felt he had been breathing the cloying hospital atmosphere for far too long and inhaling the outside air was like taking a drug, immediately making him feel more alert and alive. Not quite in the league of taking his boat out of Puerto Rico harbour, but under the circumstances it was OK – until a fleeting thought about Maria Santiago flipped through his mind, reminding him she would never be there to share anything with him again. Over summer she had been helping out with tourist trips from Santa Eulalia on Ibiza and the days had been long and languid, full of love and passion.

The memory hit him hard, made him want to crumble, but he raised his chin and thought again about how best to escape from custody, because being free was the only way in which he could even begin to devour that cold dish of revenge.

Molly watched the short procession file past her, avoiding any eye contact with Steve Flynn. From now on it was going to be all professional alertness and she scanned continually for any signs of danger, even though she fully expected this to be an incident-free journey.

The logistics were that Flynn would be in the back seat of the Galaxy alongside Mike Guthrie, whose partner would do the driving.

Molly was going to drive the Mondeo with Robbo alongside her in the front. They would follow the Galaxy and it was expected the journey would take no more than twenty minutes at that time of day, with very little traffic on the roads to hold them up.

They were going to go up on to East Park Drive, head south to Preston New Road, the A583, and simply follow that all the way to Preston itself. An easy journey across the agricultural flatlands between the two towns.

She was content to drive. It gave her something to concentrate on other than Alan, her disintegrating relationship and how she was going to pick up the pieces of her life.

The Galaxy moved off. Molly selected first gear and followed it up the hill past the Accident and Emergency department and left on to East Park Drive, suddenly feeling weariness overtake her.

She shook her head to clear her mind and focused on the back of the Galaxy to get the job done, get home to bed and sort out her existence.

They reached Preston New Road and filtered left, shortly thereafter crossing the motorway roundabout and heading past a huge DIY superstore on the right before dropping on to the clear run all the way into Preston on the A583.

Molly gripped the wheel, travelling about thirty metres behind the Galaxy, keeping the distance constant as the speed of both vehicles edged up to the fifty mph limit along the dual carriageway. She could see Flynn's wide silhouette on the back seat next to Guthrie, who was almost as wide but not quite as tall.

Progress was steady; there were very few other vehicles on the road. It was never an excessively busy route, though there were some hazardous sections of road where speeding and over-taking had caught out many an unwary motorist, often with fatal consequences.

Flynn sneaked a glance over his shoulder, saw Molly's car following then faced the front again when Guthrie scowled at him, an expression which seemed firmly screwed on to his face.

Flynn wasn't particularly enjoying the journey through an area he knew well from his time as a cop. Much of his early service had been in and around Blackpool and its environs and he had a good knowledge of the local geography, knowing they would soon be bypassing the market town of Kirkham on the left after negotiating the roundabout at Nookwood, where a huge house-building programme was underway adjacent to the road.

Then the blood drained from Flynn's face as he realized what he had just seen when he'd looked back at Molly. His head jerked around again and his eyes widened with horror at what looked like a huge black articulated tractor unit closing up fast from behind.

In a concurrent thought of sudden realization, Flynn knew that this roundabout was probably the last best point on the whole route to Preston to launch an attack as less than a mile to the north was a junction for the M55 motorway – and a quick escape.

Flynn's head twisted forwards again, his mind racing now.

His thoughts were that if this *was* an attack of some sort, then they wouldn't just be coming from behind – there would have to be a frontal assault and possibly one from the side if there was to be any chance of success. Or maybe it was just a lorry driver on his phone, not concentrating and Flynn was letting his imagination run riot.

The roundabout was perhaps two hundred metres ahead.

'Fuck you looking at, pal?' Guthrie demanded crossly.

The two police cars were slowing down now to negotiate it.

Flynn ignored Guthrie, hoping he was wrong in his assumptions.

But as he raised his head to peer over the passenger seat headrest and through the front windscreen, Flynn saw a second tractor unit burst out from the junction on the right and bear down towards the side of the Galaxy, which had just paused on the give-way markings on the roundabout.

At the same time he spotted the figures of two men lounging by the roadside on the left, as if waiting to cross.

They weren't.

Flynn knew it.

Confirmed when both men simultaneously pulled on black balaclava masks and threw back their overcoats to reveal the stubby machine pistols – handgun-style, magazine-fed, self-loading firearms capable of fully automatic or bursts of single fire – concealed underneath the material. Flynn recognized them as Czech-made Skorpions.

The phrase 'shit sandwich' jumped into his mind as he opened his mouth to scream a warning, but the words remained trapped in his throat as from three sides a world of terrible violence closed in on them like the jaws of a monster.

The first crashing, metal-crunching noise came from behind as the truck following Molly's car smashed into the back of that vehicle and drove the car into the back of the Galaxy.

Flynn then watched it all happen, piece by piece, microsecond by microsecond.

The impact of the Mondeo caught the Galaxy driver totally

by surprise and Flynn thought, *Sleepwalkers!* in reference to the cops on the escort, because they always believed it would not happen to them. He did manage to have some reaction, instinctively slamming on the brakes with a roar coming from his mouth, but the force of the impact was too immense to fight and the Galaxy was shunted out into the roundabout. The other tractor unit hurtled at them from the side and smashed into them like a raging bull elephant attacking a safari bus. There was the terrifying crash of the collision, the tearing of metal and the cracking of windows disintegrating, coupled with the sound of the big engine in the truck itself.

Flynn managed to brace himself.

At the same time, in the periphery of his vision, he saw the two pedestrians swing the Skorpions into a hip-height firing position and they strafed both police vehicles with a wave of bullets.

Flynn heard the impact of the shells banging into the side of the Galaxy and also shattering the window he was against.

As well as bracing himself, he had also pulled his body in tight.

He felt the air-whoosh of slugs above his head, but then the Galaxy was flipped over on to its nearside by the truck that had hit them on the roundabout. Flynn suddenly found himself trapped under the weight of Guthrie, whose terrified face cracked against Flynn's shoulder, and Flynn saw Guthrie had been hit by at least one of the bullets. He had a horrendous neck wound – he'd taken a hit to the throat, ripping out his Adam's apple, destroying the thick blood vessels and causing blood to fountain all over Flynn's face.

Momentarily, Flynn was disorientated and tried to clear his mind.

Then more bullets were fired in short bursts into the roof of the Galaxy. Flynn felt the impact, both into Guthrie, who had rolled sideways across him and become a shield, and into the upholstery of the seats.

The firing seemed to be unremitting.

It stopped suddenly. Reloading?

Then Flynn heard more shots being fired. Flynn recognized them as coming from a handgun – a Glock, the sound of its firing peculiar to itself, as all weapons were.

His thoughts were that maybe Molly and Robbo were retaliating and firing back.

Flynn glanced at the driver of the Galaxy who, despite his seat belt, had been tipped out of his seat and now lay crumpled and moaning in the front passenger footwell.

Encumbered by his handcuffs, Flynn hauled Guthrie off him, looking into his glazed, dying eyes for a moment, not liking to have to use him as a ladder to get across to the rear door opposite.

Which was locked.

Fucking child locks.

It's what you did with prisoners on board.

Flynn swore and, in the tight space, swung his hands sideways against the window – about the only one in the car that had not shattered – using the outer metal rim of the handcuffs to try to break the glass.

Flynn heard engines revving, more shots being fired, shouts.

And then a fresh volley through the roof of the Galaxy from the two guys on the road side who had reloaded their weapons.

The window disintegrated on the second swing and fell into thousands of chunks over him like hailstone.

Flynn, again using Guthrie's body as leverage, scrambled up through the window and dropped into the road, crouching behind the Galaxy, disorientated slightly but trying to get his mind around what had happened in the last twenty seconds. There was no time to analyse anything and think about tactics, though he could see that, behind the Galaxy, the Mondeo had been crushed but was still upright, whereas the Galaxy was still on its side.

Flynn crouched.

He could not see Molly at the wheel of the Mondeo, though Robbo was still in his seat, but, crushed up to the dashboard and although he was injured, he was conscious and struggling to get free.

Flynn felt the stitches split in his leg.

Then he heard the sound that had reminded him of a charging elephant again as he rose slightly and spun. The tractor unit that had burst from the junction had reversed away and was now thundering towards him, the driver intent on crushing him to death between the front grille of the monster and the underside of the Galaxy.

Flynn froze as the front of the truck grew quickly in size, then felt the impact of someone from behind diving into his lower spine like a bad rugby tackle as Molly piled into him and pushed him out of the path of the truck, which missed them both by inches and slammed into the underside of the Galaxy, sending it spinning and grating across the road. Flynn and Molly tumbled inelegantly to the ground, limbs everywhere.

'Come on!' Molly screamed at him. 'Fucking move!'

Flynn scrambled to his feet, Molly dragging him and keeping low as more bullets flew overhead and the drivers of the tractor units leapt down from their cabs with guns in their hands.

Molly had her Glock in hers and her MP5 slung around her neck. She fired a couple of shots on the run at these men, who ducked and dived as the slugs embedded or ricocheted into and off their vehicles. With Flynn in tow, she raced across towards the small wooded area known as Stable Wood which nestled in the triangle of the junction formed by Ribby Road and Blackpool Road.

She leapt into the undergrowth with Flynn following suit, then scrambled through the deep, damp leaf mould into the centre of the small wood, where she dropped to one knee behind an oak tree. Flynn thudded down beside her.

'It's you they want,' she breathed.

'They got Guthrie instead, though. I think he's dead.'

'Shit, shit,' Molly cursed.

Flynn held out his wrists. 'Get these off,' he said of the handcuffs. 'If they come after us I'm no use with cuffs on.'

She nodded and found her key ring on her utility belt, holstered her gun and fumbled with shaking fingers to slide the key in and release the cuffs.

Flynn watched her as she worked.

'You've done good,' he said.

She looked ferociously at him. 'Fuck off, Flynn.'

The second cuff came free and Flynn flung them aside.

'Now give me the Glock,' he said, opening his right palm.

'No way.' Her hand covered it defensively and gripped the stock.

Flynn arched his eyebrows, and was about to insist, when an

arc of bullets crashed into the trees and foliage around them. They ducked low.

'They're coming,' he warned her. His jaw was set tight. He glanced at his leg, saw blood seeping through the paper suit from the reopened wound. He ground his teeth.

Molly made a decision. She drew the Glock and flipped the gun around in her hand so she was holding the barrel and held it out for Flynn. 'There might be five or six left, I lost count,' she admitted as she brought the H&K MP5 around her front into a firing position. In the flurry of staying alive, Flynn was impressed that she'd had the wherewithal to grab this second weapon before getting out of the car. 'Just say I dropped it and you snatched it up, OK?' she said, referring to the Glock. She was already preparing herself for the inevitable questions that would be asked. If they both survived to tell the tale, that is.

Flynn said, 'I will.'

More bullets crashed into the trees.

There were shouts from the attackers as they entered the woods.

'They're gonna put us up like pheasants at a turkey shoot,' Flynn grimaced, cleverly mixing his metaphors.

Molly ignored him and spoke urgently into her PR, telling the control room succinctly but breathlessly what had happened and what was now taking place.

More slugs ripped into the undergrowth.

Flynn looked warily back through the leaves for their pursuers.

He guessed they would give it one sweep and then be gone. They would have a getaway car waiting close by. To waste time with a manhunt would not be sensible because, as of right now, cops from two divisions, plus the helicopter, dog patrols and other ARVs would be converging like fuck on this area. The attackers were not in this to end up in a cell but would be gutted that their first assault hadn't nailed Flynn.

Flynn's left hand shot out and covered Molly's mouth, preventing her from talking into her mike.

His lips formed a silent *shh* as he peeled his fingers away slowly.

But then the radio itself squawked loudly. 'Say again, Alpha-Romeo Seven,' the voice of the operator called shrilly.

This seemed to make Flynn move like lightning. He shot up

from his crouching position, burst through a mass of thin, inter-woven branches and leaves and leapt at the figure of a man he had seen sneaking towards Molly's position.

The man was armed – Flynn recognized him as one of the hooded men from the roadside shooting party – but he was angled just slightly away from Flynn and crouched in a combat stance, holding his Skorpion ready to fire again.

Flynn crashed against him without finesse, at the same time checking on the position of the others. He could not see them, but this gave him no comfort. They were there somewhere, only metres away, so he had to deal with this first man ridiculously quickly, effectively and without mercy before the others could react.

As he barged into him, he downed him with a crashing blow to the skull with the handle of the Glock. Had it been a Browning 9mm in his hand, the man would have dropped instantly, but the lightweight German pistol was not a great whipping tool; still, at least he staggered back on to his knees, but he also fought to keep his balance and swing the Skorpion around with the inten-tion of ripping Flynn in half in a hail of bullets.

Flynn moved in tight, encircled the man's waist with his big left arm, drew him right up into him as if it were some kind of tango and they might have been about to kiss before some rough sex. Instead, hoping Molly's calculation was good, Flynn put the Glock to the man's left temple and double-tapped his brain to shreds.

He died instantly, but even before he became a deadweight for Flynn he let him go, wincing slightly as the back splat of blood from the horrific wound flicked across his head and shoulders.

Then there was a moment between himself and Molly.

Molly had witnessed this killing, horrified. She was standing by the oak tree, a stunned expression on her face.

Flynn glanced at her, knowing that even this was a moment of emotional indulgence too long as another pursuer broke cover over to Flynn's left. It was one of the truck drivers and his handgun was pointed at Flynn.

Molly came to life and reacted instantly with her H&K, firing a rising stream of bullets that arced from the man's groin up to his throat, almost slicing him in half and emptying the whole magazine. He jerked backwards with the impact of each round, then fell dead.

This time, Molly stood there immoveable, completely stunned by the enormity of what she had just seen and then done.

Flynn heard more crashing through the trees, but the direction of sound was receding as the remaining attackers lost all their courage – because someone was shooting back – and they legged it. Flynn was on the point of giving chase, but then he heard car doors slam, the sound of an engine revving on the road nearby and realized his guess about a waiting getaway car had been correct.

Flynn looked at the dead man at his feet. He knew this was going to be a tight fit.

He threw down the Glock and began to strip off the forensic suit.

Molly rushed at him. 'What the hell d'you think you're doing?' she demanded.

'Getting changed. His clothes should just fit. Then I'm going, Molly.'

'No, no, no, you're fucking not.' She stepped away from him and brought up the MP5. 'Back off, back off!' she screamed. 'You're going nowhere, pal.'

'What're you going to do?' Flynn asked, pulling the suit down his body and stepping out of it. 'Shoot me?'

'If I have to.' Her voice quavered.

'With what?' he challenged her, indicating the H&K. 'An empty weapon?'

'I'll Taser you again, then.'

'Don't make me hit you, Molly.' In just his paper underpants, Flynn squatted down and began to unbuckle the dead man's baggy trousers, then pulled off the guy's trainers and yanked the pants down the legs of the lifeless body.

Molly's hands dropped her sides. The H&K hung uselessly from the shoulder strap.

'Flynn, I've just killed a man . . . You've just killed a man.'

He was busy undressing a corpse, then dressing himself. 'Both of whom were going to kill us. Quid pro quo, I'd say. Or is it Status Quo?'

'You think it's fucking funny?'

Flynn peeled off the man's coat, then unbuttoned his shirt, both bloodstained. 'Not really.' He stood up and pushed his arms into the shirtsleeves. 'But they fired first and I can't afford to stay locked up, Molly. If I do, they'll get me when I'm inside, without a doubt, but if I'm a moving target things will be much different.'

She watched him, feeling very nauseated.

'Tell Rik I disarmed you or something – or just tell him the truth. He'll get it.' The dead man's trainers were far too tight so he tied them loosely. They would have to suffice for the moment. As he rose to his full height, lastly pulling the jacket on, he said, 'You need to go and help your colleagues, yeah? They'll need first aid.'

She nodded.

'Go,' he urged her. She moved, but then he grabbed her. 'Give me your phone.'

'What? Why?'

'Give me your mobile phone, please.'

In a daze, she handed it over with dithering fingers.

'Call me,' Flynn said.

'What?' This was all getting too much, literally blowing her mind.

'Call me. But before I go, tell me the name of Blackpool's biggest drug dealer.'

She told him. He considered scooping up the Glock but it was almost empty at best. He knew Molly would have a spare mag for it on her belt, but it all seemed too complicated and time-wasting to ask her for it and he knew he wouldn't need it in the immediate future.

He looked briefly up through the trees into the sky, hearing the throb of the approaching helicopter, which wouldn't have travelled far from its base in nearby Warton, and also the sound of sirens as cops descended on the scene of carnage at the roundabout.

Without a further word, he plunged into the trees and was gone.

SEVEN

Steve Flynn had once been married, a union that had ended in disarray when his wife, Faye, had an affair with his cop partner Jack Hoyle, at the time of the shit-storm mess that was the end of his police career. He knew Faye still lived in Blackpool in the house Flynn had once co-owned with her, though she had now 'taken-up' (a phrase Flynn used with contempt) with a fairly wealthy businessman from the Fylde area. To the best of his knowledge, she was on a long cruise with the guy and therefore, Flynn hoped, the former marital home would be unoccupied.

Flynn also had a son – Craig – from the ill-fated marriage, and he knew that the lad was taking a year out from university to travel the Far East and Australia. This meant there was little chance, Flynn hoped, of either of them being in danger from the Bashkims or of him finding anyone at the house in South Shore.

That was where he was headed after deserting the shell-shocked Molly in the middle of Stable Wood with two dead bodies at her feet.

He crashed out through the trees on to Ribby Road, jogged a hundred metres or so, crossed the road and walked into the holiday village called Ribby Hall, where years before he used to take Craig swimming when the lad was just a toddler and all was right with the world. He sauntered in through the gates, passing an unstaffed security post and walked into the car park, which was almost full. There were many attractions at Ribby Hall, not just for holidaymakers, and its facilities were always popular with locals and day-trippers. He meandered through the car park until he found what he was looking for – a car he could steal with ease.

It had to be one of a certain age for him as anything too modern would be too complicated to fire up. He needed one with an old-fashioned key and ancient enough for him to rip the wires out from behind the steering column, do the business and get on the move.

He watched the police helicopter fly in low from the south, not much above a hundred feet. He stood squinting at it as it disappeared from view, then rose back into sight and hovered over the roundabout less than a quarter of a mile from Ribby Hall.

Flynn picked up a chunk of stone from a dry stone wall next to the car park and made his way back to the chosen vehicle, a 1999 Ford Fiesta. He smashed the driver's-door window and was in quickly, yanking out the ignition wires and starting the engine in about a minute.

Then he was on the move, leaving Ribby Hall, turning left and driving through the pretty village of Wrea Green and along the twisting back roads towards Lytham. En route, he was almost barged off the narrow roads by police cars racing to the scene at the roundabout in the opposite direction, blues and twos in operation.

Flynn held his nerve and tootled into Lytham, then north through St Annes into Blackpool South and made his way to the small housing estate on which his old house was situated. He did a drive past, noting that all the blinds on the windows were half-closed and the house appeared to be unoccupied.

He abandoned the stolen car about a mile away and made his way on foot, then veered off on to a path by a small children's play area which ran alongside the railway line behind the estate. He found the back fence of the house and heaved himself over the waney-lap fence, dropping into a gap between the fence and the now-slightly-decrepit shed he had built many years before.

All the blinds and curtains were fully drawn at the back of the house.

Another good sign.

He scuttled, keeping low, across the unkempt lawn on to the back patio, then shimmied down the side of the house between the fence and the garage, pulling up just short of the driveway and frowning. There was a narrow window at head height on the side wall of the garage which he backed up to, shaded his eyes and peered in to see a car parked there.

The garage was not particularly big and the car just about fitted, though it would have been a squeeze to climb out of.

It was a very nice, small BMW saloon which looked pretty new.

'Present from sugar daddy,' Flynn mused, assuming the worst of his ex-wife but at the same time pleased to see he might have access to transport.

He edged back to the corner of the garage and hoped that Faye remained a woman of regular habits.

There was a pair of large terracotta plant pots on either side of the front door, each with a precisely trimmed, orb-like bush in it.

Hopefully the key to the front door would be under the pot on the right.

Molly Cartwright raised her head. It was sometime after 9 p.m. She wasn't sure exactly.

Detective Superintendent Rik Dean stood in front of her, a mug of tea in each hand.

She thought he looked dreadful, his face gaunt and sickly, drained to the off-white hue of old parchment paper, his eyes set deep and dark and still displaying the assault he had suffered from Steve Flynn.

Not a great look.

That said, she was pretty sure her appearance rivalled his.

She had just been to the ladies' and spent not a little time in front of a mirror, considering her reflection.

Not a great look.

The two of them, Molly and the superintendent, were in Rik's FMIT office at Blackpool police station. His main office was at police headquarters where FMIT was actually based, but the department had satellite offices dotted in the major police stations around the county. This one, tucked into the corner of the high-rise block that was Blackpool nick, had an uninspiring view through the narrow, floor-to-ceiling windows (designed never to be opened) on to Bonny Street which ran parallel and one step back from the promenade, and belied its name: it was far from Bonny, a grim thoroughfare.

Molly was now dressed in civilian clothing after her uniform and equipment had all been seized for forensic analysis. She had suffered the indignity of having to undress in the ladies' locker room under the watchful eye of a female detective who had bagged and tagged each item as Molly handed them to her. Molly had changed into the spare set of clothes she kept in her locker just for emergencies: tracksuit bottoms, a zip-up hoodie top, a battered Rolling Stones T-shirt and a pair of shitty trainers.

And that was before any of the real questioning began.

It had been a long, gruelling day, not helped by the creeping onset of a genuine whiplash injury to her neck and shoulders from the smash she'd endured.

She told the honest truth because there was nowhere else to go.

The security escort had been ambushed. Many shots had been fired. Vehicles had been overturned and seriously damaged. There had been a shoot-out and she had been fighting for her life.

She had killed a man.

Steve Flynn had killed a man, then escaped from custody.

Her partner Robbo had been injured in the smash.

The driver of the Ford Galaxy had been seriously hurt, although he was expected to survive.

And PC Mike Guthrie was dead, caught in a hail of bullets, one of which had ripped out his throat.

Molly took the proffered mug from Rik. She was sitting on a reasonably comfortable chair with a coffee table next to it. Rik eased himself down into a chair opposite and gave her a washed-out smile.

She sipped the brew, holding it in both hands, enjoying the warmth on her palms and down her throat. Normally she hated tea with sugar but she'd asked Rik to lace the brew with three heaped teaspoons. She needed the comfort and sustenance.

'How're you feeling?'

'Horrible,' she said, rolling her shoulders gently. She could feel the muscles starting to tighten and contract. She recalled the impact of the tractor unit into the Mondeo and could visualize the movement of her body in response, jolting forwards, then her head jerking back like a crash test dummy. So far she had refused hospital treatment, but she knew she needed to go soon and get her condition confirmed. Not that they would be able to do anything, but a good dose of strong painkillers was appealing.

The questioning, carried out by two very experienced FMIT detectives, had taken about six hours in total. She hadn't been under arrest but had been under caution, and she knew if she decided to get up and walk out she would have soon seen the inside of a cell. That said, she did use a duty solicitor, feeling it would be prudent even though she had nothing to hide and, because this was only the beginning of a very long haul, she wanted to get it right.

'You did very well,' Rik said. 'I want you to know that.' He added, 'The force is behind you all the way.' When he saw her cynical expression, he said, 'It is, Molly. An armed ambush. Extreme violence being used. One officer dead. Two injured – plus you. Two bad guys down, tough shit on them . . . You pull a gun . . .'

'You open a door,' she finished for him, 'and you have to live with what comes through. Same applies to me,' she said flatly.

'I know, and I also know that if you hadn't responded as you did, your own life could have been lost. I'll be behind you all the way – honest,' he stressed.

'Even when the IPCC gets a grip?' She was referring to the Independent Police Complaints Commission, the body that would investigate the incident.

'Especially then.'

She sipped her tea. 'I have never been so utterly shit-scared in all my life, boss.' She blinked. 'And I don't mind saying it, but I'm glad Flynn was there and I'm glad I released him . . . just pissed off he legged it.'

'He's playing to his own agenda.' Rik was tight-lipped. Both knew what he meant.

Molly eyed him. The one thing she hadn't admitted in the interviews was that Flynn now possessed her mobile phone and she couldn't quite understand why she didn't tell the interviewers. She almost blabbed it to Rik, and also the question Flynn had asked about a drug dealer's name. That was another little snippet she hadn't mentioned, and again, she had no idea why not.

Rik looked at her curiously. 'What?'

'Nothing, nothing.'

'What do you think Flynn's up to?' Rik asked after a pause.

She shook her head. It hurt to do so. 'I don't know the specifics, boss, but I think we both know what he wants to do. And do you know what?'

Rik waited.

'I hope he fucking succeeds.'

He kept his movements around his former marital home to a minimum, not wanting to draw the attention of any of the neighbours, though he doubted they would be interested. He knew Faye kept herself very much to herself, and Flynn had occasionally crashed here when she had been here as well as when she had not, so his presence wasn't too unusual if he was spotted. He did try to keep out of sight, though, keeping all the lights off at the front of the house.

There was a certain amount of recklessness in returning here but there was nothing on police records about the house, unless his old personnel file was unearthed. He hoped this had been scrubbed from the day-to-day computer system and would only be accessible via the head of HR, who probably didn't know the access code to the archives anyway. Flynn knew these were assumptions but he did not intend to spend much time here because, once he got what he needed, he would be gone on the wind.

The key had been under the plant pot.

Once inside, Flynn locked the door then went to the kitchen, where he knew the first-aid kit was kept in a cupboard.

Once he had found that, he dropped his newly acquired pants and inspected his leg wound, peeling back the blood-soaked dressing carefully. It was bleeding because the stitches had split. Flynn dabbed it clean, squeezed a blob of Savlon into it, then, using several plasters, he pulled the wound back together and put more plasters over it to keep it in place, then finally re-wrapped a bandage around the whole thing.

It was as good as it was going to get.

Next, he went upstairs. On the landing, he reached up and released the loft hatch, which swung down. He found the ladder pole in the main bathroom and reached up with it, hooked it into the loft ladders and dragged them down.

Once in the loft, he duck-walked to the far end and found an old storage box in which he knew were some of his old belongings, including clothing. Fay had once mentioned this to him – that she still had some of his gear in the loft but couldn't be arsed to throw it out through laziness rather than for senti-mental reasons.

There were old jeans and T-shirts and a zip-up windjammer, together with a couple of old pairs of trainers, all having seen better days and all smelling slightly musty.

He came back down the ladder, replaced it and closed the hatch, then got changed. The T-shirts were fine – he liked old and baggy – but the jeans were tight around his waist. Even a fit guy like Flynn, who had spent years on a sportfishing boat, had spread somewhat with age. The trainers fitted fine.

Back in the kitchen, the kettle went on, tea was brewed and, with his old mug in hand (another thing Faye had not binned), he sat at the kitchen table and looked at Molly's phone, which was already showing a dozen missed calls (all from Alan xx), and three voice messages that Flynn assumed originated from the same source.

Flynn ignored them and dialled a number dredged up from the bowels of his memory, which he knew might not even connect now.

It rang out and was answered. A cautious voice said, 'Hullo?'

'It's me, Steve Flynn.'

'Molly?'

She spun at the voice behind her.

'Alan,' she said coldly.

She had just walked across from the police station into the multi-storey car park and was almost at her car when Hardiker stepped out from behind and called her name softly. Up to that point, she had been walking in a trance following her chat with Rik Dean. From his office, all the way to the car park, a rising feeling of dread had grown like a death shroud over her, constricting her lungs, making her breathing laboured.

She had taken someone's life. She had been involved in what could be a life-changing incident. And now a huge manhunt was underway.

Signing on, volunteering as a firearms officer, there was always the possibility of that happening, however remote.

She had once pointed a gun at a person in anger, an armed robber who'd swung a sawn-off shotgun at her, a situation that had ended peacefully. She wasn't sure if she would have pulled the trigger then, but assumed she would have done given the fact she had now killed someone.

Now that moment of decision would be scrutinized and picked through meticulously. That microsecond would be pulled apart, dissected and put back together like the most intricate Airfix model imaginable.

She knew she had nothing to fear.

Her actions had been lawful in the circumstances, the use of force reasonable. She wasn't even too concerned by the probing questions that would be asked of her in relation to giving Flynn her Glock. They had been under attack and it was the only thing she could have done to protect them.

She would live with the criticism.

What she wasn't certain of was how to handle the killing of a man, even if he deserved it. It was a subject often discussed and analysed by firearms officers and their appointed counsellors, but now Molly realized that no training, however realistic, was preparation for the real thing.

These thoughts had crowded her mind as she walked towards her car, but all dissolved on the sound of Hardiker's voice.

She turned slowly. 'You need to stop hanging around in car parks. You could get your bollocks kicked up into your throat on a regular basis.'

'I know, I know.' His hands made a conciliatory gesture. 'Look, I've been calling you. I'm just glad you're OK. You haven't been answering your phone.'

'Been a tad busy,' she clipped.

'Yeah, yeah, fair do's. But you're OK, are you? It must have been horrendous.'

'It was horrendous,' she confirmed. 'You don't know the fucking half of it.'

'Y'know, if you need a hug, I'm here for you,' he offered pathetically.

Molly was glad to note that there wasn't even the slightest nanosecond of reconsideration on her part, no weakening, no thinking that to fall back into his arms would be a good thing.

'I'd rather hug a roll of barbed wire.' She held up her right hand in a stop sign. 'I'll handle it myself, OK?'

She saw the expression on his face mutate from wet sand into concrete.

'And seriously, do not hang around in car parks.' She spun round and headed to her car.

Flynn was pleased that his errant ex-wife's habits hadn't changed much in the years he'd been away as he raided her secret stash of money – a plastic sandwich box stuffed with ten-pound notes he had once discovered during a period of marital turbulence, hidden in the back of a kitchen cupboard. He hadn't let on he had found it, but had occasionally helped himself to funds. Why she had continued to keep it post-divorce, he could not fathom, maybe just the habit of a lifetime; however, here it was, a nice butty box stuffed with cash – rolls of tenners to the value of a hundred pounds each. Flynn counted £1600 in total and took four rolls for his upcoming expenses.

Then he left the house under the cover of darkness and walked in the direction of South Shore, keeping to the shadows but not seeing any cop cars or any sign of the law. He emerged on to the promenade near to the Pleasure Beach, feeling the chill wind from the Irish Sea, and walked into the Dragon & Horse pub on the nearby seafront.

He ordered a mineral water and slid into a chair by the big bay window overlooking the promenade with his glass.

He did not see the woman approaching, only knew she was there when she perched down on the seat opposite.

Flynn swallowed.

Sue Daggert was at least ten years younger than him and looked as stunning as when he had first encountered her almost twenty years before and fallen into bed with her to begin a torrid but short-lived and very perilous affair with a woman who was the girlfriend and later the wife of one of the north-west's biggest, most violent drug kingpins.

'Flynn,' she said throatily. Her blue eyes sparkled at him. 'Never thought I'd see you again.'

'Nor I you. How are you, Sue?'

'Can't lie.' She displayed the rings on her fingers, a glittering but subtle collection of expensive jewellery, then touched the diamond pendant on her necklace, nestling just above her cleavage. She pointed past him outside the pub to a stunning Bentley convertible on the car park.

'And Jack?' Flynn asked.

'All legit now, after ten years inside thanks to you.'

Flynn smiled. 'That's good to hear.'

'He still wants to kill you, though,' she informed him.

The tyres on Molly's Mini squealed as she powered the little car out of her parking space and made Hardiker jump aside as she screwed it past him and aimed the car down the ramp, out of the car park. The first time she checked the rear-view mirror was when she reached the junction with Richardson Street and saw that it was smashed. As she twisted to look at it over her shoulder, the pain of whiplash made her cry out.

Flynn bought Sue Daggert an Orange and Passionfruit J2O from the bar – with a shot of Grey Goose vodka – and placed it in front of her as he retook his seat. She sipped it, looking across the rim of the long glass through hooded eyes.

'You're looking well,' Flynn complimented her.

'Thank you. And, up to a point, so are you.'

Flynn gave a short, double-edged laugh. 'I'm assuming hubby doesn't know of this little tryst?'

'No, he doesn't. He's in Spain for the duration anyway . . . property, y'know.'

'That's his business then?'

'More or less.' She pouted. 'So, Steve Flynn, ex-cop, I can't say it isn't nice to see you again – it is – but we had our time. Fun, dangerous . . .' she said whimsically.

'Especially the time I hid in your attic and Jack came a-huntin' with a double-barrelled shotgun.'

'Oh, that was fun.' She chuckled at the memory. 'But that was the tipping point for us. He had his suspicions but couldn't prove anything. If we'd've kept going he would have found out, though – and we'd both be dead.'

Flynn nodded. It had been a wild time, truly on the edge, playing people, messing with emotions, running the gauntlet with

Jack Daggert, one of the most dangerous men in the country. Exciting and ultimately unsustainable, as both Flynn and Sue realized. Jack suspected she was having an affair but not with whom, and definitely not with a cop, the ultimate betrayal. Flynn had been mercilessly trying to elicit information from her about Jack's criminal activities but she had been shrewd, just happy to enjoy a fling, revealing nothing of value to Flynn. It all got very ugly when Jack beat her up because of his never-proven suspicions, and that made her and Flynn end the affair, but it also gave her the impetus to drop Jack in the shit yet still stay with him.

Flynn had led the raid on one of Jack's big drug deals and sent him down for a ten-year stretch with Jack stating his intention to kill Flynn: not because of the affair, of which he still knew nothing, but because he'd been caught with half-a-million-pounds-worth of cocaine and £300,000 of drug-tainted notes in his pockets.

It was a lot to lose, and Jack was the sort of man to bear a grudge.

'I take it you've come to pump me for information,' Sue quipped. 'I don't mind the pumping bit but I'm not keen on giving out information. Me and Jack are simpatico now. He's a changed man and, like I said, on the straight and narrow now . . . sorta.'

'You know I'm not a cop now, don't you?'

From her reaction, he could tell she didn't.

'No reason why you should, I suppose. I left about twelve years ago.'

'So what's this then?' She shrugged and flipped her hands to indicate the situation, clearly puzzled.

'I'm on the run and I need some information.'

Rik Dean thought it would be impossible to describe the impression on his face. It was an eclectic mix of stress, worry, excitement, doubt and tiredness, all mixed into the crock pot that was his countenance. He guessed it did not look pleasant.

He was sitting behind his desk in this FMIT office at Blackpool, long after Molly Cartwright had left.

He held a document in his hand: Steve Flynn's passport.

He was wondering what he should do with it.

It had come into police possession together with a holdall full of Flynn's clothing and other belongings found in Flynn's hire car that he had been using before the now-deceased Brian Tasker had abducted Flynn in order to make him witness several brutal murders, including the most horrific one of all – the beheading of Maria Santiago.

Rik Dean was furious with Flynn.

Because the ex-cop had taken it upon himself to administer summary justice on Tasker by breaking the man's neck (something Tasker deserved, Rik secretly acknowledged), it had left Rik with a horrible, horrible mess.

Rik got it.

He got it that Flynn wanted revenge on the Bashkims, who were behind the whole thing. He got it – grudgingly – that the best the cops could do, and there was no guarantee even of this, was to make arrests and to try and dismantle the Bashkim crime family by legitimate means.

He got it that this wasn't good enough for Flynn.

That Flynn wanted to feel more necks breaking.

But . . . If only Flynn hadn't killed Tasker, because that meant Rik Dean had had to do his duty and arrest Flynn for murder (and for assaulting him).

What Rik had severely underestimated in all this until now was the utter, cold-blooded ruthlessness of the Bashkims in their hatred of Flynn and their ability, at such short notice, to carry out such a daring and brutal ambush on a police escort.

To steal two tractor units, to have the manpower and the brutal willpower to actually force the escort off the road, kill a cop and injure two more in the process of attempting to take out Flynn was terrifying.

What they hadn't reckoned on was Flynn himself, and also the professionalism of Molly Cartwright under fire, which had left two of the attackers, as yet unidentified, dead and Flynn a free man again.

The prospect of Flynn being at large did not really bother Rik. What did worry him was how the Bashkims had learned that Flynn was being conveyed from the hospital to the cop shop.

Rik tapped Flynn's passport on his desk and wondered if the

terrible headache that had just started to tear his brain apart was
his first ever migraine.

The virtually silent Bentley drew into the side of the kerb in
Claremont Road in North Shore. Steve Flynn climbed out, then
leaned back in through the door and looked into Sue Daggert's
eyes.

'Thank you,' he said.

'Steve, you've got yourself into a whole heap of shit with
these guys. You need to watch it, OK?'

'Got you.' He gave her a mock salute.

She sighed. 'Best sex of my life,' she said ruefully.

'And mine,' he admitted. But didn't add, 'Wild and scary, too.'

'The car will be here in an hour,' she promised. 'Old but clean,
keys under the passenger-side visor, OK?'

'Thanks again.'

He closed the door. It locked with a dull, expensive-sounding
clunk and the big car pulled away. Flynn watched it disappear.
He zipped up his old jacket then plunged on foot into the network
of terraced streets in the area, intending to call on someone from
his past who he hoped would be as accommodating as
Sue Daggert.

As he stepped off the pavement, Molly Cartwright's mobile
phone started to vibrate in his pocket.

He didn't take the call.

EIGHT

Although she didn't know it, Molly was less than a mile
away, as a Blackpool herring gull flies, from Steve Flynn
when she parked her damaged Mini in the reserved spot
outside her flat, then climbed out very slowly and gingerly,
inserted her key into the door and walked equally carefully
upstairs to her first-floor flat.

Her first port of call was to the stash of Co-codamol in a
kitchen cupboard. She necked three, then poured a large glass

of cheap Sainsbury's whisky. She was about to drink it in one gulp but the glass stopped at her lips, knowing she wouldn't appreciate it until she freshened up.

She crept to the bathroom, shoulders ever tightening, and had a very hot, long shower with the jets focused on the back of her neck. That combination – hot water and painkillers – did have some soothing effect and she stepped out of the shower feeling slightly better but not much. She pulled on a fresh pair of jogging bottoms and a loose T-shirt. Before leaving the bedroom, she rooted through a drawer in the dressing table and found a sandwich box containing a selection of her old mobile phones she'd replaced over time but never thrown out. She laid them out in a row and picked an old pay-as-you-go Nokia she thought might still have some credit on it. She flipped off the back, saw there was a SIM card in it, then reassembled it, found the charger and plugged it in.

She waited a moment, then dialled the number for a credit update and listened with a grin. £1.76p remained.

She unplugged it and took the phone and charger into the living room where her whisky awaited – as did Alan Hardiker, who was sitting in the only armchair, checking his own phone with an air of comfort, as though he lived here and had every right to be in her flat. Even his legs were crossed.

He looked up and smiled ingratiatingly. 'Nice shower?' He noticed the old phone in her hand. 'Phone broken or something?'

'This is getting beyond a joke, Alan,' she said, trying to keep the tremor out of her voice.

He slid his own phone on to the coffee table in front of him, something he'd done unthinkingly many times during the course of their relationship.

'Get out,' Molly added. 'And give me the door key.'

His face twitched. He licked his lips. His nostrils flared with temper and a curious look came into his eyes.

'I said *get out*,' Molly restated, finding more conviction in her voice at what felt like an invasion of her private space. Not long ago he would have been welcome. Not now. She held up the phone. 'I'll call the cops.'

Hardiker rose slowly. Molly shrank away slightly. He walked

towards her. She stood with her back against the living-room door frame and he positioned himself directly in front of her. Close. Inches away.

Her breathing stopped. A chilly sensation skittered down her insides, like crushed ice falling down a ravine.

'You and me are not finished, girl,' he breathed into her face unnervingly. His eyes drilled into hers but she did not retreat from his glare.

'Give me your key and go, Alan.'

He blew a gust of breath into her face. His right hand dropped into his jacket pocket and extracted a single Yale key which he held out between his finger and thumb – then dropped it deliberately on to the floor before turning and walking out. She stayed where she was, still holding her breath, listening to his footsteps descending the stairs to the front door, then the slam of it as he left.

Only then did she exhale, check if he had really gone then pick up the key.

She went down the steps to the door, opened it and tried the key from the outside just to make certain it was the right one for the door, because she would not have been surprised if it was just a nasty trick. It fitted, although she knew he could easily have had a duplicate cut.

Molly stepped back inside, locked the door with the snick and drew the single, inadequate-looking bolt across.

Back in the lounge, she sat down slowly, plugged the charger into the old mobile phone and then picked up the waiting whisky which she sank neat in one, without ice. With her hands dithering, she took up the phone again.

Her thoughts turned to Steve Flynn.

As a cop, Flynn had often operated on a knife edge, not least where the running of informants, or human intelligence sources as they were properly known was concerned. He had run several completely unofficial ones, totally against procedure and policy, because he knew that the individuals would have run a mile if he'd suggested to them they should be formally registered and allocated a handler who would not be him. Yet they were too valuable to lose and he did protect them and the information they gave him, and not one, he could have boasted (had he been allowed to) had ever been compromised or put in danger.

One such man went by the nickname of Rank Xerox, although his real name was Arthur Benfield. In another life, Arthur had been a jeweller and watch repairer, but when his employer – one of the most respected jewellers in the country – began to notice that some of the minute diamonds used in watch mechanisms were unaccounted for, Arthur was sacked.

He transferred his skills for great detail to the dark side and began a successful career forging documents, although the advent of online and downloadable documentation such as insurance and MOT certificates slowly put Arthur out of business, mostly. He did possess one skill that kept him in some work and that was forging passports, taking genuine, blank ones, usually stolen from official sources, adding fraudulent details and ensuring they appeared genuine to customs and law enforcement databases via contacts he had in various government departments.

Flynn liked to keep Rank Xerox – named after the old copying machine company – warm and for a healthy remuneration he fed Flynn details of false passports he'd made for drugs dealers, from which Flynn could keep track of the comings and goings of kingpins and mules alike. When he pounced he always ensured the trail was far enough removed from Arthur not to arouse any suspicion that he had provided any information to the cops whatsoever.

Arthur led a quiet life in a terraced house in Blackpool North Shore. The house, Flynn recalled, was outwardly dreary, but inside it was expensively furnished and kitted out and his workplace, a desk, was hidden, folded away in a wall.

It had been over ten years since Flynn had any dealings with Rank who, even then, had been sixty years old. Flynn knocked on the front door, hoping the old guy hadn't moved on.

Flynn felt a little jittery being out in the open. His eyes constantly roved, expecting a police support unit to suddenly come crashing down on him.

He knocked again, then after waiting a few moments he bent low to the letter box and flipped it open. 'Rank, it's me, Steve Flynn. Open up, mate.'

He peered through and along the narrow entrance hall, seeing light around the edges of the kitchen door, saw a shadow move at floor level and someone behind that door.

Flynn stood upright and clattered the letter box again, his impatience growing.

A moment later the front door opened and an old man peered out through wire-rimmed spectacles.

'Arthur, it's me, Steve Flynn.'

Rank Xerox shook his head. 'I don't recognize you. What d'you want?' His tone was unfriendly.

'Can I step in?'

'No.'

'Listen, you silly old fuckwit,' Flynn blurted as Rank stepped back and began to slam the door in his face.

Flynn jammed his right foot down, preventing the door from closing. 'I need a favour.'

'Go away, mister whoever you are.'

'I'm Steve Flynn, Arthur, don't you recognize me? I know it's been a few years.'

Rank opened the door again and looked blankly at Flynn, who was starting to get bad vibes.

'I need a passport, mate. Quick, like.'

'What?' Rank screwed up his nose. 'What are you talking about?'

'You know – a passport.'

'I know what a passport is. You can't have mine.'

Flynn groaned inwardly. 'You don't remember me, do you?'

Rank shook his head and shrugged helplessly. 'Should I?'

'No, maybe you shouldn't.'

'I know I'm at home, though. I know this is my house,' Rank said helpfully, clearly pleased he had remembered something.

'I know, Arthur, I know.' Flynn extracted his foot from the door. 'Sorry to have troubled you.'

'No worries.' The door closed gently. Flynn leaned against the wall of the house and said, 'Shit. Alzheimer's, that's all I need.'

In his pocket, Molly's phone vibrated as a text landed. He took it out and saw it was from a number not listed on the phone's memory. Out of curiosity, he read the message: *The next call will be from me. Please answer. Molly.*

* * *

Rik Dean had planned to go home, get his head down for at least four hours – bliss – but instead had found himself trying to brainstorm an investigative strategy for the next, crucial seventy-two-hour period. He knew those three days would be chaos and there would be very little time to rest, so he had to have a tight grip on everything that was going to happen, with contingency plans for the unexpected on what would probably be the biggest investigation of his career. He could not afford to fuck up.

He said a little prayer: *Henry Christie, please frickin' help me!*

Time was spent drawing spider diagrams, flowcharts and jotting down one-word launch pads for ideas until his head was spinning, and then he tried desperately to simplify the whole thing.

Still, it didn't work.

He'd been standing by the dry-wipe board in his office with three felt-tipped marker pens, red, green and black. At first, he'd had an idea that each colour would represent a particular thread of the inquiry, but by the time he finished the board was full and virtually meaningless, resembling the doodlings of a crazy professor. On speed.

He stood back and critically surveyed the board – the inner workings of an exhausted mind.

In a fit of disgust, because he could not make head nor tail of it, he threw the three pens up in the air. In a passing thought, he wondered that if they all fell together in some sort of pattern, maybe he'd be able to read a message in them like a witch doctor emptying chicken bones on to the ground.

They landed far apart.

No message there, then.

He looked at the board once more, his eyes homing in on the name written in red, FLYNN, and another in black, BASHKIM.

The two most important threads in the whole quagmire.

He shook his head, stepped out of the office and locked the door behind him. There was one last job to do before heading home. He jogged down the stairs and entered the custody office, which for once seemed peaceful. He asked the custody officer about the two possible Bashkims in the cells who were still yet to be identified and was told they were fine. Arrangements, Rik knew, were in hand for interviews and translators later in the morning. He then had a quick skim through their custody records to make sure all was in order. Cases had often been lost or at least faltered at court because of nooky questions surrounding custody records. They had to be impervious to any scrutiny and were usually watertight. Custody sergeants prided themselves on the state of their bookkeeping.

Even so, it was part of Rik's job to check them.

There seemed to be nothing untoward. Everything that had happened to each prisoner since their arrival had been scrupulously recorded and each entry signed as required. Which was good. Nothing to be concerned about on that score.

He closed one record, then stopped and reopened it; his brow furrowed as he ran his forefinger down the entries, then shrugged and closed the record again.

Puzzling, but it could wait.

As he walked out of the custody complex, his mobile phone rang. No surprise there. It had probably rung about a hundred times in the last few hours. He was a man very much in demand.

'Superintendent Dean,' he answered, not recognizing the number on screen.

'Hey, pal,' came the male voice with the mid-Atlantic drawl which Rik instantly recognized.

The man's name was Karl Donaldson.

The classic Mini Cooper screeched into the side of the road and the passenger door was flung open.

'Get in.'

Steve Flynn folded his wide frame into the seat and the car accelerated away.

'Nice car, broken window,' he commented, having noticed the cracked rear window as he tugged the seat belt across his chest, noting the car was so old it did not even have inertia-reels.

'1964. Belonged to my dad. I inherited it when he died, looked after it ever since. It was his pride and joy, now mine.'

'How long ago was that?' Flynn asked.

'About ten years, just after I joined the job,' Molly Cartwright said, shoving the car into third as she gunned it off Gynn Square roundabout and headed inland along Warbreck Hill Road.

Flynn looked at her profile as she drove, seeing she was holding her whole body tight and erect, unnaturally so.

'What's going on? This isn't very wise, you know.'

'I could simply be luring you back into custody. I might be driving you into the waiting arms of an ARV team and Rik Dean.'

'That's true,' he conceded. 'Which would make you one hell of an actor – at least, a radio actor.'

Flynn had reluctantly answered her call as his nosiness got the better of him. He'd found himself talking to a very distraught Molly, almost unable to speak coherently through her tears and sobbing. Flynn had calmed her down and promised he would meet up with her in half an hour at a location of his choosing because he – slightly – did not trust her.

She agreed and he spent the next twenty minutes staking out the car park of the Hilton Hotel on the promenade before Molly called again and he told her where to meet up, 'within the next five minutes or not at all'. In that short space of time, no cops descended on the location.

Flynn kept his eyes on her, sitting upright behind the racing-style steering wheel. It gave her a kind of regal appearance. In the light cast as they zipped under street lamps, he saw a tear blob out of her eye and trundle down her left cheek like a transparent bug.

'But you weren't acting, were you?'

'No.'

'And you've also got whiplash, haven't you?'

'Oh, yeah.' She sniffed up.

'So, where are we going and what are we doing?'

She was in excruciating pain, but she wanted to drive – and fast – out of Blackpool on the road to Poulton-le-Fylde, then beyond in the direction of Garstang along the A586, a fast, winding road with little traffic but requiring total concentration at the speeds Molly was driving to get it right, take the correct line on corners and not end up in a field. Although Flynn hung on to the seat belt, he did appreciate Molly's skills behind the wheel.

She slowed on reaching the village of Churchtown, then after that turned on to the A6, where she leaned back a little and stuck to the speed limits as she headed towards Preston, obviously having driven a demon out of her system.

'Better now?' Flynn queried.

She nodded. 'Needed a blast.'

'I get that.'

'Do you, Flynn? Do you really?' she demanded harshly of him. She slowed from fifty to forty mph through the village of Bilsborrow. 'How? Come on, how do you get it? 'Cos I fuckin' don't! I cannot,' she said as her lips tightened across her teeth, 'even begin to understand, comprehend what I did yesterday morning. I. Killed. A. Man. Fuck, Flynn, I killed a man. I almost hacked the bastard in half with my bullets.'

Flynn watched more tears tumble down her cheeks.

'I can't get my head round it.'

'It's not easy,' he said inadequately.

'You say that, but you're finding it easy,' she accused him. 'You killed a guy and then stripped the bastard for his clothes.'

'If you think that . . .' His voice trailed off.

'What? If I think that, I don't know you?'

'Something like that.'

'No, no, you're right. I don't know you . . . yet. How many people have you killed in your illustrious life, Flynn? Does it get easier or something?'

'Which bit do you want me to answer?'

'All the bits,' she snapped.

They were back on the coast and somewhere, far to the east across Lancashire, the beginnings of dawn were starting to crack the sky open.

Molly had driven on to the M55 at the Broughton junction and then powered the Mini towards Blackpool, but had exited before reaching the resort and curved inland across to Fleetwood to the north of Blackpool, where she had pulled up on the seafront close to the well-known Beachfront Café and then wandered down on to the beach itself with Flynn, where she linked arms with him and they strolled in soft sand.

The journey from Bilsborrow had been in silence.

Flynn had brooded darkly as Molly drove the Mini, unable to formulate any answers to the questions. As they walked, he began to talk falteringly – and didn't even know why. He knew he shouldn't be doing it but there was something about Molly that touched his inner being and, with all the events of the last few days, maybe it was time to let a few things out.

'I'm not a killer,' he began, 'but I have killed.'

Molly's arm tightened.

'I was a Marine, then a cop. I was in special forces for a time, then I was a cop. In special forces—'

He tried to explain, but she cut him off and said, 'Like what? SAS or something?'

'Special Boat Service. SAS with dinghies.'

'Go on.'

'Sometimes you are pitted against people who will kill you without compunction and you have to take them first. You don't want to have to kill anyone but sometimes there's no choice.' He stopped, not wishing to expand further on that insight. What he had done in the SBS was for no one's ears.

'And that's what happened to us?' Molly asked.

They had stopped walking. Now they stood side by side looking out across the grey expanse of Morecambe Bay towards the hills of the Lake District, which were just becoming sharp as morning continued to creep in.

'You did what you had to do, Molly. Mike Guthrie showed you that.' Flynn felt her tense up at the name of her murdered colleague. 'As did your other injured workmates. These guys were happy to mow down anyone who stood in their way. That's the equation, the balance, Molly. Yep, I've killed people and I had to kill someone yesterday. Him or me. You or them. It's not rocket science.'

'But I feel so . . .' She struggled to find the words but Flynn understood.

'And you should. Whatever you're feeling, you should.'

'But you don't!' she accused him.

'Yes, I do – and some nights it comes back to haunt me, like a ghost with a gutting knife.' He paused. 'Look, Molly, I never asked for any of this. I never asked to become involved with the Bashkim family, nor for Brian Tasker to break out of prison with murder and revenge on his twisted mind. I know I should've held back from killing Tasker, and when or if Rik Dean catches up with me, I'll face a court and take it on the chin. I lost everything through those men . . . but, hey, you know the saying. They pulled a gun, opened a door and guess what?'

'What?'

'I was standing on the other side of it.'

They sat close to each other on the sea wall, their feet dangling. Flynn had his arm around her shoulders and held her against him.

'Just tell the truth about what happened,' he encouraged her. 'Don't worry about me. You tell them what happened again and again and that process will help you deal with it, rationalize it, come to terms with it, then move on.'

She nodded as he talked.

'You've nothing to worry about. As that TV cop show says, it was justified.'

'I'll never be given a firearm again. I've already been suspended from the team . . . and I'm not actually sure if I want to pick one up again.'

'They'll let you back in time. When it all comes out in the wash, the department will realize they have a bone-fide real-life hero in the ranks, a valuable asset, someone who actually had to pull a trigger. You'll be giving talks to trainees for years. Career sorted.'

She chuckled. Flynn thought it was a nice sound.

With painful difficulty, she turned her head to him, 'You can come back to my flat with me, if you like. You could lay low there.'

'Nah, thanks but no thanks. I have things to do.' The potential of a warm body and solace through sex was appealing on one level, he had to admit.

'Such as?'

'Kick doors down – metaphorically speaking, or maybe literally.'

'She was a lucky woman to have you,' Molly said quietly.

'But I wasn't there for her. I feel like I sent her to her death.'

Her eyes played over Flynn's face. 'Thanks for meeting me. I know it puts you in a delicate position, on the run and all that.'

'Maybe best if you don't tell anyone – now that *would* take some explaining on your part.'

'I know, I won't. Oh, just one thing: can we swap phones?'

She pulled the old PAYG mobile out of her pocket. Flynn handed her iPhone over.

'I'll ditch it soon anyway. By the way, that boyfriend of yours keeps harassing you on this number,' he said. Molly's mouth twisted. 'I didn't call him back to tell him I loved him.'

'Mmm, I think he's going to be hard work.'

'Ditch him good and proper,' Flynn advised, not for the first time.

She nodded.

Molly dropped him off outside the Hilton.

He watched her drive away and she watched him in the rear-view mirror, through the cracked screen, distorting his image. He gave her a little wave.

Both were certain they were unlikely to see each other again.

NINE

When Molly was out of sight, Flynn limped up to Carshalton Road looking for a green Ford Focus parked by the roadside. 'T' registered, he had been told. He found it straight away. Sue Daggert had been true to her word.

The car was unlocked and Flynn slid into the driver's seat and fumbled for the ignition key which, also as promised, was slotted under the passenger-side sun visor. He fired up the engine, which ticked over like lumpy porridge but sounded just about OK. Then he reached under the seat and his fingers brought out a very old-looking six-shot revolver of indeterminate make. Flynn flicked out the cylinder and saw six bullets loaded into the chambers, .38 calibre, which he ejected into the palm of his left hand to inspect them. They were commercially made, which gave them a good chance of actually working – always a bonus. There were no spares, so if it came to a shoot-out he would have to make each one count.

He closed the cylinder empty and did a couple of dry-fires to check the mechanism was working. Although doing this was not good for a firearm, it was the only way of testing the weapon. It was OK. Then he checked the hammer action, thumbing it back one click so it was on single shot. He touched the trigger lightly and the hammer crashed into the empty chamber. Fine. Then he tried double-action and that too was fine.

He reloaded, thumbed on the safety catch and weighed the gun in his hand.

It was a six-inch barrel and cumbersome, not easy to conceal but it would have to do. Just as long as it made whoever it was pointed at shit themselves, it was OK by him.

He wondered what its provenance was. How many bullets had it fired in its history? Had it taken someone's life? Had it been used in robberies or drug deals gone bad? Were there ballistic reports out there that would be flagged up if he was forced to use it?

Probably.

Placing it back under the driver's seat, he fastened on his seat belt and set off, calling in at a twenty-four-hour garage and an Asda superstore on the way to make a few purchases.

'Where the hell've you been?' Alan Hardiker demanded of Molly as she inserted her key into the front door of her flat. He had appeared like a spectre but she had almost been expecting him so, while unpleasant, it was not a surprise.

'Fuck all to do with you,' she informed him.

'I've left my phone in your flat,' he told her. 'I want it back; it's my personal one.'

'No, you haven't. It's not here, I can assure you,' she told him, thinking this was just a pathetic ruse to gain entry again, pushing the door open, stepping inside with a little pirouette and slamming it in his face.

She climbed the stairs slowly and painfully as the whiplash seemed to intensify.

Inside the living room, she immediately spotted Hardiker's phone on the coffee table, picked it up and pressed one of the keys, bringing the screen to life. She saw two missed calls and a voice message.

With a sneer, she tossed it contemptuously on to the armchair and went into her bedroom.

* * *

Steve Flynn had never heard of Mark Carter, the name of the big-time drug dealer given to him by Molly Cartwright. Once he had known every dealer in the resort when he was just a PC on the beat. He'd made it his business to get to know each and every one of them from street corner shit-heads to the guys – and the occasional woman – who controlled the localized businesses. When he gravitated to being a detective on the drug squad, his field of vision had widened regionally and nationally, his *raison d'être* then being to bring down the kingpins of the trade. Sometimes local dealers moved up the chain, but usually they got stuck where they were.

It sounded as though Mark Carter was on his way up.

When asked, Sue Daggert had told Flynn a little about Carter's background – a young lad who had inherited his brother's drug business when said brother was sent to prison for a very long stretch. This was all a few years after Flynn had quit the cops, hence his lack of knowledge about Carter.

But Mark Carter's life story didn't actually matter very much to Flynn.

He just wanted information – intelligence on this man for one thing alone, the kind of golden knowledge that only someone like Sue Daggert could provide. It was stuff that, had Flynn still been a cop, he would have chopped his right hand off for, figuratively speaking.

After his errands, Flynn drove out to the south-eastern edge of Blackpool on to the notorious council estate called Shoreside. Flynn had dealt with many criminals from here, some of whom had turned a once-decent area into one plagued by drugs and crime, an estate where even a parade of shops had been demolished by rampant, uncontrolled kids driving out shopkeepers, some of whom actually fled for their lives.

He drove on to the estate, past the concrete wasteland that had once been the location of the shops.

He knew that, historically at least, much of the crime was controlled by the Costain family whose influence, according to Sue Daggert, was waning because of a concerted effort by the police under the leadership of a certain, but now retired, detective superintendent called Henry Christie. He had made it his job to dismantle the Costain operation and had made a pretty good fist of it, by all accounts. The Costains were in ruins but, as always happens in these cases, someone else had stepped into the void.

Mark Carter.

Flynn crawled slowly past the house owned by the Costains, a knocked-together semi which now looked dilapidated, helpless, lifeless.

He continued on to the perimeter of Shoreside to Mark Carter's house, where Sue had told him Carter lived with a girl.

It was a semi-detached council house, purchased by the occupier and nicely done up. Nothing special or spectacular, just what a sensible drug baron's home should be: under the radar, hiding the wealth.

Flynn cruised past. The only obvious bit of money was the black Range Rover in the driveway, all greyed out windows and personalized number plate.

So Mark Carter did like to flaunt some of his cash after all.

The house was in darkness, no sign of anyone being up.

Flynn parked up a few houses down the cul-de-sac and sat low in the car for about half an hour, slumped behind the steering wheel, using his mirrors to watch the house. A couple of cats sneaked across the road but there were no human movements.

According to Sue Daggert, Carter had done some security work inside the house with doors, locks and blinds. It was therefore doubtful if Flynn could force his way into the property, nor was it likely that Carter would simply open the front door to a stranger hammering on it at any time of day, let alone at dawn.

Flynn knew that his method of luring Carter out of his bed and house would have to be much more subtle, or brutal, depending on your perspective.

Satisfied the cul-de-sac was unwatched by anyone, law or crims, Flynn did a three-point turn and parked facing out close to the junction. Then he quietly removed his recent purchases from the hatchback – a plastic petrol can filled with ten litres of premium unleaded, a cigarette lighter and a box of matches. He shoved the pistol into his waistband, pulled his balaclava over his head and walked swiftly to the front of Carter's house.

The Range Rover wasn't really parked on a driveway, just a section of the front garden that had been flattened and laid with a few paving stones to accommodate the beast off the road.

Flynn knew there was no telling how such a thing as this would pan out, but he had to give it a try.

He quickly splashed petrol all over the lovely car, instantly seeing the fuel begin to burn the paintwork like acid. He finished by pouring a puddle underneath the petrol tank at the rear of the car.

Then he tossed a lighted match under it.

Almost instantly, the fuel erupted into flame with a maniac crackle and then, with a breathtaking whoosh, the whole vehicle was engulfed in blue and orange dancing flames and the pool of fuel under the car caught light with a guttural roar.

Flynn had quickly retreated to the corner of the house, out of direct line of the flames, but even so he was amazed by the heat generated, which sent a wave of boiling air spiralling around him.

He wasn't too concerned that the car might explode. As a cop, he had seen many stolen then abandoned cars go up in flames and never once blow up. It took a particular set of circumstances, mainly associated with trapped vapour, to make petrol explode, and setting fire to a car rarely had that effect. It was often spectacular but rarely dangerous if you kept your distance.

Once he was happy the vehicle was well alight, Flynn swung around to the front door and began to beat it with his fists and feet.

Behind him, the flames licked high. The heat was almost singeing his back.

He continued to whack the door.

An upstairs light came on. A face appeared through a crack in the curtains at the bedroom window. A shout. More lights. The sound of footsteps rushing down stairs.

The car fizzled and burned.

Flynn thumped the door again. A key turned.

Flynn swung away just as the door opened and the dancing flames lit up the face of a young man dressed in a baggy T-shirt and shorts with a frightened-looking woman behind him, gripping a tiny, yapping dog of some sort to her bosom.

'Jesus, shit!' the man blurted, stepping out barefoot on to the front step, but then crumpled to his knees as Flynn came at him from the side and smashed the old revolver on to the back of his head with just enough force, Flynn hoped, to poleaxe him and keep him unconscious long enough to haul him to the Ford Focus.

Behind him, the young woman's screams mingled badly with the howling of her pooch.

With his free hand flat against her chest, Flynn pushed her roughly back into the hall.

She stumbled back and Flynn grabbed the unfastened cord of her dressing gown and yanked it out of the loops before bending down over the unconscious man's feet, lifting them and dragging him down the garden away from the burning car. He was light, nothing like a 1,000-pound heavy marlin. At the back of the car, he opened the hatchback and lifted him in, then used the dressing-gown cord to quickly bind his wrists to his ankles before slamming down the lid and jumping in the car.

As he drove off the estate, Flynn did not see any of the emergency services on their way. He knew that around here dialling 999 was the last thing most people wanted to do because it got them involved, which was not good. Most would happily watch the Range Rover burn and forget they might have seen a man being abducted from his own house. In fact, Flynn was counting on it.

Blood streaked down Mark Carter's face. There was a gaping, ugly wound on the back of his head, exposing the shiny blue-grey of the skull under the scalp. It would require many stitches. His eyes, caked in drying blood, opened and, despite the pain and predicament, he glowered at the menacing figure of Steve Flynn standing in front of him.

Carter looked around, working out where he was.

He was sitting on the ground propped up against the front wheel of a car. His hands were bound tightly behind him. The car was on an unlit road bounded by trees with the glimmer of light beyond from a series of buildings that Carter recognized as the eastern side of Blackpool Victoria Hospital. He knew the resort well. He'd been brought up here, spending many of his younger years bike-riding around with mates.

The screech of a monkey confirmed the location.

Then the deep, throaty roar of a lion.

He was sitting on his backside leaning against a car on the road leading up to Blackpool Zoo.

All this was mind-processed quickly.

'Fuck d'you think you're doing?' he growled at the silhouette.

Flynn had now removed the old balaclava and his face, though in shadow, was revealed to Carter.

Flynn slowly squatted down on his haunches in front of Carter, careful not to split open his bullet wound again. He was just slightly above Carter's eye level, keeping the psychological and physical advantage.

'You set my car on fire.'

'Attention-grabber,' Flynn said.

'You got it,' Carter said pragmatically. Until he knew where this was going, he would play the game and hold back on threats. He had become a negotiator and businessman and had risen to prominence with very little violence, but if there had to be some he could dish it out if necessary. 'What d'you want? I don't even know you.'

'No, you don't . . . business loan,' Flynn said.

'You could've emailed me.'

'I need an instant response, bit like a payday loan but without two-thousand-per-cent interest. Free, in fact. Not a loan.'

'Just tell me, fuck d'you want?' Carter said, impatient now.

'I want to improve your business for you.'

'And how would that be – by destroying my car?'

'Look, pal, I don't want to get into huge dialogue with you . . . just to say I need cash and I need it now.'

'Wonga, then,' Carter said.

'You're my Wonga.'

'Go fuck yourself.'

'It works like this, my friend,' Flynn said patiently. 'Me and you now go to one of your counting houses . . . ah, ah, shut it . . . I know you have six dotted around the Fylde and I know the location of each one. You will take me to the one where you have the largest balance of cash and you will simply give me a holdall full of it . . . Shush!' Flynn said as Carter opened his mouth to protest. He withdrew the revolver from his waistband and let Carter see it. 'I'm a desperate man, Mark Carter, but I know this will be of interest to you.' He shoved the muzzle into Carter's cheekbone, just below his left eye. 'I need operating money and you are my fairy God-banker. Thing is,' he went on mock-affably, 'if you don't agree to do this, several things will happen.'

Carter stayed tight-lipped.

'I will personally visit each counting house, burn them down after stealing all the money and destroy everything in them. You will watch me do this. Then I'll take you home, Mark. I'll burn your house down like I burned your car, but not your girlfriend – who looks well pretty, by the way. What I'll do to her will be far worse. You'll watch me do this. Then we'll come back here to the zoo and, one way or another, I'll throw you into the tiger enclosure and watch you get mauled to death. Now then, Marky-boy, is there anything you don't quite understand?'

Flynn screwed the muzzle deeper into his skin.

Carter shook his head.

'Is there anything in there you think I won't do?'

He screwed the muzzle. Carter shook his head.

'Good. Take it from me, I mean every word.'

'How is this a business loan?'

Flynn leaned in close. 'Who is the bane of your life?'

'What d'you mean?'

'Who keeps treading on your toes?'

'Cops?' Carter suggested.

'No, bad guys. Which bad guys are moving on to your turf? Who is giving you more grief than all the others put together?'

Flynn saw something dawn in Carter's eyes.

'Bashkim,' he breathed.

Flynn nodded.

Carter said, 'You're one of the Bashkims?' completely misunderstanding.

'No, dimwit. I am going to bring them to their knees. I'll get them off your back and off the back of a ton of other shit dealers and then your loan to me will look like money well spent.'

'Who the fuck are you?'

Flynn gave Carter what he hoped was an enigmatic smile.

* * *

In reality, Flynn had been bluffing. Firstly, he did not know the location of any of Carter's counting houses, those usually well-hidden, well-guarded premises where income from drug dealing was amassed, counted and then filtered into the money-laundering system in a variety of ways. Sue Daggert had told him how many houses she thought Carter owned but not where they were.

Secondly, he had no intention of subjecting Carter's girlfriend to a fate worse than death.

All other promises, however, were for real.

If Carter hadn't fallen for the bluff, the addition would have been breaking his fingers one at a time and, if that hadn't succeeded, he would have been big cat food quickly and Flynn would have re-thought his strategy.

He was sure Carter believed him to be as good as his word, having already laid the ground rules with a spot of arson and a soupçon of kidnap.

'Who will we find in here?' Flynn asked.

Carter was in the passenger seat of the Focus, fastened in by his seat belt, his hands still tied uncomfortably behind him and his ankles bound. He had directed Flynn to the basement of a terraced house in South Shore close to the Pleasure Beach. Like many houses in this neck of the woods, it was huge, well built and had once been a genteel hotel. Now it was a hive of grotty flats above the basement, all apparently owned by Carter, and was no doubt a collection point for the money accumulated from the drug dealing that was a feature of life in certain sections of South Shore. There was a lot of money to be made in the area.

'Two guys.'

'Who?'

'Cheech and Chong, I call them.'

'What? Chinese guys?'

'Nah, just a pair of dim brothers from Blackpool. Dim but loyal – and handy.'

'How much money?'

'Last delivery was midnight. Something north of forty grand, I guess.'

'All in pounds sterling?'

'Dunno. Usually about ten per cent in euros.'

'Is the place secure?'

'Fort fuckin' Knox.'

'And the monkeys? Are they armed?'

'Yuh. They're looking after the cash until I pick it up later this morning. They got a handgun each. And knives. And knuckledusters.'

Flynn nodded and looked at Carter. The gash in his head had stopped bleeding, though it remained open, the skin flapping. The blood had dried on his face, having streaked down his neck, back and chest like war paint.

He was being cooperative for the moment but Flynn didn't trust him. He knew he would take any chance given and that he, Flynn, would have to be wary.

Carter waited for Flynn to speak.

'It's a simple trade,' Flynn said. 'Your money or your life.'

Carter swallowed. 'You're a bull in a fucking china shop.'

'Been said before, but just remember you're the china shop, pal. So we get out, walk down the steps, you do your secret knock and tell your two chimps to throw out a nice bag full of money, say twenty grand, then we reverse away and I'm gone, you're a free man and, sometime in the near future, your business will be trouble-free.'

Carter grunted with scorn. 'You really think you'll bring down the Bashkims?'

'Already started,' Flynn said. In his previous run-in with the clan he had razed three of their brothels to the ground. It was therefore no boast.

'OK, whatever you say,' Carter said with disbelief.

Flynn got out, walked around to the passenger side and opened the door. Carter swung out his legs. Keeping the gun aimed at Carter's face, Flynn tugged at the bindings around his ankles and the quick-release knot unfastened with one pull. Flynn pulled him to his feet, then pushed him forwards and down the basement steps.

Carter faced the door. Flynn stood at right angles to him and placed the muzzle of the revolver against his ear. He cocked the weapon and said, 'Very sensitive trigger, this,' as a warning. 'I don't know how much you know about guns, but the slightest twitch of my finger will fire this weapon and will remove most, if not all, of your brain. Nod if you get this.'

Carter nodded. 'How am I supposed to knock?' His hands were still tied behind him.

'Got feet, haven't you?'

He glanced down and saw his bare feet. He kicked the door. Flynn listened, could hear movement inside.

An eye-level letter box flipped open and a pair of eyes looked through the rectangular hole, like a speakeasy from the days of prohibition.

'Open up, Cheech.'

'Boss? Is that you?' came the voice from behind the door.

'Open the door, Cheech – and don't do anything stupid.'

The eyes flickered left and saw the barrel of the gun shoved into Carter's ear. The letter box clattered shut.

A key turned in a lock. Bolts were drawn back. The door opened inwardly. Flynn could see that the inner surface of the door was reinforced steel plate and industrial-sized hinges, probably capable of stopping a shotgun blast.

The door opened but the men inside stayed well back from the threshold.

'Whaz going on, boss?' Cheech asked.

Flynn stepped smartly behind Carter, keeping the muzzle in place. Carter's face was set in a permanent wince.

'Shit,' Cheech said.

Flynn saw the two men inside. The door opened directly into a living room combined with a dining room furnished with a shitty three-piece suite and a rickety-looking kitchen table and chairs. Beyond was an open-plan kitchenette. Sparse and grim.

There were two Nike rucksacks on the table.

'Put the bags at my feet,' Carter said.

Flynn watched the men, both young and slim, with deep eyes and unkempt features. Each had a gun at his side.

'Drop your guns first,' Flynn called over Carter's shoulder.

Neither man complied until Flynn banged the muzzle of his revolver against the side of Carter's head.

'Just do it, guys,' Carter said.

'Boss, you just drop down to your knees and we'll take this cunt out,' the heavy standing next to Cheech said. This must have been Chong, then.

Flynn's mouth came close to Carter's ear. 'You can if you like, but then all three of you will be dead.'

Carter nodded slightly. 'Gently toss the bags out, Cheech – after you've dropped the guns.'

Neither liked what they were doing. Cheech bent down and placed his gun on the floor, as did Chong behind him, then stood slowly back up. Flynn did not like either of these two and was certain they would chance their arm if they could. Neither did he completely believe that two handguns were the only weapons in the room or even on their persons. They looked sly and dangerous and the least time spent in their company the better, Flynn concluded.

Cheech took hold of the nearest rucksack and hefted it across the gap, where it thudded in front of Carter's feet.

'How much is in it?' Carter asked.

'Twenty-two grand, and some,' Cheech informed him.

'All sterling?'

'About five in euros.'

Carter nodded and asked Flynn, 'That do?'

'Get down on your knees,' he ordered Carter.

'But you said . . .'

Flynn pushed him down by the shoulder. He sank to his knees. Flynn grabbed the rucksack and pulled it to one side, his eyes staying with the two henchmen. He fumbled with the zip and opened the main compartment, revealing it to be packed with rolls of bank notes. He re-zipped it and said, 'Back on your feet,' to Carter.

The drug dealer pushed himself upright as Flynn slung the bag over his right shoulder, having to slot his gun hand through the strap as he did and heave the heavy bag into place. But he slightly misjudged the weight – heavier than he'd anticipated – and the strap slid back down his arm, catching the revolver, which was the moment Carter had been waiting for.

Seeing the very slight struggle and Flynn's eyes momentarily distracted, Carter hurled himself through the open door of the basement, screaming at his two men to get their weapons and kill Flynn.

They scrambled for their discarded guns as Carter lurched sideways once in the room, so as not to be in the line of fire.

Flynn cursed, dropped the rucksack and spun into the doorway.

Cheech reached his weapon first, scooping up the gun, trying to get it into his grip, although it seemed to have a mind of its own and want to jump out of his hand like a slippery bar of soap.

The voice inside Flynn's head wanted to shout at them not to be so stupid.

But they were and he didn't have time to reason with them now.

He fired at Cheech as the man jerked up with the gun finally in his grasp. Flynn's old gun, with the hammer cocked, blasted loudly, and Flynn braced his wrist for any recoil because he was holding the gun with only one hand. The bullet tore off most of the right side of Cheech's face, his cheek and ear, spinning him around.

By this time Flynn had readjusted his aim to Chong, who had also managed to retrieve his gun, but was flinging himself behind one of the armchairs for protection.

Flynn shot through the piece of furniture twice, punching holes in the upholstery and, as soon as he had done it, he brought his aim back to Cheech, who had fallen heavily against the edge of the table, grabbed it and tipped it over.

Flynn put another bullet in his neck just as Chong slumped sideways from behind the armchair with a look of horror and surprise at the two black holes in his chest, in his heart, from the two slugs that had passed through the furniture.

Neither man then moved.

Flynn stepped into the room.

Carter watched him, now fearful.

'You could have avoided this,' Flynn said.

He raised his gun and fired the remaining two bullets into Mark Carter's head.

TEN

Despite eating painkillers like smarties, the ever-growing throb of pain in her neck and shoulders kept Molly from sleeping at all. There was no remotely comfortable position in her figure-hugging mattress, or place to rest her head on her fancy pillows without agony.

In the end, she got up, realizing a visit to A&E was a long-overdue necessity now, just in case there was something more serious than whiplash to contend with.

She swallowed another Co-codamol, then poured another large shot of whisky which she sipped as she eased herself down into the armchair and stretched out her legs on to the edge of the coffee table.

She checked her mobile, now crammed with missed calls, text messages and voicemails.

Some were from Alan but most were now from friends and family wanting to catch up with her. She wanted to respond to them all individually really, but instead she composed a text stating she was fine and would be in touch soon and thanks for asking. She sent it off to all.

She had hoped to find one from Flynn, but there was nothing. She was amazed and cross with herself at the same time that this fact disappointed her so deeply. She placed the phone on the chair arm, but it slipped down between the arm and the seat cushion, so she retrieved it and at the same time found Alan's phone in the same place.

Sipping the whisky, she considered the phone with narrowed eyes and then found that the curiosity bug eating her insides needed to be fed.

Because he'd been promised that the Focus was clean, Flynn fought his instinct to set it on fire, because that would just draw in the cops too quickly and they might start to make links with the killings at the counting house. Instead, hoping that the likelihood of any witnesses coming forward was fairly remote, he simply parked up a few streets away from his former marital home and left it there. He walked back with the two hefty rucksacks over his shoulders and Asda carrier bags in his hands.

Once back at the house, he went in through the front door and closed it behind him, standing still on the rubber welcome mat where he stripped off all his clothing, including shoes and socks and underwear, and stuffed it all into a charity collection bag he had noticed behind the door on his first visit. He did the same with the clothing he had taken from the man he had shot in Stable Wood. It seemed an ideal way to dispose of clothing worn during the commission of a crime and he felt a flush of charitable pride when he tied the knot in the bag. It was due for collection the next day.

Taking the Asda bags with him upstairs, he then went for a shower. Before venturing out he had turned on the immersion heater and the water was hot and reviving. Also, because the combi-boiler wasn't in use, there was no external evidence of him being in the house from emissions via the flue.

He washed thoroughly, several times, having wrapped one of the carrier bags around his thigh to protect his leg wound.

He emerged with crinkly skin and found a large bath sheet which he tied around his middle. When dry, he got dressed in the clothing he had bought from Asda on his way to Mark Carter's house. New underpants, socks, jeans and a T-shirt, plus new trainers, then went down to the kitchen and took the rucksacks with him, which he placed on the table.

He'd bought some bread on the Asda trip, which he toasted, lathered with butter and ate with a can of chicken soup heated in the microwave. Then he made a mug of tea, sat at the table and tipped out the contents of the rucksacks.

He looked at the piles of cash, about £40,000 in total, knowing he didn't need so much. It would be difficult to carry around and conceal in such bulk anyway, and getting it through customs would be problematic, even though technically it shouldn't be. Stuffing a few pockets with it would be the only practical option really, maybe carrying five or six grand, half in euros, which would probably see him through. He did intend to keep the remainder but decided it needed a good home to go to.

His problem at that moment was, besides being on the run, the lack of a passport.

Taking a second brew up to Faye's bedroom but keeping fully clothed, trainers included just in case he had to do a sharp exit, he lay down, sipped the tea, finished it then fell asleep pondering the passport predicament.

'He's out on a job,' the detective constable, whose name was Johnny Connors, told Molly.

It was ten a.m. and she was back at Blackpool Police Station, having gone via an early call at A&E for a doctor to check out her whiplash, which was giving her real pain. She could hardly move from the perpendicular and was walking as though the proverbial broom handle had been shoved up her bottom. Her neck had been X-rayed but there was nothing untoward showing despite the pain. The serious painkillers the doctor had palmed to her were having some effect, though.

'In fact, everyone's out on a job, except me. I'm dealing with the overnighters,' Connors whined.

Molly glanced around the CID office, which did have the look of the officers' mess of the Mary Celeste.

'What's the job?'

'Mark Carter's met his maker,' Connors said. 'They're already calling it the counting house killings,' he added creepily.

All the fluid in Molly's mouth instantly dried up. 'What?'

'Mark Carter? Big drug dealer?' Connors said. 'And two of his crony low-life gofers . . . looks like there's been a turf war fallout and Carter and his goons've come off second best.' Connor pointed his right hand at her and made a gun shape. 'Bang, bang.'

'Who . . . what? Suspects?' she blurted.

Connors shrugged. 'Dunno. I've been down in the traps dealing with the dregs of Blackpool's gene pool. Mr Dogsbody, me.'

'Who's heading it?'

'FMIT. Rik Dean for the moment but I think he's handing it over to another super 'cos' – Connors tweaked the first and second fingers of both hands in invisible speech marks around his next words – 'he's "sooo busy", the soft-arse. Wants to get his shit down to those cells. Now that's busy.'

'And Alan's out with them?'

'All hands on deck,' Connors confirmed.

'OK, ta.' She walked away from Connors to the detective sergeants' office in which there was a desk for each of the four DS's in the department. Molly sat down at Hardiker's and took his mobile phone from her shoulder bag. She looked at it with disgust, then dropped it on the desktop on his jotter pad, in front of his computer screen.

'Bastard,' she said quietly, then picked it up again, sighed deeply and slid it back into her bag.

What she had discovered on Hardiker's phone had made her feel physically ill.

There were several voice messages from a woman named Laura and one from Tina (*for fuck's sake*, Molly thought). Also a lot of explicit texts and a couple of Snapchat photos of boobs and female genitals, including a horrendous arsehole shot that must have been incredibly hard to take. Hardiker's response to these in his sent folder were shots of his cock, more erect than Molly ever recalled seeing it.

Molly had not looked at, listened to or read everything because she had become nauseous quite quickly, dropping the phone as if it was a turd.

She considered leaving it on the desk for Alan but now realized she wanted to hand it back in person accompanied with a knowing look, so she stood up and wended her way out of the CID office, almost colliding with a young woman coming in clutching a handful of files. She was one of the members of the intelligence unit.

Her name was Laura Mathers.

Molly stood in front of her, the blood draining from her face as the identity of the woman called Laura on Alan's phone dawned on her.

Laura smiled innocently.

'Laura? You seen Alan at all?' Molly asked, keeping her face sweet.

'Er, no. I think he's out on a job.'

'OK, no probs.'

'Can I help at all?' Laura offered.

'No, no, it's OK . . . He . . . uh . . .' Molly hesitated, but then went for it because of the image seared into her mind like a branding iron of Laura's cunt and arsehole on Snapchat. She held it together as she held up Hardiker's phone and said, 'He left his phone at my place last night. I was just returning it. I didn't want to just leave it on his desk.'

Laura's perfect, heart-shaped lips made a little popping sound and Molly relished the comical expression on her face, one resembling a rabbit caught in the main beam.

'I . . . I'll give it to him if you like,' Laura stuttered.

'No, it's all right, Laura. I think you've already given it to him, haven't you?' Molly's eyes looked meaningfully into Laura's as she continued, 'I'll give it to him personally.' She walked stiffly past Laura who stepped aside, ready to be punched out. From the corner of her mouth, Molly couldn't resist saying, 'Nice Brazilian, by the way.'

Flynn woke at about ten a.m., feeling fresher even though his leg was extremely sore. He made himself some more toast and another mug of tea and switched on the TV in the kitchen. There was a national news bulletin being broadcast, followed by a local update. Flynn sat upright when reference was made to the police in Blackpool attending the scene of a triple shooting at a drug dealer's house. Details were scarce, the newsreader admitted. Flynn turned off the TV and sipped his tea thoughtfully, then glanced down at the phone Molly had given him, which began to ring.

Molly took the lift, which rattled up to the sixth floor of the police station, and stepped out to join the queue of people in the dining room. A few folk asked her how she was and she made a little small talk, although she sensed people were a little wary. After all, she had shot someone dead and was being investigated. She got toast and coffee, found an empty table by a window and sat with her back to the room.

She had a busy day ahead of her.

First, she was due to see the chief inspector of operations who ran the armed response units, followed by a chat with her divisional commander, then another meeting with Rik Dean before the one with two detectives from West Yorkshire Police, who'd been briefed by the IPCC to interview her as part of the investigation into the incident. After all that she was going to visit the two surviving AFOs who were still being treated in hospital.

It would be a challenging day, at the very least. She knew she had to get her story straight, keep it simple, a bit emotional and lie by omission rather than words.

She was very screwed up about the issue of her phone and the late night/early morning tryst with Steve Flynn. As a good cop, she had always told the whole truth, but she wasn't happy about the prospect of revealing that Flynn had taken her mobile phone, nor that he had asked her to name Blackpool's biggest drug dealer, now murdered.

She swore. Sipped her tea. Rubbed her forehead then looked at the phone she had retrieved from Flynn, having replaced it with one of her old ones.

On top of all that was Alan Hardiker. And Laura. And Tina, whoever she was. The immature temptation was to start posting pictures on social media and really fuck the bastard up. A sore temptation and one she almost succumbed to.

In the end she decided to hold on to the phone a while longer because it could come in handy as a bargaining tool.

As for Flynn, she wasn't so certain.

She slid Hardiker's phone away and then stared at her phone on the tabletop before picking it up and going through to the TV lounge which, as usual, was empty at this time of day, the TV on blaringly loud. She turned it down, sat on an easy chair and found the number last dialled.

It was answered, but only by silence.

'Flynn?' she asked the void.

There was no response.

'I just had to know it wasn't you.'

'What wasn't me?'

'Three deaths. Tell me it wasn't.'

'I don't know what you're talking about.'

She sighed with guarded relief.

'You shouldn't call me . . . but now that you have . . . I really do need a favour.'

Molly sat in front of a desktop computer in the report room, her mouth dry again. She was about to log on to her own page on the system, but stopped herself and then decided that a change of location would be sensible because she didn't want to leave any cyber fingerprints that might come back and point at her. She uprooted herself and went back to the CID office, which was now completely devoid of staff, including DC Connors.

She sat at Hardiker's desk and typed in a password.

Not hers. His.

And then she sat back as the Lancashire Constabulary intranet network came online, welcoming DS Hardiker and automatically listed his last three searches on the system.

Molly saw the name: Bashkim.

She leaned forward, held the cursor over the name and clicked on it, opening an intel file that she personally did not have the necessary authorisation to access but which Hardiker, by dint of his rank and role, did.

Molly's bottom tightened as she leafed through extensive pages of information and intelligence about the Bashkim crime family, its known structure, wealth, its reach and suspected operations in Lancashire and the north of England. Molly skimmed through and sent a lot of the information to the printer shared by the DS's.

All the while, she was asking herself one question: why was Alan even looking at the Bashkim file?

Mere curiosity, just because he was allowed to?

That, surely, could be the only answer. The Bashkims were the flavour of the day and she guessed a lot of cops suddenly wanted to know more about them.

She collected the printout and slid the sheets into a folder. As she was about to collect her bag, Hardiker's mobile phone rang in her pocket. She fished it out and looked at the screen, expecting to see Laura's or Tina's number, but it was neither. The caller ID indicated someone phoning from abroad.

She answered it.

A deep, accented male voice said, 'Sergeant Hardiker?'

'No, I'm answering his phone for—' The line went abruptly dead before Molly could say the word, 'him.'

She shrugged. It could have been anyone calling.

The appearance of a couple of detectives walking into the CID office hastened her to get a move on, but the sight of Alan Hardiker behind them made her come to a cold halt. She took a grip of the file and virtually marched out past him, ramrod straight, with a sneer on her face.

'I'm going to see the IPCC now,' she said. 'We'll speak later.'

Hardiker's eyes seemed to grow dark as they followed Molly's progress out of the office.

He walked into the detective sergeants' office at the moment the printer came to life and spewed out one sheet of paper.

Hardiker picked it up and looked at it. It was from a file on the Bashkim family, the last sheet from a report related to prostitution in Lancashire.

Hardiker slumped heavily at his desk, trying to work this out, his brow deeply furrowed. He tapped a computer key and the screensaver de-pixelated. He had expected to see his log-in page, but the screen went straight to his personalized homepage. He was certain he had logged out before attending the triple murder. Positive, in fact.

It was a gruelling day for Molly. She seemed to be passed from one person to the next and spent three hard hours being interviewed by the IPCC detectives who delved deeply into her version of events and were particularly interested in how Steve Flynn had acquired her Glock and, oddly, she thought, they probed into her relationship with Flynn. It was purely a fishing trip because up to that point there was no 'relationship' with him. She'd met him for the first time the other day when she'd Tasered him, then guarded him in hospital, then conveyed him halfway to Preston, when things became ugly.

'So you gave a prisoner a gun?' one of the detectives asked repeatedly, shaking his head in disbelief.

'And released him from his handcuffs?' the other added.

'Yes to both. We were under attack and if I hadn't done something drastic we would both have died. I don't regret it, whatever you might think.'

'Were you having an affair with Flynn?' the first one asked. Molly couldn't even recall their names.

She laughed. 'No . . . and what a stupid question!'

'We have to ask,' detective number two stated.

It was at that point she named them, in her mind, Piss and Shit, Number 1 and Number 2.

'So then he killed one of your attackers and you killed the other?' Piss asked.

'Yes.'

'And the others ran off?' Shit asked.

'Yes.'

'And so did Flynn – after stripping the clothes off the one he'd shot?'

'Yes.'

'And you didn't stop him?' Piss then asked.

'No, I'd just killed a man. I wasn't feeling up to it.'

'Please, don't be facetious,' Shit said.

'You know you'll never carry a firearm again, don't you?' Piss told her.

Molly shrugged.

She kept to her story and eventually Piss and Shit relaxed. For the time being they had gone as far as they could, and they allowed her to leave the interview room with a warning to talk to no one about the matter. Without telling anyone, she left the police station and took her Mini to a garage to get the rear window replaced. While waiting she went for a saunter through the streets of Blackpool to clear her head and slid into a greasy spoon caff, ordered a sausage barm and a mug of tea which she devoured at a table by the window, then made a phone call.

'It's me. I've got something you might want to read.'

Flynn had hardly moved all day. He had set up a little living space in the kitchen at the back of Faye's house, kept the blinds drawn, brought down a quilt and pillows from the bedroom which he laid on the floor and stretched out on while he watched the kitchen TV, the media frenzy and public outcry about the ambush, and quite a lot on the triple murder in Blackpool.

He had been glad to rest up. He wasn't certain of his way ahead but knew he would need all his strength and as much time as he dare take for the gunshot wound to heal before he got moving.

He also knew that remaining holed up, literally on a blanket, as per the old mafia terminology, was inviting a knock on the door from the cops or other bad people. He wasn't going to assume he wasn't in the frame for the Mark Carter killings, having left three dead bodies in his wake, but at the very least he was on the run for escaping from custody and the murder of Brian Tasker; he would also have some explaining to do about taking Molly's firearm and shooting one of the men out to get him.

All those things, but not necessarily in that order.

Bottom line: the police would be very happy to have him in their clutches.

And if he was, then any thoughts of taking on the Bashkims would have to be shelved.

So remaining at liberty was crucial but remaining where he was, at his ex-wife's pad, was inviting trouble because they would eventually get to it.

Flynn did have a fairly cynical view of the investigative abilities of cops. He remembered a PC he once knew years ago who said to him that if he ever lost his job, he would simply come back as a burglar because the police were virtually useless at capturing crims. It was a view that Flynn more or less shared. He knew that most offenders were caught because they were dimmer than the police. The ones with slightly more intelligence were rarely nailed.

Not that he underestimated Rik Dean's capabilities. He'd known Rik for a long time, from way back when Rik was a PC on patrol in Blackpool, and recalled him being one of the best thief-takers he had ever known. He had taken that ability on to CID with him . . . and because Flynn knew Rik, Rik also knew Flynn.

It wasn't as if they had been great mates or anything, just that each knew the other as a colleague and a little about each other's personal lives.

Flynn knew Rik had been a great charmer in his younger days, a legend at being able to lead ladies astray. In turn, Rik knew Flynn had been married to Faye, and because of that it would not be long before Rik came a-knocking just to check the address, and if there was any suspicion that Flynn was hiding here, doors would fly off their hinges.

At least being solvent meant Flynn now had the option to move out and find somewhere in the jungle that was Blackpool, a place where anyone could go to ground and never surface if they so wished, or go further afield.

For the moment, he decided to rest up a little longer, at least until he'd seen Molly again and read what she had managed to download for him.

His eyes focused on the TV, on which he saw a familiar location and a reporter speaking earnestly to camera about the horrific discovery of three men shot to death in a basement flat in Blackpool, not far away from where Flynn was holed up.

He turned up the volume just as Rik Dean came into shot for

a quick soundbite to the camera. Flynn recognized it for what it was: a holding statement to keep the media at bay.

Rik confirmed the discovery of the three bodies but did not identify them and said that it was the very early stages of an investigation, so the police were not jumping to any conclusions at the moment. It was a triple murder; the young men appeared to have been shot dead, money may have been stolen and there was the possibility of links to the underworld.

The reporter, who obviously knew more details than he was allowed to reveal, asked if the premises in which they were murdered was actually a drug dealer's counting house. Rik said he did not know at this stage. When pressed as to whether the police had any suspects, he again said he did not know anything at this stage.

The reporter also asked Rik if there was any link to an arson attack on a Range Rover on the Shoreside estate, but Rik gave the same answer and said that more details would follow later, and then made a plea for any witnesses to come forward, call the police at Blackpool or speak to Crimestoppers. Either way, they would be protected.

For a man who looked completely exhausted, Flynn thought that Rik did quite a good job. He turned the TV off and closed his eyes for a moment. He was hungry and thirsty.

Molly Cartwright's not-good day continued and then concluded with a trip back to the hospital to pay a visit on her partner, Robbo, and Mike Guthrie's partner. Both were in the same side ward, sitting up. They looked battered but seemed in good spirits.

Guthrie's partner was surrounded by his family and Molly said a quick hello and gave him a sad hug before moving across to Robbo, who was alone but expecting his wife and kids to land any time.

Molly, still whiplashed, gave him a gentle but extended embrace. They had been partners on the ARV for about eighteen months and worked well together. Molly perched on the bed and interlocked her fingers on her lap.

Robbo's injuries were not too serious: whiplash coupled with a broken rib, and a very battered face, having headbutted the dashboard. He expected to be able to leave hospital the next day.

Molly updated him on her condition and the sort of day she'd had.

After a short silence, Robbo said, 'You know, you did very well, Moll.'

She narrowed her eyes. 'I just reacted, I suppose. Did what I had to do and all that.'

'I'm not sure I could've done the same,' Robbo admitted. 'I'm almost glad I was unconscious. You are far fucking braver than me.'

'I'm in the shit, though, brave or not.'

'No one can blame you for what you did.'

'Even giving Flynn my gun?'

'Even that. Under the circumstances, it was reasonable . . . trust me.'

She wasn't convinced and had been wavering inside about it since her interview with Piss and Shit.

Robbo sensed it. 'You'll have doubts, Moll, 'course you will. Human nature, but it'll all turn out OK.'

'Mm.' It was a doubtful murmur. 'I'm not going to be an AFO any more.'

'You'll be in demand, though,' Robbo said. Then went quiet before saying, 'That said, I won't be either. I'm going to jack it in. It's done my nerves, this . . . and I have a family to think of.'

Molly touched his hand and he gripped her fingers. 'You're a good cop and AFO, Rob. I understand what you're saying but I'd go into any dangerous situation with you behind me or I'd follow, you know that.'

'I know, but something like this is a game changer.'

'Yeah, yeah.' Molly's eyes began to moisten.

'There is one thing, Molly.'

'What's that?'

'Who knew we were escorting Flynn to Preston? Not many, I'd lay odds. It was basically done on the hoof, which poses a very worrying question to me, lass.'

'Listen, Grandad, this man Flynn is very dangerous. Too dangerous. We should let it go now, otherwise other things will be compromised. We've made our point; let's leave it at that.'

Viktor Bashkim regarded his last remaining grandson with undisguised scorn. 'You never had the stomach for this, did you?'

'It's not that, Grandad.' Niko sighed down his large nose, frustrated by trying to get his point across.

'What exactly is it, then?'

'We are not in the Albanian hills any more. These are not the old days when you took a man's life just for looking at you. Please, let this go.'

They were on the lower rear deck of *Halcyon*, once more berthed in Zante. The evening was warm and the scent of hibiscus hung in the air.

'You were always the weak one, Niko,' Viktor said stubbornly. 'Good at adding up the money but no real feel for the business.'

Viktor had been sitting on a leather armchair, waiting for news.

When it came, via Niko, Viktor had been of a mind to string up one of the staff and baseball bat him to death. Niko had managed to talk him down and try to reason with him.

Now Niko's eyes played over his grandfather's face. 'We have enough assets now to live the rest of our lives in luxury.' He stopped suddenly, realizing he had said the wrong thing when Viktor's eyes flashed ferociously. But he went on, 'You can live in luxury . . . you live in luxury . . .' He waved his hands at the boat. 'You don't need anything else.'

'And you don't understand,' Viktor said. 'This has now become about pride and honour, not about the accumulation of wealth. This man has devastated my family, directly or indirectly, and I will only rest when he pays the price.'

The cool box was on the deck next to Viktor's feet.

He slid his fingers underneath the lid and lifted it off.

He looked down at Maria Santiago's severed head. It was packed with ice that was continuously replenished, but the flesh was beginning to deteriorate and the aroma of death could be smelled against the scent of flowers.

Viktor looked up at Niko. 'You know what I want.'

Niko nodded.

'Bring me Mr and Mrs Jackson.'

ELEVEN

I t was late and felt even later as Detective Superintendent Rik Dean walked into the Tram & Tower public house close to Marton Circle on the outer edge of Blackpool and ordered a much-needed pint of Stella Artois with a Bell's whisky chaser and a packet of peanuts.

Instead of letting the whisky chase, though, he swallowed it first because he wanted to clear his airways, nose and throat of the stench of death.

Next he snaffled a palmful of peanuts then swigged about one third of the pint.

Only then did he relax a little and glance around the bar, spot a deserted alcove which he made a beeline for, sat down and exhaled.

He had been on a post-mortem marathon, lasting most of the afternoon and well into the evening.

Three bodies – one cop and two crims, the latter still unidentified.

It had been drummed into Rik Dean by his predecessor, Henry Christie, that there were some duties a senior investigating officer could not duck.

One was delivering the death message to whom it may concern – wife, husband, lover, whoever; the other was to be in attendance at the post-mortem of the victim(s).

Both duties were emotionally draining, especially when one of the victims was from the 'police family'.

Rik had taken it upon himself to deliver the message of PC Mike Guthrie's death to his wife, now widow. It had been traumatic.

That had been yesterday.

Today he'd attended Mike's post-mortem plus those of the two offenders who had been part of the gang that ambushed the police escort. One had been almost sawn in half by bullets from Molly Cartwright's MP5; the other had massive head wounds from her Glock, fired by Steve Flynn.

They had been relatively straightforward PMs, the causes of death obvious from the get-go, but they had to be carried out thoroughly and all forensic and ballistic evidence had to be collected for further examination. Post-mortems did not stop on the slab.

He drank more beer and wondered how he had got through the last few days on such little sleep.

The last thing he needed were three more bodies to add to the tally, those belonging to local drug dealers.

Rik had taken and covered the call because he was on duty and the closest SIO, plus the Fylde was his area of responsibility, even though there was no way in which he could take on this new investigation and run with it. The plan was for him to cover the initial stages then hand it over to one of the FMIT DCIs – Jackie Dangerfield, a more than competent detective who was champing at the bit for a big job. Rik was more than happy to hand it over.

He had dealt with the initial press briefings but Dangerfield would be handling everything else from now on.

Rik had more than enough on his plate with the whole Flynn/ Bashkim/Tasker scenario and did not have the room or energy to take on anything else, no matter how juicy it looked. And the Mark Carter triple killing looked very interesting indeed.

He downed the remainder of his pint, bought another plus chaser and resumed his seat in the alcove, happy that the smell of death was no longer in his tubes. The beer and spirit tasted good but he knew this was his limit. He had to get home, get some sleep and be back at work at six a.m. the next morning to get his mind around the complexities of the investigations.

There was a lot to do if he was ever going to bring down a crime syndicate such as the Bashkims, who were behind every- thing that Steve Flynn had been sucked into, confirmed by the phone call he'd received the day before from a man with an American accent and a conversation that revolved around the future of Flynn.

Rik reached into his jacket and pulled out Flynn's passport, flipped through the pages and had a very tough argument inter- nally, one of many presently tumbling through his mind at that juncture, until eventually all thoughts came to roost on the moments prior to Rik receiving the phone call from the American, when he had been leafing through the custody records . . . At which point, as he sipped his lager thoughtfully, Rik's phone rang again.

In a similar way in which Rik Dean's brain was in freefall, so was Molly Cartwright's. There were two main threads, interlocking and twisting, which were causing her untold grief, confusion and suspicion.

The first related to Steve Flynn and surrounded a conflict in her dendrites about him. Although fighting it, she did feel a huge attraction to him in spite of their age difference and the fact he was obviously a rogue. For some unaccountable reason, she had felt able to open up to Flynn both when she was guarding him at the hospital and subsequently after the attack when she'd sought him out under circumstances that could have got her into very serious trouble (and still might), and driven him across the breadth of the Fylde in order to further unload her emotions on him. He had listened, given good advice, opened up to her a little and even turned down her genuine offer of a warm – but stiff – body for the night. His refusal had moved him even higher up in her estimation.

But then, the murder of Mark Carter and his two heavies.

That was where her respect for Flynn began to falter.

Was it a coincidence?

Molly seriously doubted it. In her lower gut, which ached like trapped wind, she knew Flynn had killed them because she knew he needed money in order to get out of the country.

She'd been happy to gloss over the fact that Flynn had taken her mobile phone but now she realized she had to put a block on her feelings for him. Her duty as a cop came first.

The other conundrum sloshing around was Alan Hardiker. She was absolutely positive she did not love him any more, did not even like him after what she'd found on his mobile phone. What she had discovered on his work computer disquieted her – Hardiker searching the intel database for details of the Bashkims. It was just an uncomfortable feeling – that plus the very strange phone call he'd received on his mobile phone from abroad.

That is why she then made a call to Rik Dean.

She had an awful lot to confess.

Flynn hadn't really expected to hear from Molly again, so when she called he was quietly pleased, yet wary.

'It's me. I've got some stuff you might want to read,' she opened up straightaway.

After a short conversation and a lot of reassurance from her, he agreed to meet at her flat in Bispham later that evening, just before the witching hour.

Despite Flynn's cynical view of the police and their ability to catch crims, he knew he had to be cautious. Even if Molly wasn't luring him into a trap, and he believed she wasn't, it wasn't beyond the realms of possibility that she was under surveillance herself and didn't know it. When something as serious as an ambush on a police escort happens, even the cops involved had to be thoroughly checked out and maybe followed. Inside jobs were not unknown – and in this instance, Flynn would have put all the money he'd taken from Mark Carter on very bad odds and still won. Details of the escort must have come from a police source, he believed.

Finding it would be tricky.

Molly had told Flynn what her movements would be that evening and he managed to pick up her tail when she left the hospital after visiting Robbo. He was in the 'clean' car that Sue Daggert had provided for him, but knew for sure this would be the last time he would ever use it. He had wiped it down and was wearing surgical gloves while driving it.

He tailed her back to her flat and found a parking space close by where he could keep an eye on the door. Nothing occurred that gave him any cause for concern. No suspicious vehicles parked up and no one walked past, other than himself when he decided to stroll around the block to see if he could spot anything or anyone untoward.

He was convinced she wasn't being watched because, even in the world of hi-tech, the human element of keeping tabs on a target was still crucial and Flynn saw no such evidence.

After one more drive around and one more stroll, with his newly purchased hoodie from Asda pulled over his head, he affected to walk past Molly's front door, then, at the last moment, veered down the short path and rapped on the door.

Seconds later, he was in.

She looked even more wasted and drawn since he had last seen her in the early hours of that same morning. She was clearly on pins, had been crying and her hand shook as she gave him a shot of whisky. Her eyes seemed deep and hunted and, as much as Flynn was glad to see her, he was nervous, wondering if he had walked into a set-up.

'I'm glad you came,' Molly said as he took a sip of the whisky then placed the glass down. She was standing just a couple of feet in front of him, looking up into his face. 'Will you hold me again, please?' she whispered.

He nodded. They came together and he wrapped his muscled arms gently around her as she started to sob and he had to do his best to hold back his own tears. Now he was sure he had not been lured into a trap as he held her close, feeling the shudder of her body with the side of his face close to her ear.

She exhaled long and hard, the breath juddering out of her before she pushed away from him. She tucked her hair back and gestured for him to take a seat, which he did on the armchair across from the settee where she sat.

'Nice place,' he said appreciatively.

'*Bijou*, I think is the term.'

'Whatever that means.'

'Yeah, I'm not sure either, but it sounds good.' She coughed, cleared her throat. 'What have you been doing?'

'Not much, Lying low, considering my options. You? I'll bet it's been a killer of a day.'

'It has, more than you could know.'

'Have you been interviewed by the IPCC yet?'

'Yes, it was grim but, y'know, stuck to my story.'

'Best way.'

'And I got these for you.' She pointed to the file on the coffee table. 'From the intelligence database. Stuff that's confidential and sensitive. Stuff I shouldn't be showing you.'

'Thanks.'

'It could put me in a very awkward position.'

'I know. I won't blab.'

'There is one thing, though . . .' She hesitated and her eyes became steely, like the cop she was. No pushover.

'That would be?'

'Mark Carter.'

Flynn said, 'Who?' unconvincingly. He was a fairly simple man and did not lie well, often giving things away with his body language, as in this case. He dropped his eyes and shifted uncomfortably on the chair. Out of sight, his arsehole contracted. It was one thing making a denial over the phone; in person it was a whole lot tougher.

'Mark Carter. Drug dealer, the one whose name I gave to you; the one who is now dead, together with two of his sidekicks.'

'Oh, Mark Carter!' Flynn shrugged. 'Drug dealers end up dead. It's a risk they run.'

'I know I've already asked you, but did you kill him – them?'

'How did they die, remind me?'

'Shot to death.'

He brought his gaze up level with hers. 'I don't have a gun.'

'So did you or didn't you?'

Flynn sighed impatiently. 'No.' It was always best, as a solicitor friend once told him, to deny, deny, deny. 'I don't get where you're coming from.'

'I told you his name, now he'd dead. Just adding up, y'know?'

'No, I don't,' Flynn said witheringly. 'You've got something for me.' He looked at the file, changing the subject without subtlety.

Her mouth was pursed tight as she stared at him, then her shoulders wilted. 'Yeah, stuff on the Bashkims. Quite high-level stuff above my authorization level.'

'How did you get it?'

'Logged in as Alan Hardiker. He once told me his password,' she fibbed.

'Clever . . . May I?'

Molly reached out to get the file. Her fingers had almost got to it when there was a knock on the front door at the bottom of the stairs. She stopped moving like a mannequin, then tilted her head slightly. Her face was a mask of guilt.

Flynn recognized it, tipped his head back and said, 'You bitch.'

'I'm sorry, Steve.'

*   *   *

Flynn sat in the armchair with his head in his hands, cursing his naivety. He had checked the flat wasn't being watched which meant his gut feeling must have been telling him not to trust Molly and he should have listened to it. She was a cop, after all, and her first allegiance was to herself and her job. Now he should be a hundred miles south of here on a coach or a train with the intention of blagging his way across the Channel and into Europe. Not sat here being set up by a deceitful female, which is now how Flynn cynically thought of Molly.

She had paused at the lounge door to look at him before going along the short landing and down the stairs to the door. Her mouth had popped open to say something contrite but no words came out because there were none to say. She knew what she had done.

Flynn had almost reverted to his primal state because when his back was against the wall, his usual urge was to fight – and then fly. He didn't want to hurt Molly so he decided to see how it panned out, understanding her perspective. She owed him nothing. She was a cop. He was a murderer.

Fuck.

He heard her footsteps clump down the stairs, heard the click of the latch being unlocked, then the creek of the door opening.

Feeling like the worst traitor in the world, Molly unlocked the door, expecting to see Rik Dean. She was taken aback to see Alan Hardiker standing there, his shoulders hunched, his head angled towards her, his eyes glaring menacingly.

'Alan,' she said, but in a parallel thought she realized she'd shown her hand to Flynn by assuming it was Rik at the door. To find Hardiker there meant a very difficult time ahead with Flynn, who realized she had asked him there under false pretences.

Hardiker's hands were thrust into his trouser pockets. His eyebrows rose and fell. 'Molly,' he responded. 'It's me.'

Already, his demeanour concerned her.

'You've still got my phone.'

'Oh, yeah, sorry . . . things got busy.'

'What do you know?'

'About what?' she asked.

'I'm assuming you've been through it, seen the photos? Especially after that little quip at Laura.'

'No.'

'Even with that one word, you're a bad liar.'

'Look, I haven't been through your phone, but I have left it at work in my locker. Can I return it in the morning? I'm in real pain and need to get some proper rest.'

Hardiker simply stared at her. 'What were you doing on my computer?'

Molly's heart went cold. 'What do you mean?'

'The computer on my desk. In my office. You were on it this morning.'

Molly shrugged and shook her head, feeling the pressure. 'I wasn't . . . Why do you think that?'

Hardiker pulled his right hand out of his pocket with a folded piece of paper in it, which he opened. 'Sometimes the printer plays up. Doesn't always print everything at once. Like this.' He showed it to her, part of a file referring to the Bashkims.

'Not me,' she insisted feebly.

'So I'll ask again, Molly.' He scrunched the sheet up into a ball. 'What do you know?'

'Like I said, about what? Look, I haven't been on your phone and I haven't been on your computer. Clearly you're paranoid about something. Now, I need to get to bed . . . I was involved in a serious incident where a cop died and I shot someone, as you know, so I'm not feeling tiptop and I'm also wondering about how the people who ambushed us knew about the police escort. That, Alan, is what is screwing up my mind, not your computer or your phone.'

She stepped back, intending to close the door on him.

Hardiker flung the screwed-up piece of paper into her face. It caught her by surprise, but then he came in behind it. His left arm shot out and forced the door out of Molly's grip, and his right hand went straight to her throat. He pushed her back against the wall and came in close and tight right up to her. Breath in her face, reeking of garlic, onions and alcohol.

Molly realized he had been brooding about this, drinking in a pub.

The back of her head cracked against the wall and Hardiker's fingers tightened around her slim throat, instantly restricting the blood flow to her brain. The whole of her body, from the neck down, bawled in pain as her whiplash injury jarred.

'What do you know?' he snarled into her face.

She pawed at his forearm and hand, trying to wrench it free and, as she did, she realized for the first time that he was wearing skin-tone latex gloves.

In a thought: *He's come to kill me.*

His grip tightened, squeezing.

She brought up her right knee, intending another ball-crushing slam, but he was ready for this one, had his legs together and was twisted slightly away from her.

'Not this time,' he laughed harshly.

His eyes were on fire.

His grip tightened even more.

'What do you know?' he repeated, spittle from his mouth flicking into her face.

In spite of the pain, she writhed and struggled and kicked, tried to scream out, not to succumb.

'Nothing,' her voice grated.

He moved in closer, more intimate, pinning her against the wall with the width and weight of his body, still squeezing, his face contorted, sweaty.

Molly managed to swing her left fist into the side of his head, but it was a glancing, ineffective blow.

He laughed again.

'You'll have to do better than that,' he challenged her.

The next punch to the side of his head sent him into instant unconsciousness.

His grip came free from its hold on Molly's throat as his whole body went limp and he slithered to the floor with a dull, 'Urgh' escaping from his mouth as all his bodily functions short-circuited.

Molly fell forwards on to her knees, coughing and spluttering.

Steve Flynn, the deliverer of that blow, knelt beside her, one hand resting on her back as she sucked in oxygen and her senses, which had been fading, returned.

'I had him, y'know?' Molly coughed. 'I had him.'

'I know. I put him down to save him from you,' Flynn said
jokingly, shaking his head.

'Help me up.' Molly reached out and Flynn brought her slowly
back to her feet. 'He's got latex gloves on,' she said.

'I know.' Flynn looked down at Hardiker, who was groaning
and squirming slightly.

'He's not dead, then?' Molly asked.

'No.'

'Brain-dead?'

'No. I hit him just hard enough to put him down.'

'You can do that?'

'With practice.'

Massaging her neck, she regarded Flynn. 'Thank you.'

'Well, whatever . . . I'd better be off. Whoever you were really
expecting might turn up. Wouldn't want that, would we?'

'I'm so sorry, Steve.'

'Forget it.' Flynn swallowed something back in his throat –
probably regret and sadness and disappointment, though he wasn't
entirely sure what he could realistically have expected from her.
He took another look at the moaning Hardiker, held back an urge
to kick him repeatedly, then stepped across him over the threshold,
only to find his way blocked by Rik Dean.

In that first look, Flynn did not see anyone accompanying Rik,
which he thought was strange but good, though it wasn't something he had time to analyse. If Rik had decided to come alone,
then more fool him. It made it so much easier for Flynn.

He did not hesitate.

Using the momentum from stepping over Hardiker, Flynn
lurched at Rik and drove a hard, deep punch into his guts, almost
making the man's eyeballs burst out of their sockets as he doubled
over and gave Flynn a look of surprise and horror, then went
down on to one knee, crippled and winded.

Flynn knew he needed more of an advantage than that.

He needed time to get to the car and put at least five minutes'
driving time between him and Rik. Five minutes at that time of
night would put him on the outer rim of Blackpool, maybe even
as far as Poulton-le-Fylde and within spitting distance of the
motorway.

With that calculation in mind, he delivered a punch to the side of Rik Dean's head which was similar to the one he'd just put on Hardiker.

Flynn did not even look back. He ran as quickly as his injured leg would allow, ignoring the shout from Molly. As he turned into the street on which his car was parked, the area seemed deserted. The car was still there and he ran into the road to get to the driver's side – the moment he knew he was not alone.

A big hand grabbed the back of his neck and slammed his head down on to the car roof, trapping his face sideways, left cheek scrunched down while the muzzle of a pistol was twisted into his temple. Flynn tried to squirm free but he was held in place by a man of similar stature and strength to himself, whose face loomed into view.

'Hi, Steve, we meet again,' the man said into Flynn's upturned ear.

TWELVE

He sat alone in a room. One door, no windows. A solid door, steel construction like a police cell. Maybe it was a cell, but not like one he had ever been in before. There was the chair he was sitting on, pulled up to a sturdy table, both items of furniture screwed to the floor by heavy bolts with shaved heads. A pair of manacles hung from the wall by the table and ankle bindings were fitted to the front chair legs. Flynn was not shackled, though. Two free-standing chairs were on the opposite side of the table.

There was no bed in this room, or a toilet.

Just the furniture, illuminated by a strip light on the ceiling protected by a wire mesh.

There was a red panic strip at waist height on three of the walls. The door had an inspection hatch, which was shut.

Tucked high in one corner was the lens of a security camera protruding from the ceiling. It was behind a Plexiglas protective screen.

It was cold.

Flynn shivered.

He knew this was a secure interrogation room, but was not sure of its location.

Not in any police station, that was clear.

The man who'd pinned him to the car roof had been joined by another from the shadows and together they had worked quickly and expertly to put a black cloth over Flynn's head, bring his arms around his back and secure his wrists with plastic cuffs.

As they were doing this, a vehicle had slid up. Doors opened, Flynn's head had been pushed downwards and he'd been bundled into the back of a van, forced to sit on a bench seat. Doors had slammed shut, the van moved off. No one had spoken.

Blinded by the hood, Flynn had been aware that there may be two other individuals in the van sitting on the bench seat opposite.

They had been good, quiet and efficient. Flynn knew not to mess.

He'd said nothing, but instead relaxed and tried to work out where he was being taken to. The van had driven up to the junction with the promenade, made a left and headed south, then almost immediately slowed and went left. Flynn knew they had turned into Red Bank Road in Bispham and were therefore travelling inland. He had felt the lurch on a roundabout, then a series of short runs, left and right turns and had begun to lose track of the journey, but there was no way he was being taken towards Blackpool nick.

They'd been on the road for about three-quarters of an hour and the last thirty or so minutes were motorway driving, straight, long and fast, the tyres booming on the surface, so they had to have been travelling east down the M55 to start with, away from Blackpool.

Flynn had driven along this stretch of road many times at many speeds and knew that from one end to the other at a constant seventy mph, which seemed to be about the speed of the van, would take twelve to fifteen minutes tops. From there, the motorway curved either north or south as it filtered into the M6, a manoeuvre that could be achieved without slowing down, but because of the bend of the carriageway and how he had to brace

himself to stay sitting upright, Flynn knew that at the end of the
M55 the van had merged south on to the M6.

First exit from there was junction thirty-one at the Tickled
Trout Hotel on the River Ribble, maybe three minutes away
travelling at the speed they'd been going.

The van had begun to slow down and Flynn knew they were
on the exit ramp and the left turn where that met the roundabout meant they were now travelling towards Blackburn on
the A677.

Why, he'd had no idea, so he'd sat back and tried to keep
track of the direction, though he was less familiar with the
geography in this part of Lancashire. They'd travelled a further
ten minutes fairly quickly and along mostly straight roads, but
eventually the van had slowed, turned left, slowed right down
and gone left again until it had been creeping along and he'd
heard the tyres squealing despite the slow speed. He'd guessed
they were on a concrete surface, possibly in a car park. Then the
van had stopped and Flynn was sure he'd heard a shutter door
close with a crash.

Destination reached.

Flynn had tensed under the blackness of the harsh hessian
hood.

The van door had opened.

Wordlessly, hands had grabbed his arms, one rested on his
head and he'd been eased out of the van, standing there unsteadily
as the hood had been whipped from his head.

No bright light, but he'd blinked and seen that he was standing
inside a large industrial unit – shiny concrete floor underfoot – in
which about twenty vehicles of many shapes and sizes, ages and
condition were parked. At one end of the unit were doors which
he'd assumed led to the offices.

The man who had accompanied him had stayed behind him,
kept hold of his shoulders and guided him between the vehicles
towards one of the doors. Beyond it he'd seen a long, sparse
corridor, three doors on each side. The first door on the left was
open and he'd been ushered into the room, noticing the solid
nature of the door as he passed through.

The two men had pushed him towards the chair on the opposite
side of a table, removed the plastic cuffs and sat him down on

the chair. They'd left without a word but closed the door behind them, locking it.

Flynn had then continued to wait patiently at the table, listen and plan.

Christ, his leg hurt.

Now there were footsteps outside in the corridor, the mutter of voices, a key in the lock, the door opening and a man stepping in.

The man who had kidnapped Flynn.

He closed the door softly, walked across the room and sat opposite Flynn.

'Hope you weren't treated too roughly?' he said. He had an American accent, obvious but maybe diluted by too many years spent in the UK.

'I always love having a gun shoved into my face,' Flynn said sourly.

'I figured it was the best and quickest way to get and keep your attention.'

'A drink in a pub would have sufficed.'

'I doubt it.'

'So,' Flynn looked around the room/cell. 'Where am I and what the hell's going on?'

'First, you don't need to know; second, we'll come to that soon.'

The door opened and a man entered carrying a cardboard tray rather like an egg box, in which were slotted three large paper cups with lids from Starbucks. The man slid the tray on to the table and sat down in the vacant chair, looking acidly at Flynn. His face was a swollen mess, red raw and sore looking. He sniffed something up his nose.

'I wish you'd stop assaulting me,' Rik Dean said.

The American's name was Karl Donaldson. Flynn had come to know him through Donaldson's friendship with Henry Christie and had first encountered him in the village of Kendleton in north Lancashire when Flynn and Christie found themselves in the middle of a blood-soaked feud between gangsters, Donaldson along for the ride. He had met him a couple of times since, the last occasion being when Donaldson appeared just as Aleksander

Bashkim was about to put a bullet between Flynn's eyes. Donaldson had materialized from nowhere, killed Bashkim and then disappeared into the mist.

Flynn had never really fully discovered the whys and wherefores of Donaldson's welcome intervention but he thought that there was now every chance of some explanation because he could not really see any other reason for the American sitting opposite him.

Flynn didn't know a great deal about Donaldson, other than he worked for the FBI at the American embassy in London. The few dealings he'd had with him suggested he was much more than a legal attaché.

Flynn also, grudgingly, accepted a couple of other things about Donaldson.

That he was a big, tall, wide, good-looking Yank with a square Superman jaw and he guessed that women swooned over him.

Second, that he was a very handy guy. There were not many men or women Flynn looked at and thought he would be reluctant to tackle if needs be. Karl Donaldson was one of those, which was one of the reasons why Flynn had acquiesced so placidly to this 'kidnap'. Particularly in his current state of health with the wounded leg.

'Coffee?' Donaldson lifted one of the cups out of the tray and pushed it in Flynn's direction. 'Latte, skinny, decaf, wet and extra hot – I guessed.'

Flynn took it, eased off the lid and took a sip. Tasted good.

Donaldson took one himself and Rik helped himself to the remaining cup.

'We have a lot to discuss,' Donaldson said.

Flynn blinked. 'You first.'

A shimmer of a smile played on the American's lips, then his face became deadly serious. 'OK, I'm very sorry about the death of your lady friend, Maria Santiago.'

Hearing her name was like an electric shock to Flynn's system. He kept his face impassive, took a quick sip of the coffee but his hand quivered slightly. He gave Donaldson a little nod.

'I know the background now,' Donaldson continued. 'The Brian Tasker element, his seeking revenge on you and some of your old cop colleagues for putting him away, how while in prison he linked up with the Bashkim family with whom you were having dealings, shall we say?'

'Understatement,' Flynn said.

'And who, it seems, were happy to go along with Tasker to revenge the deaths of certain family members, allegedly at your hands, part of that revenge being to kill Maria in the most brutal way imaginable. An eye-for-an-eye, that kinda shit. I've seen the footage.'

Flynn sipped more coffee. 'I upset a crime family I didn't ask to become involved with and now they want their pound of flesh. That's my summary, and now I want mine.'

Donaldson nodded. 'Sounds about right.'

'Let me think about this,' Flynn said, staring at Donaldson. 'You are part of a multi-agency team investigating the activities of the Bashkims . . . hence why you showed up at a very opportune moment and prevented Aleksander putting a bullet into me – and you are still part of this team.'

'Something like that,' Donaldson concurred. 'In spite of your onslaught against the Bashkims, they are still very much operational and I have a vested interest in bringing about their demise.'

'To which onslaught are you referring?' Flynn asked. He glanced at Rik, who was glaring at him.

'Let's just leave it at onslaught,' Donaldson said knowingly.

'Yeah, let's leave it at that. So, what's your vested interest?'

Donaldson's face twitched – a thought, a memory. He seemed to brace himself. 'The FBI was running an undercover agent in the Bashkim setup. He went off-grid six months ago.'

'Off-grid?'

'Uncontactable.'

'Dead?'

Donaldson nodded. 'The remains of his body were found floating in Grand Harbour, Valetta, Malta. I say remains . . . he'd been decapitated. DNA confirmed his ID. His head was never found. I was his control. I lost him.' Donaldson's voice sounded bleak.

'Ahh,' Flynn said.

'Exactly. He was a friend of mine.'

'Even shittier, but that doesn't begin to answer what I'm doing here, unlawfully detained, presumably at the pleasure of the President of the United States.'

'At the moment, Steve, it's the lesser of two evils where you're concerned.'

'How so?'

'You could be at Her Majesty's pleasure,' Rik said.

Flynn's eyes flicked between the men opposite him. He waited, between a rock and a hard place.

'Time you made all this clear,' he then suggested.

'OK,' Donaldson said. 'The Bashkims, the FBI are certain, had our man murdered – and I'll come back to that in a minute. As an organization and as a civic duty, we wish to dismantle the apparatus of this family.'

'To be honest,' Flynn said, 'I had thought the demise of Aleksander Bashkim had achieved that. Clearly I was mistaken.'

'Yes, you were. The Bashkims are still operating big style, people smuggling, drugs, women, you name it. This is because Aleksander and his two sons, all now deceased, were key members of the family, but not the only members.'

Flynn closed his mouth. It had been sagging open like a fly trap.

'They are in fact headed by an old man called Viktor Bashkim, now in his eighties. He is the absolute leader of the clan, has been for over sixty years. There is also one grandson left, Niko, who is Aleksander's third and last remaining progeny.'

Flynn listened, astounded.

'Niko isn't anywhere near as violent as his siblings were, but he and Viktor have been keeping the ship afloat just as success-fully as before. Thing is, Steve, old man Viktor is not one to forgive and forget. He's very old school, which is why we find ourselves in this position.'

'The position being?'

'That the pursuit of lawful justice is at an end.'

Rik Dean shifted uncomfortably.

Karl Donaldson smiled evilly.

Steve Flynn wondered what the hell was coming his way.

'OK, you won't be upset if I'm a bit wary, will you, guys?' Flynn asked. 'I don't know where this is headed' – he arched his eyebrows pointedly at the two men – 'but I'm not being drawn to say anything in this environment that might incriminate me. I've been abducted at gunpoint, brought hooded to an unknown location in Blackburn' – here he saw both men react to that, even though all it was only an educated guess – 'and I don't want to be verballed up.'

'I understand your reticence, Steve,' Donaldson said calmly, 'but let me assure you of several things. First, our conversation will not be recorded in any way, shape or form because what we will talk about is entirely off the record and I don't want anything I say to be heard anywhere else, either.'

Flynn glanced at Rik and prompted him with another arch of his eyebrows.

'Me, too,' he said sullenly.

'So we will be honest with you,' Donaldson said.

'OK, tell me exactly where I am right now.'

Donaldson took a breath. 'What we say is entirely confidential, between ourselves.'

Flynn nodded.

'Just to show I trust you, I'll tell you: you're in an industrial unit on the outskirts of Blackburn, which I think you already worked out. It is as secure as it can be and is a joint facility used by the FBI, CIA, MI5 and the SIS.'

'For what?'

'To hold certain people incognito.'

'Terrorists?'

'Terror suspects.'

'And interview them?' Flynn asked.

'If appropriate. Some people who have been detained here have subsequently found themselves in other locations in which they can be held without charge.'

'Rendition, then,' Flynn said.

Donaldson shrugged.

'OK,' Flynn said. 'Cross my heart and promise not to blab, though I'm still not convinced this chat of ours won't be recorded.'

'It won't, I assure you,' Donaldson said.

Flynn's eyes turned to Rik. 'It won't,' the detective said.

'Can I have that in writing?'

'No!' both men responded together.

Flynn shrugged.

Donaldson said, 'I'll tell you why. Once we've established the ground rules here, what we will then tell you, if it became record, would put us both in danger of losing our jobs, and I have too many years invested in it for that to happen.'

Rik said, 'Me, too. I want to retire on a superintendent's pension.'

I'll bet you do, Flynn thought cynically. *Commute over a quarter of a million tax-free and a half pension around the forty grand mark*. A full police pension was something he himself had been denied and it still rankled.

Rik shrugged on seeing Flynn's expression. 'I don't make the pension rules.'

'Guys,' Donaldson interceded, sensing tension. 'OK, what we are about to discuss is off the books. My bosses know about it and have sanctioned it because that's part of their jobs, but it is completely deniable. Rik's chief constable is also aware but, if it comes back to bite our asses, you can bet shit will slide downhill.'

Flynn stayed silent.

'The, err . . . slight bugbear in all this, Steve,' Donaldson went on, 'is that you were in custody for murder and it's not as though that can be written off.'

Flynn remained silent.

'I'll come back to that but Rik probably needs to speak now.' Donaldson handed over to the superintendent, whose face seemed to continue to swell visibly. He wasn't looking well.

'A few things,' he began. 'Obviously you killed more than Brian Tasker, such as one of the guys who ambushed the police escort. You took Molly's gun off her and shot one of them. She shot another.'

'No actual denial there, just mitigating circumstances, such as we were fighting for our lives.'

Rik held up a hand. 'I know that and I'm certain it will not go to trial. There will be an inquest but not a trial. The result will be justifiable homicide. I can make sure of that.'

Flynn waited for more.

'I have to know something else,' Rik said. 'Mark Carter, our local drug lord. Did you kill him and his two associates?'

'Who?' Flynn said.

'That'll do,' Rik said. 'Looks like a gang war to me.'

'Still leaves the issue of Brian Tasker,' Flynn said.

'You're a wanted man. I can't suddenly rescind that and make it go away. You also assaulted me, stole a police van and wrecked it.'

'What could you do?' Donaldson asked.

'I could bury it,' Rik said simply. 'Fudge it, delay it.'

Flynn said, 'Why would you do that?'

'Because,' Donaldson answered for Rik, and this was no surprise to Flynn to hear it, 'you could be useful to us.'

'What? In a greater good kind of way?'

Donaldson leaned on the table. 'You have intimated to Rik and to PC Cartwright that you haven't finished with the Bashkims.'

'I'm good at intimating things.'

'Thing is – do you have a plan?' Donaldson asked.

Flynn shrugged. 'Suck it and see.'

'So, no plan,' Rik said dryly.

'Correct,' Flynn affirmed.

Donaldson leaned back. 'In my estimation, piss-poor planning, as they say, will screw you over. And you can only plan if you have knowledge of a subject. Agree? Which I think is what you intended to get by coercing Molly Cartwright to download confidential information for you from Lancashire Constabulary's intel database, for which she could be in big trouble.'

Flynn didn't respond to that either. As it happened, Molly didn't really need to be coerced, but he understood she had spoken to Rik and was now trying to save herself by telling him about the misdemeanours she had committed and then luring Flynn into a honey trap of sorts. Cover your own backside, Flynn thought, which is what he'd told her to do anyway.

'Look,' Rik said, seeing Flynn's hesitation, 'I know all about it – she told me.'

Flynn sighed. 'So what are you proposing, guys?'

Donaldson's eyes narrowed. 'You don't have a plan?'

'No, OK? No plan,' Flynn admitted.

'So how did you intend to deal with the Bashkims?'

Flynn leaned forwards now. 'I have no idea. So far everything has been purely reactive.'

'Well, a good plan . . .' Donaldson commenced to say before Flynn cut in irritably, 'You're a stickler for planning, aren't you?'

'Far from it,' the American said, unoffended. 'But what I like to have is knowledge; yeah, I do formulate plans but they're always flexible.'

He stood up. Flynn watched him with a furrowed brow as he untucked his shirt and lifted it, exposing his stomach and lower chest area. Tanned, obviously, and still with a hint of a six-pack. Just under his ribcage was an ugly, puckered wheal of flesh as though he'd been stuck by a red-hot poker tip which had then been twisted.

Flynn knew a gunshot wound when he saw one. Indeed, he had his own currently in his leg.

'A man wanted on terrorist charges almost killed me.' Donaldson pulled down his shirt. 'The planning was good but, like all plans, once someone shoots you they tend to go to rat shit.'

'What was the other guy's fate?' Flynn asked.

'Not pretty,' Donaldson said wryly. He sat back down. 'Look, all I'm saying is this: you want your revenge for Maria's death. I want my revenge for my agent's death. My hands are tied, pretty much, although there are always things going on in the background. You, however, are pretty much a free agent. We can brief you on the Bashkim organization, then it's down to you. You'll have more intelligence and information than PC Cartwright could ever access for you – from the FBI database and others – and you can use it to formulate your . . . plans . . . if you have any.'

'So you want to feed me then let me loose? Is that the deal?'

'In a nutshell,' Donaldson confirmed.

'What if I say no?'

'Then you'll be coming with me to the nearest cop shop,' Rik said.

'And if I say yes, then I walk out of here and disappear into the night?'

'You won't,' Donaldson said.

'But what if I did?'

'Your call, but you won't.'

Flynn weighed it up. 'So in essence, this is a briefing?'

'Kinda,' Donaldson said.

'In that case, it's a long time since I was at a briefing, but I seem to remember that a prerequisite to every single one I ever attended was bacon sandwiches and lots of coffee. This isn't any different.'

THIRTEEN

The three men left the cell and made their way upstairs to the first level and a large conference room, big enough to hold about thirty delegates if they squashed in. There were several rows of chairs each fitted with a swing-over desktop, reminding Flynn of his early days as a probationer PC on courses at Hutton Hall. The classrooms there were all then kitted out with such furniture for the new bobbies. At the front was a raised stage and on that was a desk with an open laptop. Behind this was a smartboard and the image displayed on it was the laptop screensaver, a view of a beautiful but unidentified mountain valley.

Flynn took a seat at the front, as did Rik Dean, but several seats apart. Donaldson went to fiddle with the laptop, then stepped away from it using a wireless mouse. He sat next to Flynn, two very big, physically fit, powerful men squeezed into chairs too small for them.

Donaldson pressed a button.

The smartboard screen came to life with the first slide of a PowerPoint presentation entitled simply: THE BASHKIM FAMILY – black writing, white background.

The next screen had the same title but smaller, and a list of bullet points followed.

The first one said, *The Albanian Mafia.*

The next, *Albanian History/Geography.*

The next, *The Bashkims.*

As this last one came on screen, the door to the room opened. Flynn glanced across, disinterested, but suddenly sat upright on seeing who entered.

Molly Cartwright.

She was carrying a tray with four fresh Starbucks coffees slotted in it and four paper bags each containing hot Starbucks all-day breakfast sandwiches.

Flynn watched her walking painfully, handing out a coffee and sandwich to Rik, Donaldson, then finally him. As she gave him the food she half-smiled. He smiled back, noticing the red marks on her neck from Hardiker's assault.

She sat on the other side of Flynn, who said, 'What's going on?'

Donaldson said, 'Bit of a decision on the hoof . . . We'll explain soon.'

Flynn sat back, flipped his desktop over his lap and opened his all-day breakfast. He could smell its aroma immediately and it did the job on his senses. He bit into it with joy and a sidelong glance at Molly, who pretended not to notice him as she opened her food.

Once each person had eaten a few mouthfuls and sipped some coffee, Donaldson got back to the briefing.

Flynn actually did know quite a lot about the Bashkims. They were one of many criminal gangs operating out of Albania and their sphere of operations stretched across the whole of Europe and included some connections with Mexican drug cartels. They were heavily involved in people and drug trafficking, the latter being a line of business far more lucrative and less dangerous for the gang than the drug trade. Flynn had believed that the ultimate boss – or *krye* – was Aleksander and that his two sons, Pavli and Dardan (known as *kryetars*) – were his main henchmen.

Which had been true, up to a point.

What Flynn hadn't known was that Aleksander had another son, Niko, and that his still-living father, Viktor, was the actual boss of what was known as the *Shkodra Clan*.

He had wrongly assumed that the deaths of Aleksander, Pavli and Dardan would be the end of their story and he would live happily ever after.

Wrong. It seemed that the old man had been prodded back to life with bleak thoughts of revenge on his mind and that the Bashkim enterprise was still a thriving concern with many lesser family members now involved.

'So as you can see,' Donaldson explained, 'taking Aleksander and his two sons out has not put the beast down.' He paused and clicked the mouse. A face materialized on the smartboard. A young man with a lock of thick black hair falling over his eyes who reminded Flynn of a young Frank Sinatra, but the look was pure Bashkim. 'Circa 1956, this is the young Viktor Bashkim.'

Flynn sat forwards and saw the arrogant expression in the two dark eyes as they looked down his long nose at the camera lens of what was definitely a police mugshot. Flynn saw a heavy chain around his neck.

'Arrested by the police in Tirana for stabbing another youth to death. Charged but never reached court. Story is that the gold neck chain he's wearing belonged to his victim.'

'Good-looking boy,' Flynn said.

'We have a few more photos over the years.' Donaldson flicked through a series of shots showing an ageing Viktor until finally pausing on one taken by a long lens of old man Viktor leaning on a boat rail. 'This is him now.' He looked at Flynn. 'No doubt he ordered Maria's death.'

Flynn kept a straight face and shovelled the last piece of his sandwich into his mouth.

'And this is Niko, by default suddenly second-in-command of the Bashkim family,' Donaldson said as another photo came on the screen. 'He'd been on the periphery of things really. Enjoyed the good life and the money and the women and, although he can be extremely violent when roused, he's more of a bean counter but has stepped up to the mark.'

Niko was a good-looking man, reminding Flynn strongly of Aleksander and of Viktor.

Donaldson continued to narrate. 'Stepped up to the mark certainly in terms of people trafficking. Word is there's supposedly going to be a concerted pre-winter push to bring as many people across the Med from North Africa before the weather turns. Up to a thousand just by the Bashkims, so somewhere around the three million euro mark for their coffers.'

'Why don't you stop 'em?' Flynn asked.

He knew it wasn't a realistic proposition. Stopping people smugglers was like trying to plait fog. It wasn't as though the migrants all waited patiently to board a nice ferry in Libya and disembark in Italy. Hundreds of different, tiny, usually unsafe boats would be used. A few might be intercepted but that was just the tip of the iceberg, and it was too late anyway. By the time a boat was stopped or overturned by waves, the smugglers would have their money in their pockets.

Donaldson just scowled at Flynn for the stupid question.

Another picture came on the screen. At first Flynn could not quite make out what he was looking at. He twisted his head slightly and the image was revealed.

A body floating in water, minus its head.

The next photo was, Flynn assumed, the same body naked on a mortuary slab.

No head.

'My agent,' Donaldson said. He clammed up, stared at the photograph, then took a quick sip of his coffee.

'Bastard,' Flynn said, his thoughts on Maria.

Another picture came up, this time much more pleasant, of a very sleek and expensive-looking powered motor yacht, moored in a marina Flynn did not recognize.

'This is *Halcyon*,' Donaldson said.

'Nice.' Flynn sat up. He had been slouching.

'It belongs to Viktor Bashkim.'

Flynn blew out his cheeks. 'Take a lot of migrants to pay for that.'

'Somewhere around the forty million euro mark, give or take,' the American said.

'Wow.' Flynn was impressed and angry at the same time.

'And it's on this boat that Viktor Bashkim now lives, plodding mainly around the Aegean Sea and eastern Med.'

'Not in the hills of Albania?'

'No. A life of luxury at sea, surrounded by armed guards. It's easy enough to be incognito, which is what he likes. Currently in and around the Greek island of Zante.'

Flynn knew Zante, had once been there on holiday with Faye.

The smartboard went blank. 'That's about it,' Donaldson said.

'Not that much,' Flynn commented, 'and yet . . . I still think you know even more.'

'What makes you say that?'

'You used the word "supposedly" when you talked about

Viktor's push to bring as many people as possible across to Europe before winter. To me that indicates knowledge . . . and a source,' Flynn concluded.

More coffee had arrived from Starbucks, this time delivered by one of the guys who had escorted Flynn to this location. He seemed less aloof now and even smiled at Flynn as he handed the coffee over, then left the briefing room.

'Slip of the tongue.' Donaldson grinned.

'No, it wasn't,' Flynn insisted. 'You've got a source, haven't you?'

Donaldson chewed his lips and regarded Flynn. 'You got me,' he admitted.

'Who?'

'Can't say.'

'Where?'

'Ditto.'

'On the boat,' Flynn guessed. 'Crew member, maybe.'

'Can't say.'

Flynn rolled his eyes and uttered a disapproving gasp. 'So much for information.'

'Their safety. You know how it works. The more people who know, the more likely a leak and a beheading.'

Flynn shrugged acceptance but not happiness. It meant things were happening without his knowledge.

'We have something else, too,' Rik Dean piped up. 'But not sure how we can use it to our advantage.' He looked at Molly as he spoke, then his eyes shifted to Flynn.

Before anything could be revealed, there was a knock on the door. The man who had just brought the coffee stuck his head around and addressed Donaldson. 'Sorry to interrupt but I need a word, Karl. Urgently.'

Donaldson rose from his chair, saying to Rik, 'Tell him,' and to Flynn and Molly, 'I'll be back.'

He left the three behind.

Rik Dean looked quite ill. Flynn said, 'Sorry,' meekly, in reference to his injuries.

'Whatever . . . Anyway, one or two things have come together.'

Molly said, 'He's talking about Alan Hardiker.' She rubbed her neck gently on saying the name.

'Who is still being treated at A and E and may be there for some time . . . NHS waiting times and all that. The first thing that's helpful in this situation is that he didn't see you coming down the stairs and is convinced that it was Molly who punched him, so that's good.'

'He didn't see me?' Flynn said.

Rik shook his head. 'He has no idea what really happened.'

Flynn smiled broadly at Molly. 'You must pack a good punch.'

'I do,' she said proudly, 'so watch out.'

Their eyes intermingled. Rik saw something affectionate pass between them and coughed to break the moment. They looked guiltily at him.

'Like I said, some things have come together,' he said. 'First is that when I was checking the custody records for the two unidentified lads in custody who were with Brian Tasker, and who we believe are Bashkims, neither of whom are still saying anything, incidentally, I saw that one of them had been taken out of his cell for fingerprinting, DNA and photographing.'

'Not unusual,' Flynn said.

'It is when it's an officer completely unconnected to the case who does it, unless having been instructed to do so.'

'Hardiker,' Flynn said, feeling his stomach churn.

Rik nodded, then looked at Molly, who picked up the tale. 'He left his personal mobile phone in my flat by mistake. Other than the obscene photos and texts to and from his various lovers, there were also texts to an overseas number and a voicemail from an unidentified male.'

'Which said?'

'Something along the lines of, "Your information has been gratefully received". Then I found out he'd been accessing force intel on the Bashkims through his police computer.' Molly shrugged. 'Not that it necessarily meant anything in itself.'

Rik went on, 'Molly gave me the number of Hardiker's personal phone and I found that a call was made on it from Blackpool nick at the time he was in the fingerprint room with the prisoner. Obviously we can't pinpoint the exact location it was made from, but it does link with the time he was in with the prisoner.'

Donaldson had re-entered the room during this conversation.

'Who did he call?' Flynn asked.

'A mobile phone on Viktor's boat in Zante,' Donaldson said, picking it up. 'It's not a number we know – the Bashkims drop and change their cell phones like their underpants – but the call from the cells in Blackpool was made to a phone on the boat.'

'Shit,' Flynn said.

'He's made others, too, and sent texts to various phones, all on the boat,' Rik said. 'And received calls also from on-board the boat.'

'He's the police source then,' Flynn said.

Rik nodded gravely. 'Also, we've been reviewing CCTV footage from the cameras on the multi-storey car park at Blackpool Victoria Hospital. Hardiker was seen to drive on to the car park half an hour before you were taken to Preston and he went shortly after the escort left the hospital. We don't know what he did in the car park, but he could have used one of the upper floors as a vantage point. There is footage of him driving off the car park shortly after the escort set off. And he made a phone call from that location to another mobile phone in Zante at the exact time the escort moved away from the hospital.'

Flynn gave a sharp laugh and tapped his hands together in a nervous gesture.

'He's in debt, like I told you,' Molly said. 'Maybe he saw it as an easy way to make some money back.'

'Do we know if he received anything?' Flynn said.

Rik looked at Donaldson, who nodded. To Molly, he said, 'You don't know this, but he received a wire transfer from a bank in Paris to his personal account at Barclays . . . £2,000. We're still trying to trace the named holder of the French account, but it's likely to be one of the legitimate accounts fronting the Bashkims.'

Flynn looked at Molly. 'Served you up on toast. And me.'

'I know,' she said softly.

'One of our own,' Rik said bitterly.

'Question is now on a practical level – how do we play him to our advantage, because at the moment he doesn't know that we know anything about any of this,' Rik said. 'He just thinks he went round to Molly's flat to harass her and get his phone back, and she punched his lights out.'

'I think he had something worse planned,' Molly said. 'Why wear latex gloves?' She shivered.

'Again, let's not divulge we know anything about the gloves,' Rik suggested. 'I think we play it all down, give him a bit of an unofficial warning with a nod and a wink – all guys together kind of thing – pretend to smooth it all over, tell him he got what he deserved and he's lucky you're not making a complaint . . . that sort of thing, and then have him and his phone under twenty-four-hour scrutiny, maybe feed him a few morsels about you, Flynn, and see what he does. Just spit-balling here, folks. All ideas gratefully received.'

'I like the sound of it,' Flynn said. 'Letting him hang himself. Molly?'

'Yeah, yeah, I can go with it . . . paint me as the hysterical female in all this.'

'If the cap fits,' Flynn quipped, and got a punch in his shoulder for it.

'And there has been another development,' Donaldson announced, 'which might affect matters.'

'You ever heard about this place?' Flynn asked Molly.

They were taking a fifteen-minute comfort break, the excess coffee taking its toll on their bladders.

Donaldson had given the nod for Flynn to go get some fresh air and Molly had accompanied him up a set of metal stairs on to a flat roof area, screened from any onlookers by a smoked-glass barrier and covered by a fine wire mesh. It reminded Flynn of an exercise yard, although he doubted if any of the transitory detainees filtering through this facility were accorded such privileges or dignity.

He still hadn't been told exactly where he was, but he could hear the close hum of early rush-hour traffic and still thought they were on an industrial estate on the outskirts of Blackburn, possibly in the Whitebirk area by the arterial road.

'I don't even really know where I am,' she admitted. 'One of Donaldson's guys brought me over.'

'It's probably best to expunge it from your memory,' Flynn advised. 'How are you? Recovered from your ordeal?'

'Not really.'

Flynn hesitated. 'You thought it was Rik Dean at the door, didn't you?'

A little chastened, she nodded. 'I'm so sorry.'

'You were saving your skin. You've got a career and a pension to think about. You have to make moves to protect those things.'

'Maybe, or maybe I was just being a coward, but the Mark Carter thing got to me. I gave you his name, next thing he's dead!'

'Coincidence.'

'Honestly?'

He nodded, not having a career or pension to think about.

'So are you going to do this?' Molly asked.

'Their dirty work?' he said. 'Fortunately, it's very similar to my dirty work.'

On their return to the briefing room, Donaldson and Rik were looking grim, discussing something quietly with a sheet of paper between them. Flynn sat with Molly next to him, still not certain as to her role in all this. She hadn't been forthcoming during their little sojourn to the roof and he hadn't pushed her.

Donaldson clicked the remote mouse and the smartboard came to life, showing the home screen of the laptop.

'I mentioned a development,' he said. 'You might want to watch this.'

Flynn saw the cursor on the screen hover over an icon and then a new PowerPoint opened. There was no title to it and the first slide was blank.

Donaldson said, 'I showed you photographs of my agent floating in Grand Harbour . . . these are some more images I think you should see. Brace yourselves.'

He clicked the mouse.

The next slide contained a gruesome crime scene of two people decapitated in a back alley.

'Paris, Latin Quarter, last year. These two were business rivals of the Bashkims. Beheaded, as you can see,' Donaldson explained.

Flynn took in the horrific image.

The next few slides were more angles of the same scene. Huge amounts of blood, wheelie bins, litter, sleaze.

Then there was another. A dead man on a sandy beach. Headless and naked, feet in the water. More shots of the same scene followed. 'Benidorm, six months ago . . . Lots of organized crime in Benidorm. This man was also a rival of the Bashkims.'

'Head?' Flynn asked.

'Never found.'

Donaldson carried on with two more similar executions, one in Oslo and one in London, until Flynn said, 'OK, we get the gist. Where is this leading, Karl? I accept that Maria met her death in a similar fashion and obviously there's someone out there who gets their kicks by chopping people's heads off.'

'Where am I going with this?' Donaldson posed, angling his face to Flynn. 'Our intel suggests that the same people committed these crimes on behalf of the Bashkims. I mean, it takes some doing to chop someone's head off. Putting a bullet into someone is one thing but hacking off their head . . .' He was lost in a moment of thought. Flynn's feet twitched impatiently. 'We had a message from our source on *Halcyon* to say that a couple fitting the description we have of the suspects in these killings arrived on the boat a day or so ago.'

'A couple? What, two men?' Flynn asked.

'No, a couple as in a man and a woman,' Donaldson corrected him.

'So we're thinking the people who might have murdered Maria are on Viktor's boat right now,' Flynn said animatedly.

'Were, but not now.'

'What d'you mean, not now?'

'They've left the boat, seemingly in a hurry following a short meeting with Viktor. My source has heard only snippets of the conversation, but your name was mentioned and I can only guess at the context.'

Flynn jolted upright.

'There are a lot of imponderables in this scenario,' Donaldson warned, 'but I think they're coming for you, so maybe we should serve you up on a plate.'

FOURTEEN

Flynn sat alone in a cell at Blackburn police station, staring blankly at the point where the off-white wall met the off-white floor. Some wag had managed to etch 'fuck all cops' into the wall, a sentiment Flynn wholeheartedly agreed with. He had been incarcerated for eight hours – long enough for someone to jet halfway around the world if they so wished – and he was getting irritated.

He needed to get going, be on the way, and going through this rigmarole was interminable.

A key turned in the door. He watched the inside of the lock turn and the door opened outwards – cell doors always opened outwards to prevent prisoners being able to barricade themselves inside – and the civilian gaoler stood there. He jerked his head.

Flynn stood up. The gaoler stood aside and Flynn sidled past along the corridor towards the custody office, where he took up a position at the desk and faced the sergeant opposite.

Flynn looked sideways as Rik Dean came alongside. Flynn smiled.

'You're going to be released without charge for the moment, Mr Flynn.'

'That's good to know.'

'However, enquiries are still ongoing and I have no doubt that at some stage in the not-too-distant future I will have amassed enough evidence to re-arrest and charge you.'

'Look forward to it.'

The sergeant listened to this exchange and wrote it on the custody record. Flynn signed for his property, including all the items that had been seized from his hire car. He was relieved to see his passport coming back his way plus a holdall containing clothes and paperwork and the e-tickets for the flight he had booked – and missed – for his intended return to Ibiza that had not happened. But soon he would be on the way there to collect his boat.

His boat named *Maria*.

He was eager to get going to reconnect with one of the loves of his life, sail out of the marina at Santa Eulalia and head back to the Canary Islands where he lived. It was a journey he was anticipating, a journey on which he would grieve for Maria and be at one with the sea. If he got the chance. And at the end of that journey, put himself out as bait, like a tethered goat, for the two killers who had murdered Maria. He was sure they would come. He was looking forward to it.

He signed on the line, as requested by the tapping finger of the custody sergeant, and heaved the holdall over his shoulder.

'I'll show you out,' Rik said.

Flynn followed him out of the custody office and through a door leading to the side of the police station where a black van was waiting. Rik opened the sliding door and Flynn clambered in. There were three rows of seats and Flynn slid into the centre one next to Molly Cartwright.

Donaldson was in the front row and Rik climbed into the back one.

The driver and front-seat passenger were the two guys who had originally driven Flynn from Bispham to the secret FBI facility. He was getting to like them, though they weren't the most talkative chaps in the world.

Donaldson was sitting sideways, his left arm draped over the seat back.

'How did it go?' he asked.

'The cops had nothing on me,' Flynn said.

'Good. I knew it would end well.' He elbowed the back of the driver's seat and the van moved off, joining the early evening traffic on Whitebirk Drive. He went right and picked up the M65 motorway for Preston and ultimately Blackpool.

Flynn had no desire to talk. He leaned back, closed his eyes, pulled up the shutters and went immediately to sleep.

'I find it very hard to come to terms with this,' Rik Dean confessed to Flynn. 'Letting a murderer walk whatever the circumstances.'

Flynn patted him patronizingly on the shoulder. 'You'll get over it.'

'I have a lot of things to fudge,' he said, miffed.

'But a lot of things to keep you busy,' Flynn said.

Rik shrugged. Very unhappy. As much as possible, he had always tried to do all police work by the book and had been a good cop. 'Henry Christie once confided to me,' Rik said, seeing Flynn's face twitch at the name, 'that if you can bring a murder charge against an individual, then you can sure as hell do the opposite.'

'So I've got him to thank?'

'No, you've got Karl Donaldson and this whole scenario to thank, but if it goes tits up and looks like an alligator's snapping at my arse, things might change.'

'I think you were mixing your metaphors then,' Flynn chided him, even if he only had a vague idea himself what a metaphor was. English language wasn't his strongest subject, closely followed by maths.

Rik shook his head sadly at him.

Flynn, Rik, Donaldson and Molly were clustered around the car Flynn had been using, the one supplied by Sue Daggert which she claimed was clean, but Flynn was ever so slightly nervous about it in case Rik ran it through the Police National Computer and it came back of interest, or if a car of a similar description had been seen in connection with the Mark Carter killings, in which case he might change his mind about letting Flynn slip through his fingers. There was nothing worse for a cop than watching a good job walk away – and if Rik suddenly chose to have a quick root through it, the forty grand in two rucksacks stashed in the boot might also sway him.

The car was still where it had been parked when Donaldson had lifted Flynn, just around the corner from Molly's flat.

'Anyway,' Rik relented begrudgingly, 'good luck. You're going to need it.' He thrust out his right hand and they shook.

Donaldson, who had been leaning on the car, pushed himself upright and shook hands too.

'You asked about Molly's role in all this?' Rik said.

'Yeah, she's never been fully explained to me.' Flynn grinned at her.

'She's off sick at the moment with stress and whiplash injuries, and that's how I want her to remain,' Rik said. 'Slightly off-grid.'

'I'm going to fix her up with a super-duper new computer with access to certain areas, shall we say, in order that she can do some research,' Donaldson said. 'She will be your point of contact. She'll be able to track your phones and remain the conduit through which we stay in contact and feed you any information you might need to know.'

'What phones?'

'You'll be given two when you reach your destination, both with tracking devices installed. Please keep in touch, Steve . . . Don't go rogue, otherwise we'll not be able to protect you in any way, shape or form.'

Flynn almost choked on his chuckle.

'Molly will drive you to the airport,' Rik told him. He slapped the roof of the car and declared, 'Well, that's me . . . bed . . . Good luck.'

Donaldson slapped Flynn on the arm then left with Rik, both climbing into the van with sliding doors, leaving him with Molly.

They looked at each other.

'Flight's in six hours. I've been told to give you this.' She handed him an envelope which he peered into, seeing a thick wad of euro notes. 'Two thousand. Operating costs, apparently.'

'Very nice. Look, Molly, I need to get a shower and a change of clothes . . . Could we meet back here in an hour?'

'You could shower at mine,' she offered hopefully.

'That's kind of you, but I'll be fine. One hour?'

She looked crestfallen but said, 'OK.'

Flynn jumped into the car as Molly walked back to her flat. He drove back to Faye's house in South Shore, not too concerned about concealing himself from neighbours this time. He heaved the money-laden rucksacks and his holdall into the house. Then he went up for a long, hot shower to cleanse out the grit which seemed to be in every pore, crease and orifice. Being in custody was a grimy affair. He changed into the clothing he had in his holdall and went back to the kitchen to make a brew, which he supped while tipping money out of the rucksacks.

He divided it into eight equal piles and put one of the stacks into the paella dish on top of the kitchen cupboards. He would contact Faye sometime in the near future to thank her, let her know he had paid for his unauthorized stay at her home and ask her to give half the money to Craig. He trusted her to do this.

Finding a couple of plastic supermarket carriers in a drawer, he split the remaining money into them, deciding he would try and get one of the bags through customs, but he had a plan for the other bag.

He was then about ready to move.

He replaced the door key where he'd found it under the plant pot, then drove back to Bispham. He would text Sue Daggert to tell her where to pick up the car and that there was payment in it for her troubles (and to send someone trustworthy to collect it for her). The revolver wouldn't be in it because he had disposed of that piece by piece in various drains throughout Blackpool.

A few minutes later, he was knocking on Molly's door.

She drove him to Manchester airport in the Mini Cooper. The journey took about an hour and a half and she parked on the short-stay car park at Terminal 2. It was here she handed him the e-ticket and boarding pass for a flight leaving in a couple of hours for Ibiza.

'You don't have to come in with me, you know,' he told her.

'I know. I won't. I just didn't want to feel rushed by pulling up on the drop-off point.'

They regarded each other in silence, their faces half-hidden by shadows thrown by the fluorescent lighting.

'It's funny when you meet someone and you just kind of know,' she said.

Flynn smiled.

She went on, 'I know this couldn't possibly go anywhere and it would be nuts to think it would.'

'Completely nuts.'

'You're grieving. I've just ditched a bastard . . .'

'I've just punched that bastard's lights out.'

'That, too.' She smiled. 'I'm very young,' she teased him, 'and you're very, very old.'

'Mm,' Flynn murmured dubiously at that one.

'And you're going to go up against a highly dangerous criminal gang without a plan. You could be dead in two weeks.'

'That, too.'

'But, like I said, it's funny when you meet someone and you just kinda know.'

'Maybe when this reaches its conclusion we could . . . see how the land lies.'

'Good idea.'

Once more, they looked at each other. A kiss could easily have happened but both knew it would be a mistake as neither was really ready to plunge into anything yet, despite the temptation for reckless abandonment.

'I'll be going then.'

Flynn climbed out of the Mini, walked to the car park exit opposite departures and did not look back.

The plane was delayed about an hour, giving Flynn plenty of time for a meal and a drink and then time for reflection, although this wasn't one of his strengths. However, he did think how short a time had passed since he had arrived at Manchester airport, coming in the opposite direction from Ibiza with Maria Santiago at his side, all revved up to do something about the murders of his former colleagues and current friends.

That had been the end of a magical summer for Flynn and Santiago.

She had taken extended leave from her job as a cop in Gran Canaria and joined him for long days taking out tourists and exploring the bays and inlets of Ibiza, followed by long nights and a lot of lovemaking.

Flynn's almost perfect lifestyle: a boat, a beautiful woman and a steady income from day trippers.

He acknowledged he was a simple man at heart.

It had all been destroyed.

Part of him wished he was the sort of man who could be philosophical about it, let it go, let the cops get on with it.

But he wasn't.

FIFTEEN

Alan Hardiker had been admitted to hospital for observation. Although his head X-ray had showed no fractures or problems, the doctor treating him wanted to be safe rather than sorry, so he was kept in overnight and well into the following day when, after a further X-ray showed all was fine, he was discharged.

He was amazed at how hard Molly had managed to punch him.

He didn't have any recollection of the swing, nor the impact.

Just sheer panic, then blackness, then a vague recollection of being in an ambulance with darkened windows, yet able to see the street lights whizzing by.

He had been glad to remain in hospital. If necessary, it would be good evidence that he had been assaulted if it came to him having to defend himself from an allegation from Molly that he had attacked her. He could say he simply went round to collect his phone from her flat, she became instantly violent . . . no, he did not touch her . . . but she managed to strike him quite a devastating blow which had put him down. He had done nothing to deserve it. He had been completely reasonable and non-threatening.

And she had lamped him without provocation.

First, he needed to see which way the wind was blowing.

He was about to find that out when he went to see Detective Superintendent Rik Dean in his tiny FMIT office first thing that morning.

Hardiker tapped on the door and was called in.

Rik was behind his desk, head down in paperwork.

He did not look up, but beckoned Hardiker in and to the chair in front of the desk in the way superintendents did.

'Mornin' boss,' the DS mumbled.

Rik held up his left hand for quiet. He was scribbling something and trying to keep his concentration.

He finished with a flourish of the pen and a gasp of relief, placed down his pen, looked at Hardiker and said, 'Sorry about that. Just needed to finish it before my mind crashed.'

'No probs, boss.' Hardiker surveyed Rik, seeing his facial injuries from the assault inflicted by Steve Flynn – which, if anything, looked worse than before. 'I know there's a lot going on at the moment, I mean, if I can help?'

'No, all fine, Alan.'

Alan. That was good. 'Alan' was informal. 'Sergeant' less so.

'OK, you obviously know why you're here.'

Hardiker tried to look penitent. 'Molly Cartwright?' he ventured.

Rik nodded. 'Look, d'you fancy a brew or something? Up in the dining room. I know you must still be feeling a bit groggy.'

'Yeah, but I'm OK. Bit tired. Sore head . . . and a brew would be good, boss.'

'My shout,' Rik said. 'We'll find a little table for a chat.'

Hardiker nodded. This was, so far, going much better than he'd anticipated and already he was thinking, *Maybe I'll get a chance to put one over on the bitch after all.*

The men stood up and headed for the lift.

It was that time of day when there was a bit of a lull in business and for a short spell the dining room was almost deserted.

Rik bought two large coffees, getting both smiles and sympathetic grimaces from the ladies behind the counter on seeing his and Hardiker's injuries. He led the DS to a table at the far end of the room and they sat across from each other.

'You going to tell me what happened, Alan?' Rik began. He knew he had to keep the conversation non-threatening because he wanted to scam Hardiker, but also knew the DS was no fool. It was hard to do this because Rik wanted to reach out, grab his head and smash it to a pulp on the tabletop. Maybe he would get the chance in the not-too-distant future.

'Am I under caution?'

'No, why should you be?'

'I just want to know how the land lies, that's all.'

'And I want to get to the nub of the matter with as little shit flying as possible.'

Hardiker nodded. 'What did she say?'

'No, Alan, I want your version of events and then I'll balance the two. But, just so you know, my gut feeling is this is a nothing job, OK? Not going anywhere.'

'All right.' Hardiker leaned back and marshalled his thoughts. 'Has she made a complaint against me?'

'I have her story. Her side. I want yours, then I'll make a decision.'

'How come you're involved anyway, if you don't mind me asking? Surely it should be a local boss, not an FMIT super.'

'Comes with the territory,' Rik said.

'Right, right. OK, here we go . . . You probably know me and Molly were seeing each other. Well, we split up, bit acrimonious, sad and all that, but hey, relationships,' he said, being all worldly. 'Anyhow, big do's, little do's, I realized I'd left my personal phone at her flat and went round to get it. She sort of taunted me that she had it and I went for it.'

'At that time of night?'

'Well, y'know, boss, emotions running high, that kind of shit.'

'Yeah, yeah, 'course. And when the door opened, what happened?'

'I dunno, it's just a blur. She went for me as soon as she saw me and that's all I remember.'

'You didn't attack her first?'

'No, no way. I'm a DS. I have a career and a pension to think of. I realize it was a silly time of night to be going round, but I did need my phone and I'd never lay a finger on her. I'm pretty sure she was pissed, actually.'

Rik nodded. He was quite liking this.

'Er, did she allege anything else?' Hardiker asked delicately.

'Such as?' Rik sipped his coffee, which was pretty good.

'Oh, nothing, nothing.'

'So, she opened the door and went for you . . . and then?' Rik prompted.

'A lucky punch, I suppose. Next thing, ambulance and A and E. A hell of a lucky punch to be precise, to put me down like that. Right on the nail.' He touched the side of his head tentatively while Rik thought, *You don't know the half of it, matey.*

'OK, that's what I thought, to be honest,' Rik lied. 'I've spoken to PC Cartwright and between you and me and the gatepost' – Rik winced and leaned forwards conspiratorially – 'I've got to say it's a hysterical female thing.' A look of sheer relief flitted across Hardiker's face, the 'I've bloody well got away with this' look. 'I do think your judgement is in question for going round to her flat at stupid o'clock, but she definitely overreacted and things got messy. My view, as it stands, Alan, is that it's probably six of one, half a dozen of the other. Couples breaking up can be messy but police involvement is something that should be a last resort, even if it's cops involved . . . get my drift?'

'Yeah, yeah,' he said too eagerly.

'You know, if you made a complaint and she made a complaint and it went to court . . . very messy in my opinion. No winners. Not you, not Cartwright, not the constabulary. You can if you wish but I'd really advise against it. What are your thoughts, mate?'

Mate! Hardiker liked that. He pretended to consider the option before him. One thing for sure would be that if he made a complaint, all the shit would surface. People like Rik Dean would start to delve into his life and uncover crap. He could not afford for that to happen.

'I won't make a complaint if she doesn't.'

'Best way,' Rik agreed. 'It'll have to be recorded in some form, but to me it's just going to be verbal advice given to both parties. How does that sound? And you'll have to keep away from each other.'

'Sounds good to me, fairest all round. One thing, though . . . I've still not got my phone back.'

Rik fished the offending device out of his jacket pocket. 'This, you mean?'

He laid it on the table between them. Hardiker visibly tensed up and nodded cautiously.

With the tip of his forefinger, Rik slid it towards the DS.

'Don't leave it behind again.'

Hardiker was desperate to know if Rik had been into it, or if Molly had said anything about what could be found on it.

Instead, with shaking fingers, he took it and slipped it quickly into his pocket.

'Thanks, boss.'

'No probs.' Rik took a drink of his coffee, eyeing Hardiker

over the rim of the mug, despising the sleazy creep of a man more with each passing moment. To keep the conversation going, he said, 'Got much on? I'm presuming you're back in work?'

'Oh, yeah, busy, busy, busy . . . stuff stacking up, but not like you. Christ, what a shitload you have on at the moment,' he said, glad of the subject change. 'If you'll pardon my French.'

'Oh, yeah, very busy, too.'

'That ambush!' Hardiker whistled in awe. 'That was some violent thing. Was it all about that Steve Flynn guy?'

'That's the assumption still.'

'Hell, two dead bodies! And two offenders escaped . . . But at least you got Flynn back in custody, I hear.'

'Didn't you know?'

'Know what?'

'He's back out.'

'Really?' Hardiker was genuinely astounded, but a predatory look came over his face. 'How come?'

'Long story, hard decision,' Rik said mysteriously, 'but I'll be seeing him again.'

'On bail? With conditions?'

Rik shook his head.

'Isn't he a flight risk?'

'He's under no illusions about where he stands. In some respects he's peripheral to the whole shebang and I've made an appointment for him to come back with a brief in about a month. Told him to bring an overnight bag and no expectations about going far.'

'Think he'll turn up?'

Rik nodded.

'Where is he in the meantime?'

'Left the country. Gone to pick up his boat from Ibiza, by all accounts.'

'He's got a boat in Ibiza?'

'So I believe.' Rik was trying to sound disinterested. He really did have a lot on his plate and wanted to get on with it after having sown these seeds. 'Anyway, Alan,' Rik drank the last of his coffee, 'I need to get back to the grindstone.'

'Yeah, yeah . . . Look, boss, thanks for sorting this thing with me and Molly.'

'That's OK, but you need to keep your distance from her.'
'Got it, boss. Thanks again.'

Delay followed delay for Flynn's flight to Ibiza. Though impatient to get there, he took the opportunity to crash out at the airport while keeping one eye on the departure monitor and, when the flight eventually took to the sky, he wedged himself tightly in an economy seat, flipped the seat tray down, leaned on it with his elbows, wedged his face between his hands and, in that position, slept for most of the two-and-a-half-hour flight.

He wasn't exactly refreshed when he landed but the aroma of the island and the late summer warmth, even at six in the morning, served to revitalize him. As did his bag full of cash in his hand, which had made it unscathed through immigration.

Just before he jumped into a taxi, a man approached him and handed him a padded envelope, which he tore open to find two iPhones and two chargers, Donaldson being as good as his word. The man nodded, jumped into a waiting car and was gone. Flynn hailed a taxi from the rank and told the driver to take him to the marina at Santa Eulalia, a journey of about twenty minutes at that time of day.

As the taxi pulled away from the road by the marina after depositing him, the sun was beginning to rise and he blinked in its rays. He looped his holdall over his shoulder and walked out along the jetty against which his boat – *Maria* – was moored.

He almost cried when he saw her. Beautiful, sleek, forty-five feet long and a dream to drive, as it were. He flipped the light steel gangplank across and walked over, unzipped the protective awning covering the rear deck and stepped back into the life he loved, conditions attached.

He was in no hurry to make contact with the friend he'd been helping out that summer with the day boat charter business. He'd left him in the lurch, slightly, having thought he would be back quickly from his excursion to the UK, so he wanted to keep a low profile on the day he arrived back, just to reacclimatize, before going into the office on the quayside, grovelling and saying he was available for charters for another week before setting sail back to Gran Canaria to resurrect his fishing business. Ibiza was wonderful and classy, but the waters of the Mediterranean held hardly any fish that interested him, whereas the Atlantic around the Canaries teemed with big fish.

It had been his intention to sail back straight away but, during a period of reflection, he thought he owed it to his friend to offer to do a few more day cruises to make it up to him.

The first thing he did, after having a long mooch around the boat to see that everything was OK, was to split up his newly acquired cash reserves. He hid half deep in the engine room and the other half almost literally under the mattress in the main cabin, in a small compartment he had himself built within the framework of the bed, well-hidden enough to be missed by a cursory search, although a concerted one probably would find it.

That done, he unhooked and folded away the plastic awning, began to clean the boat and run the twin Cummins 715 horse-power diesel engines. They sounded sweet, burbling away like happy babies.

He spent a couple of hours making sure everything was all in order before locking up and wandering down to the Mirage café on the quayside for a prawn sandwich, so full of delicious sauce that most of it ended up on his face. It tasted wonderful with a pint of local lager, although sitting there alone watching the boats in the marina and tourists walking past felt strange. He and Maria spent a lot of time at this place in its excellent corner position. It wasn't that Flynn was averse to being alone in bars, but he had got used to her presence.

He did some necessity shopping at the small Spar supermarket just behind the front row of restaurants and shops, then carried his four bags back to the boat.

After informing the harbour master of his plans for the afternoon, he slipped his moorings and edged carefully to the fuel station, filled up with diesel and a few moments later was on the open sea, heading north, slowly opening the throttle while passing the Ses Estaques Hotel and making the boat skim the calm water, prow high and proud, Flynn at the wheel in his dark glasses, battered baseball cap, torn T-shirt and cargo shorts and deck shoes. He could feel the throb of the engines shooting through his soul, making him come alive.

Maybe for the first time in days, his smile was utterly genuine.

Leaving Santa Eulalia behind, he followed the coastline, passing between Punta d'en Valls and the privately owned island of Tagomago. He came in tight into the tiny bay of Pou des Lleo, translated as the 'Well of the Lion', one of Ibiza's prettiest locations with great views of Tagomago. Flynn slowed, stopped and dropped anchor, and picked up a mooring in the crystal clear water. Once happy the boat was secure, he changed into his swimming shorts. After checking the dressing on his leg wound – now no more than big plasters – he dived in, going deep to the sandy bed, holding his breath until his chest began to cry out before propelling himself like a nuclear missile back to the surface, which he broke with an explosion of water. He bobbed for a couple of minutes, treading water, then began a slow, circular crawl around the boat, which he maintained for half an hour before dragging himself back on to the rear deck. He shimmied along to the foredeck where he laid out a towel, removed his shorts, laid himself out to catch the rays of the hot afternoon sun and fell asleep.

He was back at the berth in Santa Eulalia by five p.m., sipping Spar own-brand whisky on the rear deck before venturing out for a meal from one of the many good quayside restaurants bought with cash stolen from Mark Carter.

'He hasn't learned,' Molly moaned to Rik Dean, who was standing looking over her shoulder in an office in the FMIT block at police headquarters at Hutton, near to Preston. Lounging in a chair behind her was Karl Donaldson, his long legs crossed. Molly had been driven over to Hutton and allocated an en-suite room in one of the accommodation blocks at the training centre which she could enter and leave discreetly, just fifty metres from the FMIT block. That itself had once been student accommodation but had been commandeered and refurbished for the Senior Investigating Officer team which had eventually become FMIT. It was where Rik Dean's main office was located, halfway down the first-floor corridor, and it had once belonged to Henry Christie. Since taking over, Rik had had the office completely gutted, refurbished and decorated at great expense to the taxpayer.

Molly had been given an empty office on the same corridor

which had computer links wired in, and she was now using a laptop provided by Donaldson. It seemed to have all the bells and whistles required.

She was discussing Alan Hardiker and the fact he was still harassing her in spite of the meeting with Rik Dean.

'He texted me four times, called me twice but hung up, also left two vaguely threatening voicemails and guess what?' She had her mobile phone in her hand, thumbing through the dross from Hardiker. She held the screen up so Rik could see it – a photograph that Hardiker must have taken while sitting at his desk in the detective sergeants' office of his open flies with his flaccid cock peeking out, foreskin pulled right back, in full colour, of course. 'Not even erect,' Molly said.

Rik said, 'Yuk. I'm really going to nail him to the wall when all this is done, possibly by his foreskin.'

'Only if you give me a hammer too,' Molly said.

She had been glad to move out of her flat for the time being and into headquarters, away from any possible physical harassment from Hardiker. She had left her car parked in a non-police friend's garage who was happy to let her do so without having to provide a detailed explanation. Although the facilities at headquarters were not five star, they were good and comfortable.

'Where is he now?'

Molly shook the computer mouse and a screen similar to a Google Earth satellite view came up, but it was the FBI version and it was live from orbiting satellites. It was almost a drone's-eye view of the police station at Blackpool from which a tiny red dot pulsed a signal, letting her know that, at the very least, Hardiker's doctored phone was there.

'Still in work, by the look of it.'

'And Flynn?'

Molly typed in a command and the screen flicked to an aerial view of Santa Eulalia. Green and blue lights pulsed. One was from a restaurant on the quayside, the other from Flynn's boat moored in the marina.

'He's using that one,' she said, pointing to the blue dot coming from the restaurant. 'He let me know earlier.'

Molly had followed him, on and off, all that day, from his lunch at the Mirage to his boat trip to a secluded cove and now his evening meal at El Corsario Negro – the Black Pirate restaurant, wishing she was with him all the way.

She didn't add that she had done this, nor that she had zoomed in low for a view of the marina and the name of the restaurant he was eating at, though she could not see him because it was not a live feed as such.

'OK,' Rik said. He turned to Donaldson. 'Shall we eat?'

Donaldson nodded and stood up.

'Keep us posted if anything interesting happens,' Rik told Molly. They left her alone in the office where her task, as well as monitoring Hardiker's and Flynn's movements, was to delve into police and intelligence services databases across the globe to search for anything useful as regards the Bashkims via a special portal supplied by the FBI. It was a fairly vague task but it was interesting to learn about the extent of their operations. They were vast and lucrative. She was also following up and delving into murders committed by the unknown couple who were supposed to be working for the Bashkims and who could have murdered Maria.

Molly wasn't a computer geek but she had done a short spell in the Intelligence Unit in the aftermath of a miscarriage she'd suffered when she was married, something she rarely shared with anyone. It was a bleak part of her life that had played a major part in the breakdown of her marriage. In that time on the unit she had been taught by a certain DC Jerry Tope to interrogate databases. She was rusty but it was coming back to her.

She leaned back and thought briefly about the baby she had lost. It was mid-pregnancy, there'd been ongoing complications from the start and the baby had been born almost fully formed but dead. She had named her Elise after her own mum and buried her next to her father's grave.

'Fuck,' she said, and rubbed her gritty eyes.

That had been four years ago but the pain, though well hidden, was still raw.

Her phone rang.

She scooped it up.

'Hey! You watching me? I'm standing looking up at a beautiful night sky, waving at the stars and the moon, hoping I'm being beamed to you by satellite.'

Flynn actually was standing by the water's edge, looking up, waving into the darkness with an iPhone to his ear and crowds of people on their night-time strolls splitting to walk around him but pretty much ignoring him. Silly people were not unusual in this part of the world.

'Unfortunately not,' Molly said. 'No live link for this, just GPS tracking, so I know exactly where you are but not what you're doing.'

'Maybe it's as well,' Flynn said. He stopped waving. 'How are you?'

'Been moved to HQ and shoved into one of the rooms at the training centre for the duration, so I'm OK. Alone, but OK. You?'

'Good, too. Any news on anything?' He started to walk slowly along the quayside.

'Nothing so far.'

There was a pause.

'I know it's inappropriate, Flynn, but I wish I was there with you . . . obviously only because I know you've been out on your boat today. I need a bit of warmth and I'm jealous.'

'You wouldn't have liked it,' he said. 'All that sun, all that seawater.' Then he became serious. 'And I know it's inappropriate too, but your company would have been appreciated, Molly.'

Both smiled at the thought.

'How is the boat?' she asked.

'Spot on, like unleashing a tiger.'

'And have you got any plans yet?'

'No, other than to stay here a day or two to help out my mate with the boat hire business. It should give me time to get my head straight, then I'll head back to Puerto Rico and maybe say, "C'mon, I'm here", to the Bashkims.'

There was a pause before Molly said, 'OK.' She hated the thought.

The call ended.

Flynn stopped walking and looked across the water, then up to the almost full moon again, which he considered howling at. He thought about Maria Santiago and Molly Cartwright. In his bones, he knew he was going to have to put them both behind him.

Meanwhile, a thousand miles away, Molly thought about Steve Flynn, wondering how she could make it work.

*   *   *

Molly spent another couple of hours sifting through various databases but feeling she was getting nowhere in a hurry.

She had been looking at all the murders attributed to the couple and where possible had been scanning CCTV records in and around the murder locations, then looked at ports and airports but it was a huge, thankless task for one person who had a sore neck and back, both getting gradually worse from sitting around staring at a computer screen all day.

She checked the locations of Hardiker and Flynn.

The former, according to the pulse from his phone, was now at his home, a flat in a nice part of South Shore. The latter was on his boat, from which two pulses throbbed.

That was if both men had their phones with them.

She stared at the signal from Flynn's boat, imagining being there with him, then she decided to call it a night. She hadn't been told how long she was expected to be at the computer, but surely it wasn't forever. She needed bed, urgently.

As she was about to power down the laptop, the signal from Hardiker's phone began to move.

SIXTEEN

M olly shot upright in the office chair and watched the beating dot travel along the road outside Hardiker's flat then turn on to Lytham Road. She fumbled for her phone and called Rik Dean's mobile number: no answer, straight to voicemail. Then she called Donaldson and got the same result.

'How very fucking useful,' she muttered crossly. Then, 'Shit!' and sat back down to watch the progress of the dot through Blackpool while calling and recalling Rik and Donaldson repeatedly and leaving messages on both their phones, plus a text to each: *Call me.*

Not that Hardiker's movements necessarily meant anything.

He could be going to a club or maybe, Molly thought nauseatingly, meeting up with one of his girlfriends to compare genital shots.

The blob travelled south along Lytham Road, then turned inland, east, on to Squires Gate Lane, a road which was essentially the southern boundary of Blackpool. She followed the progress past the airport and up to the roundabout where the A5320 joined the M55, at which point the dot, and presumably Hardiker, began to travel quickly along the motorway towards Preston.

Maybe that was unusual.

Molly phoned Rik Dean again. This time, it was answered.

Problem is that when obsession takes over, coupled with power, it is very difficult to curb. Which was Alan Hardiker's issue with Molly Cartwright. Sending subtly threatening texts and phone calls were things that gave him great pleasure, as did sending photos of his cock, because he knew the devastating effect it would have on her. Even though he'd had his warning from the superintendent, it was clear that Rik and the organization were firmly on his side and that both thought Molly was just an unbalanced female.

That was why he couldn't resist sending her a few more things through the ether, although he knew he would have to stop after tonight.

He had the upper hand and didn't want to lose it.

Well, maybe he would stop using this particular phone, which he intended to destroy and cover his tracks anyway. He was lucky that Rik Dean, the stuck-up stickler, hadn't even bothered looking at the content on it.

He had certainly yanked the wool over that sucker's eyes, Hardiker thought.

He had been considering pulling the plug on the Bashkim connection, but when he had stumbled more by chance than anything on information they would pay dearly for – the possible whereabouts of the one and only Steve Flynn – that changed the game.

After leaving Rik Dean that morning, Hardiker had bided his time at work, going through the motions, dealing with prisoners and delegating as much as possible. He was actually glad that he hadn't been selected for the team to investigate Mark Carter's murder, because that would have been full-on, taking up all his time, no excuses.

He made the call at five p.m., brazenly using a work landline in the DS's office. He was feeling untouchable.

He believed this little nugget of information would be a nice earner for him. The Bashkims had paid quickly for his previous help – cash followed by a bank transfer, but Hardiker much preferred cash in his greasy palm. Everything electronic could be traced. As a one-off it was fine, but he didn't want to take too many chances. This time it would have to be cash in hand. Any combination of pounds, dollars or euros would do, just as long as it all added up to five thousand pounds in total.

The phone was answered; he made his pitch.

Then he had to wait, holding the line for an answer, hoping no one wandered into the otherwise empty office, such as the DI, who had gone home for the day but had a nasty habit of forgetting things and coming back in a rush for them, dozy bint.

The wait seemed never-ending.

Then a voice came back on: a time, a location, a car make, a name and the promise of cash.

At 11 p.m. he began the journey and twenty minutes later pulled off the M55 at the Fulwood junction, the Broughton interchange, and into the car park shared by the Phantom Winger pub and the Ibis Hotel, adjacent to the motorway roundabout.

The pub was still open, busy; next to it, the lights burned at the Ibis.

The car park was crowded, which was good because he didn't really fancy meeting up with these guys in a dark alley. He had kind of done it once, had a gun pushed into his head and didn't like it, so a busy public car park was good. He crawled around it in his car until he spotted an old Volvo tucked in one corner under some overhanging trees. He had been given a make and a partial number to look for and the Volvo was it. He swung nose first into the empty space next to it, got out and walked around his car to the Volvo, seeing just one person in it.

Which was good.

Two would have made him overcautious – one he could handle.

It was a young man, good looking, fresh-faced, not really what Hardiker had been expecting. He thought he would have met a roughneck East European, brutish, square-jawed and unshaven. This guy looked like a soft-arse, more like an upper-crust

Englishman and non-threatening, maybe a pushover in Hardiker's world of racial stereotypes.

The man reached over to the passenger door and stretched to open it for the detective.

'Mr Hardiker?'

'Yes . . . Mr Jackson?'

'That's me,' the man smiled affably. 'Why don't you get in?'

Hardiker did so and said, 'You have my cash?'

'I have. Right here,' the man called Jackson said and handed over an A4-sized brown envelope which was bulky.

'You won't mind if I count it?'

'Not at all, but it's all there . . . in exchange for your information.'

'I get it.'

Hardiker opened the top flap of the envelope and peered in. It was dark, he could not see too much and to actually count it would have been almost impossible, but it was a big bundle of notes and looked to be all there.

'Honestly, it is all there,' Mr Jackson assured him. 'Now, if you please.'

'The signal hasn't moved for an hour,' Molly said.

She, Rik and Donaldson were staring at the blinking dot on the computer screen, the emission from the tracker that Rik had got the technical services department to fit into Hardiker's phone.

'Close in on it a bit more,' Rik said.

Molly clicked on a plus sign in the corner of the screen and enlarged the image, showing the signal was coming from the car park of the Ibis Hotel next to the Phantom Winger at Broughton. The image displayed wasn't real time from a satellite and just showed a deserted car park surrounded by high trees in one corner.

Molly knew the place well enough. She had eaten meals at the Phantom Winger and had once attended a murder at the Ibis. The car park was shared between the two establishments and there was a tree-lined footpath from the car park out on to the A6.

So the signal from Hardiker's phone, which gave the exact location, was from the car park and definitely not from the pub or hotel.

'Maybe he left it in the car and has gone into the hotel,' Donaldson suggested. 'Or he's gone with someone else and driven away.'

'He could be shagging in the hotel,' Molly said.

'My interest is piqued,' Rik said. 'An almost midnight tryst . . . but with who?'

'Let's go sneaky beaky,' Donaldson said. 'Use my car.' He looked at Molly. 'Are you up for this?'

'Definitely.' She almost rubbed her hands together in gleeful anticipation.

A couple of minutes later they piled into Donaldson's Jeep and, ten minutes after that, having driven straight through Preston, he was pulling up on the car park, doing a loop around. Despite the hour, there were quite a lot of cars still parked up, suggesting the hotel, which was popular with travelling businessmen, was pretty full. Molly spotted Hardiker's car parked under the overhang of some large trees in the far corner. Donaldson drove slowly past it, slotted into a gap opposite and stopped.

Molly was looking at her phone. She had logged on to the tracking system and it still showed the signal pulsing from this location.

'Not moved,' she announced. 'Phone's still in his car.' She knew it was accurate up to about two metres.

Donaldson slid out from behind the wheel and walked over to the car, noting it was parked between a Vauxhall on one side and an oldish Volvo saloon on the other. He shaded his eyes and peered into Hardiker's car. It was empty but when he tried the door handle he discovered it was unlocked.

Molly and Rik watched from the Jeep.

Donaldson shrugged at them, walked around to the passenger side of his car and Rik opened the window.

'Could have been picked up, could be in the hotel,' Rik said.

'Just seems odd,' Donaldson said.

'Maybe we should leave it,' Rik said. 'Maybe it has nothing to do with anything.'

Donaldson's mouth twitched as he regarded Rik, then looked at Molly in the back seat. 'And we all know that is garbage. We've all been in this game too long for this to feel comfortable.'

'Except if he walks out of the hotel now and sees us, our game with him is over,' Rik said. 'We're blown.'

'Agreed,' Donaldson nodded.

'I think we should challenge him,' Molly said, 'or at least you two should. I think this is odd, even for him. And the fact is we have a lot of incriminating stuff against him, so all is not lost.'

The men eyed each other and reached their decision with a nod.

Rik got out and he and Donaldson walked across to the hotel, leaving Molly in the Jeep. She sighed, wondering what the increasingly sordid Alan Hardiker was up to now. As the two men entered the hotel, Molly dropped out of the Jeep, jarring her spine and making her wince: her whiplash wasn't going away quickly. Driven by the curiosity of a cop, she went to Hardiker's car, opened the driver's door and peered inside, not expecting to find anything. She didn't, so she walked around the car and peered in through the passenger-side door. Nothing.

Her phone still pulsed with the tracker from Hardiker's phone.

She leaned against the passenger door of the car parked along-side, which was the old Volvo, narrowing her eyes and trying to think what Hardiker could be up to.

A prostitute was the most likely scenario, Molly concluded. Right up his street. Or maybe a rendezvous with Laura's fanny. Either option was a good bet.

She looked over to the hotel; Rik and Donaldson came out of the front door and made their way back to join her at Hardiker's car.

'Not booked in and no one fitting his description has entered or left the hotel in the last hour or so, according to the night porter. I think we should just leave it for now,' Rik said.

Molly wasn't happy with that, but she nodded, pushed herself away from the Volvo and followed the men back to the Jeep. It was only as she took hold of the door handle that she realized her right hand was a bit wet. Puzzled, she pulled it away slowly and brought her palm up to her face to inspect it.

Suddenly the pulse in her ears started to pound.

Donaldson had watched her. 'What is it?'

She turned her hand palm away from her so he could see it. Blood.

*   *   *

The ever-so-slight rocking of the boat in the still water of the marina, coupled with the last whisky of the night on the rear deck, combined to have a huge soporific effect on Flynn. Back in the environment he loved, he had the longest, deepest, least interrupted sleep he'd had in a very long time on the soft, wide, rectangular bed in the main cabin.

He teetered to the shower and swilled off, then replaced the dressing on his leg wound. His eardrum still throbbed, but that too was improving and was manageable with paracetamols.

After drinking half a litre of chilled water, he rooted out a pair of shorts, a baggy T-shirt and a pair of old trainers and stepped out on deck, feeling the need to get back into the groove of daily runs. He had to be fit and strong for whatever was lurking dangerously over the horizon and decided to start today with a very gentle jog on the flat around the marina, then along the seafront of Santa Eulalia as far as the river mouth, then back, maybe two miles in total. Not a lot, but a beginning.

Even keeping it smooth, the run jarred the wound and he walked most of the return leg.

He showered on the boat again, though there wasn't much hot water left in the system. After drying himself he got a pot of coffee filtering and prepared scrambled egg on toast with a glass of tomato juice, all of which he devoured like a lion – and then made himself another couple of slices of toast, poured another coffee and sat and watched a bit of life going by, trying to keep his dark thoughts of revenge at bay for a while.

He was in no great hurry to seek out his mate with the charter business, so busied himself with chores around the boat for a couple of hours.

His phone rang at eleven a.m., ten a.m. British time. It was Molly.

'Hi, still tracking me . . . feels like *Enemy of the State*,' he quipped, naming one of his favourite but now slightly dated films.

'Yes, I am.'

Even from those few syllables, Flynn picked up something very wrong in her voice.

'What is it, Molly?'

'It's Alan.'

'Oh, has that bastard been harassing you again?' Flynn said vehemently, instantly flying off the handle. 'Hasn't he learned anything? One thing I'll be doing when this has all settled is—'

'Steve, Steve – no,' she cried.

'What? What then?' he frowned.

'He's dead, Steve. He's dead.'

Flynn sank on to the fighting chair. 'What happened?'

'He was murdered. Stabbed,' she stammered. 'Maybe a hundred times.'

'Hell! Tell me, Molly.'

Falteringly, she related the tale of tracking the phone signal, finding Hardiker's car in the pub/hotel car park (a location Flynn also knew well), the blood on the Volvo, the blood inside the Volvo – lots of it – and finally checking the boot. She described in detail the lid opening and seeing Hardiker's terribly mutilated body folded up in a foetal position, stabbed multiple times, the number of which would only be confirmed when the post-mortem was carried out.

The Volvo turned out to be stolen from near Manchester airport and was on false plates.

Flynn listened, mostly horrified, slightly glad but also unhappy when Molly revealed, 'Rik Dean fed him some information about your whereabouts.'

'And the hypothesis now is that Hardiker might have shared this with whoever killed him?' Flynn ventured.

'Well, we don't know that but, y'know . . .'

'Suspects, witnesses?' Flynn asked.

'Neither . . . The security cameras in the car park had been tampered with, disabled and so far no actual eye witnesses have been traced.'

'So could he have been lured to the location?'

'Yes,' Molly said. Her voice was cracking.

Flynn said, 'Are you OK?'

'It's just shock. Can't get my head around it.'

Flynn didn't want to be flippant because he didn't wish death on anyone before their time. As such, he had to hold his tongue and not make an inappropriate remark such as, 'At least he won't be harassing you again.'

'It's you I'm bothered about,' he told her genuinely.

'I think I'll be all right. It's just so horrific . . . another terrible thing . . .'

'I understand. Since you Tasered me, guarded me, met me . . . things have really gone down the pan. I'm bad to be around.'

'No, no, I didn't mean that.'

'I think you'll find you did.'

'No, I didn't,' she said firmly.

'Where are you now?'

'Back at HQ in the bedroom they've given me. I just vomited,' she concluded colourfully. Obviously Flynn couldn't see this but she was standing by the washbasin in which she had just been sick and was miserably poking the plug hole with the handle of her toothbrush to clear away the lumpy sick which blocked it. 'Steve?' she said.

'Yep?'

'Please be careful. If this is connected to the Bashkims . . . these people are too dangerous . . .'

'Now you tell me.'

Flynn hung up, then messed about on his boat for a couple more hours, thinking about what Molly had told him and its implications. If Hardiker had passed on information about Flynn's whereabouts, then Flynn had to assume that at some stage in the not-too-distant future, one or more representatives of the Bashkim family would turn up on the jetty, knocking on the cabin door.

Flynn knew he had certain options.

He could await the arrival or he could put to sea now, head back to Gran Canaria and put off the inevitable visit, or he could take the game to them, the latter always having been his preferred option.

The issue with the first two was that whoever turned up on his doorstep would still only be enforcers – heavies sent by the Bashkims to deal with Flynn and, if he dealt with them first, nothing would change much. They were just messengers and would keep turning up until one got lucky and he was dead.

Therefore, sailing to Gran Canaria would just delay things.

So to Flynn, the only option open now was somehow to go and meet old man Bashkim and put this nonsense to bed. He had a vaguely formed idea about how this might be achieved, though he was loath to call it a plan, and he needed to know one thing for certain.

He called Rik Dean.

'I don't want any wishy-washy discussion about this, Rik,' he told him. 'Molly's informed me about Hardiker and if he did tell them anything about my whereabouts, then I reckon I've a day or two's grace before I need to shift out of here; even if he didn't, I need to know one thing.'

'Which is?'

'Is Bashkim's boat, *Halcyon*, still in Zante?'

'I'll find out and let you know.'

Satisfied for the moment, Flynn jumped on to the jetty and walked to his friend's boat charter office on Calle Sant Llorenc, a step back from the marina front and therefore cheaper to rent.

Despite the office hours being displayed as nine a.m. to five p.m., it was closed. Flynn wasn't surprised. Office hours in this part of the world were, at best, just guidance. He decided to stroll around town, catch a coffee somewhere to people-watch, come back in an hour or two and wait for an update from Rik Dean.

He heard from Rik as he sat sipping a coffee at a café overlooking the beach.

'Location currently unknown,' the detective told him. 'Definitely not in Zante.'

'No news from Donaldson's source?'

'Nothing.'

'OK. Keep me informed, please.'

Flynn thought that was a bummer. He had visualized mooring next to *Halcyon*, climbing aboard and presenting himself to Viktor.

He finished the coffee, pushed himself up from his chair and walked back to the charter boat office.

This time the door was open and Flynn stepped into air-conditioned coolness. There was a young lady who did the front of house meet-and-greet and admin sitting at a glass-topped desk and behind her in a glass-fronted office was his friend Paul Caton, talking to a couple of customers, Flynn assumed.

Paul glanced around as Flynn sauntered in and an immediate look of relief crossed his face. He said something quickly to the couple, who looked over at Flynn, and gave them a 'wait a moment' gesture, stood up and came out of the office to Flynn.

'Where the fuck have you been?' he hissed but kept a professional smile on his countenance.

Flynn blinked at him. 'Don't you read the newspapers or watch the news?'

'Nope. I hire boats for charter in Ibiza; I spend my days on them and my nights shagging the available clientele of the female variety. Why would I watch the fucking news?'

At least it made Flynn smile: the lifestyle of the louche and lush, something he once might have aspired to.

'Anyway, matey,' Paul said garrulously, slapping Flynn's shoulder. 'You're back and that's what counts.' He turned his back on the couple in the office. 'These two are desperate for you – yes, you, as it happens.'

'Me?'

'Word of mouth. A couple you took out earlier this year spoke about you in glowing terms, highly recommended, and this lovely duo, on their honeymoon, no less, want to hire you for a couple of days including an overnighter in one of the bays if possible. Yeah? Willing to pay over the odds, so I've just doubled the price . . . I'm assuming the boat's shipshape? Get a nice meal together for them to eat on board – lobster and all that crap, you know the drill. Can Maria do that?'

Flynn gasped inwardly at the mention of her name. Maria had been his unpaid helper over summer, accompanying him on the day charters, sorting out the food and drink for the clients.

'What is it?' Paul asked, seeing Flynn's odd reaction.

'Nothing . . . she just had to get back,' Flynn said, unwilling to expand. 'I'll sort it. A cold buffet type of thing, oysters maybe, the food of love.'

'Good man.' He slapped Flynn's shoulder again and gave him a double-fisted sign of encouragement. 'Come and meet them. Really nice couple . . . Tons of dosh,' he added from the side of his mouth.

Flynn followed him into the office. They couple stood up shyly but were fresh-faced and full of life, really nice looking, setting off on life's great adventure.

Paul introduced him. 'This is Steve Flynn, who you've heard about.'

The young man smiled broadly. Unkempt brown hair, blue eyes sparkling. He held out his hand and Flynn shook it.

'So pleased to meet you.'

To his side, his young wife reached out and also shook Flynn's hand. Pretty, slim, brown arms and legs, azure-blue eyes.

'So pleased to meet you, too.' She echoed her husband.

'Hi, hi,' Flynn said, all smiles, quite a good-looking bastard himself.

'It seems really odd to say this, as we're not quite used to it.' The husband glanced playfully and with love at his new wife, then back at Flynn. 'We're Mr and Mrs Jackson.'

The timing gave Flynn another afternoon and night alone, which he was pleased about. It enabled him to buy supplies, stock up the on-board freezer and fridge and prepare the boat for a two-day mini cruise. He could do a bit of planning, too. He usually took out day charters but had done a few overnighters and knew what they entailed. Look after the clients, make sure they didn't drown, find somewhere nice and calm for the night and hopefully get a huge tip.

After prepping the boat and foodstuffs, it was almost six p.m. He had not heard anything from Molly but decided not to trouble her or Rik. They would all have their work cut out with the murder of another cop. He could imagine the headless chicken routines going on plus all the explanations Rik would have to be spinning about using Hardiker as possible bait, although his murder could not have been predicted. That said, it was just another of those door things Flynn often talked about. In this case, Hardiker had opened a door to the dark side and what had come through it was not nice.

Flynn spent the evening mooching listlessly around the market stalls in the resort before finding a seat at El Corsario Negro for another paella and a couple of beers. While shovelling the paella into his mouth he caught sight of tomorrow's clients sitting at a table in the corner of the terrace, pretty much engrossed in each other, doing all the silly, nonsensical things that couples in love do: feeding each other, giggling at crass jokes, drinking through intertwined arms, the full gamut of young love. He watched them for a few moments and the young man accidentally caught his eye, whispered something to his missus and both looked at him, waved and smiled. He raised his pint to them, actually now quite looking forward to their company over the next few days, though he hoped their humping wouldn't rock the boat too much. Their attention went back to themselves.

Flynn finished his food and then strolled back to the boat and completed the evening in his usual style, with a glass of whisky before falling into bed.

He was up before the sun, doing last-minute prep and cleaning, ready for the clients who were due at ten. He redressed his wound again, still healing well, and dressed himself in a nice pair of cargo shorts, just long enough to cover the bandage, and a Fred Perry polo shirt.

His phone showed nothing from Molly, Rik or Donaldson. He'd call them later if he got the chance.

Coffee was filtering and the engines were ticking over nicely when the two guests arrived still looking fresh and full of life.

Flynn welcomed them effusively and, after he'd shown them to their luxurious cabin, he slowly manoeuvred the boat out of the mooring and turned to the open sea.

SEVENTEEN

'She's really a sportfisher, isn't she?' the man called Mr Jackson – Matt – said. Flynn nodded. 'She's got great lines.'

Flynn acknowledged the compliment. Anyone saying how good his boat was always went up in his estimation.

Matt was by his side at the helm.

'I'm just helping Paul out this summer,' Flynn said. He explained the backstory briefly and added, 'She makes a great pleasure cruiser but she really comes alive in the ocean, out fishing.'

'Not much good fishing in these parts, I guess,' Matt said.

'Not really. The open oceans are the best places for the big fish, though the Med does have its moments, I guess.'

'What's the biggest you've ever caught?'

'Personally? Marlin, just short of 800 pounds; a customer once pulled an 1100-pound one out, a few miles south of Gran Canaria, but we always tag and release.'

'Good going,' Mr Jackson said, impressed.

Flynn smiled at the memories: simpler days, maybe.

Through the windows he could see Mrs Jackson – Lizzie – sunbathing on the foredeck in a tiny bikini bottom but no top.

'Where does the name of the boat come from?' Matt asked. 'Maria?'

Flynn's face became rigid. 'Nowhere, really.'

'Oh, come on,' Matt Jackson chided. 'Gotta be a wife or girlfriend,' he teased.

'Yeah, girlfriend. Gone now, though – you know how it is.' Flynn did not elaborate but realized that if he didn't change the name this was a question that would be asked all the time and he needed a strategy to deal with it.

'Shame . . . she must have been something else for you to name your boat after her.'

'Oh, yeah.' He glanced sideways at the client. 'She was.'

Mr Jackson chose a few coves and bays he and his new wife wanted to visit and the day was pleasant and leisurely. Not a lot of nautical miles were covered but lots of dips in the sea were taken and they finally drew into Cala de Sant Vicente, where the couple sat chilling on deck and Flynn prepared a lobster, crab and oyster salad for them. He left them alone with food and wine and clambered up the ladder to the flying bridge, the platform located above the main bridge with a secondary set of controls used for fish spotting and helping to manoeuvre the boat when a big fish is being played. Up here, he ate his own food, a pasta salad.

His mobile phone rang: Donaldson calling.

'Hey, yank,' Flynn said.

'Hey, fugitive,' Donaldson said.

'Got something for me?'

'Uh-huh . . . *Halcyon* is now on its way to Grand Harbour, Valetta.'

'Malta?' Flynn said. 'Any idea why?'

'Connected with that last big push of migrants from Libya, we think. Viktor is just there to collect payment from intermediaries, not give lifts to his customers.'

Flynn tried to visualize the thousand people about to commence the treacherous journey from North Africa to Europe in search of a better life – if they made the crossing in one piece, that is, or joined the many who had died trying that year.

'OK,' he said.

Donaldson said, 'Plans?'

'Formulating,' Flynn said. 'Thanks for that.'

The call ended. Flynn finished his meal then climbed back down to the rear deck and collected the dishes from the clients, who had wolfed their food down with glee and told him how good it was. He took the dishes into the galley to wash up before serving dessert.

As he dried the dishes, his phone vibrated in his pocket. Before he could answer it he looked and saw that Lizzie Jackson was standing behind him. She had showered and was now wearing a bikini top, loose denim shorts and a see-through Kaftan. Her hair was bedraggled but she looked amazing.

'Hi.'

'Hi, there,' Flynn said back, ignoring the phone.

'How good does food taste after a day swimming in the sea?'

'Brilliant,' Flynn said.

'Look, I hope you don't mind me asking . . . it's a girlie thing . . . but you know this Maria, the girl your boat was named after? Matt mentioned her to me and I don't know . . .' She hugged herself. 'I feel a sort of connection with her.' Then she laid both her hands on her chest. 'Here, in my heart . . . like I know something, I dunno, something really bad happened.' She gave the impression she was struggling to get to grips with the feeling. 'I'm really sorry if I'm wrong, Steve, it's just an overwhelming feeling of sadness. I'm not psychic, don't get me wrong.'

He looked at her in amazement, not knowing how to respond to this intuitive woman. 'Uh . . . she died.'

'Oh my God, how tragic,' Lizzie said. 'I'm not psychic, honestly, but I do feel things here, like there's something about this boat . . . sadness but happiness too, y'know? It could be her spirit. Close. To you, to us.'

'Nah, I doubt it.'

'You're a man. You don't feel the same things as a woman.' She tilted her head. 'Can I give you a hug? Non-sexual, that is.'

Flynn hesitated and glanced at Matt out on the deck, looking across the bay and sipping his wine.

'You need it,' she prompted him, opening her arms and encouraging him. 'Human-to-human . . . much deeper than sex.' Her eyes were wide and alive, yet tinged with some kind of faraway-ness.

Flynn relented. 'OK.'

She embraced him – a tad too long, he thought – but it was kind of nice, although his embraces with women were usually a precursor to something far more basic than the spirit. When she stepped back, she looked him in the eye. 'Now I really do feel a connection. She was a good woman, that Maria, wasn't she?'

Numbly, Flynn nodded. 'She was.'

They retired early.

Flynn stayed on deck, mopping it down, generally cleaning and rinsing the towels, thinking about how instinctual women seemed to be in complete contrast to himself, a brute force of nature. Perhaps he'd take up Reiki, get in touch with his inner soul, light candles with sickly aromas and breathe deep, though, joking aside, Lizzie Jackson's connection, or whatever it was, to Maria was uncanny and unsettling.

He decided to chance a small whisky before he retired to his single bunk and it was only when his phone vibrated again that he realized he hadn't looked at it when it had done so previously.

It was Molly.

'Hey, Flynn, thought you were ignoring me.'

He laughed. 'Just been busy – in a nice way.'

'Lucky you.'

'Yeah, it's a tough job, et cetera. How about you?' Flynn took himself, the phone and the whisky to the rail.

'Busy in a busy way.'

'I can imagine. I spoke to Karl earlier.'

'About Malta?'

'Yep.'

'And?'

'Just thinking through possibilities . . . Anyway, what have you been up to?'

'Combing the Web, looking through CCTV footage . . . Did you look at the text I sent earlier?'

'Should I have done?' He sat on the fighting chair and placed his glass down on a bait box.

'Some still photos from security cameras at Manchester airport and Paris Charles de Gaulle. Manchester the day before yesterday and Paris last year. They show the Bashkim couple – the man and the woman – using the private side of those airports who could well be the people suspected of murdering that gangster in Paris that Karl talked about . . . and maybe Alan Hardiker, although we don't know for certain if two people are involved in Alan's death. I've been trying to dig into flight plans for private aircraft around those dates. Paris is a nightmare, not least because my French is crap, but Manchester has revealed something.'

'Go on,' Flynn said.

'A small private jet touched down from Zante two days ago, then hours after we found Alan's body, it left Manchester for Ibiza. I'm struggling to get names but it looks like there were just two people on board. I'm on it, as they say.'

Flynn took in the information. Ibiza, he thought. These fuckers move quick, but at least he was untouchable at this exact moment in time.

'Anyway, the Ibiza thing is a bit worrying, obviously, so you might want to really be on your guard, just in case,' Molly said. 'Again, I'm trying to access information from the authorities there, but . . . so frickin' slow, you wouldn't believe it. But at least you're OK.'

Flynn said, 'I'll have a look at those photographs.'

'OK.'

He ended the call and went on to the phone's menu to find Molly's earlier message, which he opened and tabbed through to the photographs she'd attached.

There were four. Not particularly clear ones, two showing a man and woman passing through a revolving door at Manchester

Airport and another two showing what appeared to be the same couple passing through a sliding door at Paris.

Flynn used his finger and thumb to enlarge one of the pictures.

The boat rocked ever so slightly.

There was a faint creaking noise behind him.

Flynn recognized the two people in the photograph at the same time as the piano-wire garrotte made a whooshing noise as it zipped through the air over Flynn's head and was hauled in tight around his neck, the thin wire digging deep into the skin immediately, cutting his flesh. His mouth opened, his tongue shot out, his eyes bulged and he released an ugly, rasping choking noise as the blood and oxygen were cut from his brain.

Behind him, Matt Jackson pulled hard on the toggles of the home-made, specially prepared killing tool, knowing that a solid grip would be essential to complete what was usually a straight-forward task with most people.

He already knew, but was not intimidated by the fact that Flynn was not most people. That made it all the more exciting, not like the repeated plunging of his knife into the body, head and neck of the stupid, money-grabbing detective who had outlived his usefulness. That killing had just been perfunctory. But this one . . .

However, Matt realized his first mistake was that Flynn was sitting in the fighting chair, which meant that the back of it came between him and his intended victim. Also that the chair – which essentially was a heavy-duty office chair – although fixed to the deck could obviously swivel. Consequently, Matt had to contend with both Flynn and the movement of the chair.

He hadn't expected it to be easy. Flynn was big and tough and unlikely to go down without a fight for his life. Matt had known that as soon as the wire was around his neck he would have a real struggle on his hands.

But not all killings could be easy. If they were, everyone would be at it.

Flynn dropped the phone and instinctively tried to insert his fingers between his neck and the wire, and at the same time used his feet on the deck to begin to swivel the chair and keep his attacker off balance from the get-go.

This movement seemed to catch Matt by surprise. He had

murdered a couple of people by this method over the years. Both had been seated and both, in reaction to the garrotte, had flicked up their legs and panicked like demented puppets.

Flynn, however, kept his feet on the deck and tried to run and spin the fighting chair, which dragged Matt sideways and off balance.

He kept a tight hold, pulling the wire with the toggles and digging it in, a grimace of effort on his face.

Flynn fought back, rotating the chair, making Matt move with it to keep his position behind and, in doing so, he stumbled on the bait box which had been on the deck at Flynn's feet, though he did remain upright.

As the chair spun, Flynn caught sight of Lizzie standing and watching the spectacle from the main door to the lounge. Even in that fleeting glimpse, when his face was twisted in agony, he saw a gleam of killing lust in her eye and a large knife in her hand at her side – the back-up plan.

Flynn realized that Matt had stumbled on the bait box. He stopped trying to get his fingers under the wire because they simply would not go. He dropped his left hand to the side of the fighting chair, fumbling with his fingers and finding the metal adjustment bar which he yanked upwards, causing the foot rest that had been so neatly tucked under the front of the chair to swivel up as he raised his feet, then slammed them down on the rest. This gave him extra purchase and he forced himself upright, like stamping on the brakes of a car, and he rose up and angled backwards against Matt, who was suddenly faced with having to step back and pull the garrotte at a downwards angle instead of the horizontal, losing grip and power as the physics altered. Flynn virtually back-flipped out of the chair, not like a dainty gymnast but a grizzly bear, rolling and falling with his full weight against Matt, knocking him sideways. The toggle in Matt's left hand whipped out of his grip and immediately the pressure on Flynn's neck was gone.

He didn't have time to savour, gasp and suck in air, because as he too staggered sideways, elbow-jabbing Matt in the chest, Lizzie screamed and came at him with the large knife. Flynn now saw it was not just a knife but a machete, raised high in both hands, aiming at Flynn's head. Even if she missed his skull and was unable to slice that off like a boiled egg, and connected with his neck or shoulder instead, the wound would be devastating and debilitating, a deep, bloody cut, serious enough to put him down and be at their mercy.

Flynn knew the machete would be honed to perfection – and the fight would be over if it struck him.

He also knew that, to one side, Matt was scrambling to his feet.

Flynn sidestepped right and pivoted.

Lizzie swerved with him, the machete still raised.

She was fast.

The big blade angled, slicing through the air at forty-five degrees with a swish, and Flynn knew the only way to stop it was to be faster and perfectly accurate himself, otherwise she would now just slice through his forearm and maybe take his hand off with the first blow.

Flynn's left hand shot out, his palm facing outwards as though he was changing gear from first to second. He caught Lizzie's right arm just above the wrist and grabbed it – he was in control then. With a tearing, crunching twist, he forced her arm upwards against the elbow joint and broke it. He turned into her, cupped her elbow with the palm of his right hand and then pushed upwards again, damaging the joint even more.

An unworldly scream ripped out of her warped mouth and she dropped the weapon on to the deck.

Flynn then turned again so he was face-to-face with her, keeping a hold of her left wrist. He brought his right arm back and then slammed the heel of that hand up into her nose, dislodging the septum, the thin partition of gristle separating her pretty nostrils, and ramming it upwards into the frontal lobe of her brain, imbedding it. Her eyes rolled, her legs gave way and she quivered down on to the deck like runny jelly.

Flynn released her; no time to dwell on this.

He spun to face Matt, who had regained his feet and was powering towards him, having discarded the garrotte but replaced it with a small flick knife, the blade of which flashed out as he came at Flynn, whose mind now saw everything in slow motion. This, now, was his kind of conflict, the type he had won many times and expected to win again.

A street fight on the rear deck of his boat.

It was over in a matter of seconds.

Flynn concentrated on the blade initially. He parried it away with his left hand and, before Matt could bring it back on its killing trajectory, Flynn pirouetted 180 degrees in a balletic continuum of the parry, using Matt's extended right arm as a pathway. Flynn's crooked right elbow followed it all the way up to the side of Matt's face, driving the point into his cheekbone and sending him staggering sideways. Flynn kept hold of his arm, yanked Matt back to him and goose-necked his wrist against his own chest, forcing Matt to drop the knife as searing pain forced him to open his fingers. Flynn continued to force Matt's hand down and the wrist broke with a tearing crack of bone and tendon. Flynn followed this with a powerhouse punch with his right fist into Matt's agonized face that flattened all his boyish features momentarily before they more or less sprang back into place, though his nose was now broken and distorted.

Stunned, Matt slithered down to his hands and knees with blood gushing and pooling on to the white deck underneath his bleeding face.

Flynn positioned himself and kicked him hard in the ribcage, a new ferocity overwhelming him.

Matt's uninjured arm collapsed underneath him as Flynn continued to stomp on him until finally he stopped, gasping for breath.

He stood over Matt. 'You killed her, didn't you? You murdered Maria.'

Matt rolled on to his side and squinted through already closing and swelling eyes at the unmoving Lizzie. 'She dead?'

Flynn looked across at her. She was alive but her face looked as though she had been hit head-on by a lump hammer. Her eyes were glassy, unaware.

'Not yet, but she will be.' Probably brain-dead just for now. That little shard of bone must have done its job. 'Did you kill Maria Santiago?' he asked Matt.

Behind his blood-covered features, Matt laughed harshly. 'It was easy.'

'And you cut off her head? You took it – where is it?'

'Fuck you, fuck you . . . nobody's ever . . .'

'Beaten you? Just watch this.'

Flynn moved over to Lizzie and placed his right foot on her exposed neck. He pressed firmly and kept on the pressure. Lizzie's instinctive reactions to stay alive made her claw at his calves as blood and oxygen failed to make it to her brain. She was weak and uncoordinated.

Matt said, 'You bastard,' and tried to slither though his blood towards her. Flynn watched him come, his eyes cold as granite. He did not move, simply kept his foot in place until Lizzie's flailing hands fell away, then took a step back as Matt tried to launch himself at his legs, landing party across his killing partner's unmoving form. Matt then dragged himself up her body until he was nose to nose with her.

'Lizzie, Lizzie,' he whispered through bubbles of blood. 'My Lizzie.'

His broken wrist flopped uselessly across her torso. Flynn circled them until he was behind Matt, who rolled off Lizzie and looked up at Flynn, who squatted down on to his haunches.

'Where is Maria's head?'

'Like I said, fuck you.'

Flynn nodded. 'OK.' He wiped his face, then rocked forward so that his right knee was on Matt's chest. He reached out with both hands and almost gently placed his fingers around Matt's neck and looked him in the eyes. He wanted to make this one up close and very personal.

Flynn stripped both bodies, then strapped weight belts and ankle weights around them from the diving equipment he had on board and packed them with lead. With a bait knife he slit their bellies so they would not bloat with gas, then shoved each one through the transom door on the rear deck into the wake of the boat. The bodies flipped over, did not immediately sink but did attract a whole host of shrieking and whirling gulls that were already following the boat. The birds dived and squawked and squabbled over the entrails but were finally defeated as the bodies disappeared under the churning seawater and began their slow, twisting descent to the bottom.

Flynn then listlessly tossed twenty fingertips overboard that he had also removed with the bait knife, causing a fresh commotion from the birds, then flung Matt and Lizzie's teeth into the water, having smashed their jaws to a crumble with a hammer. Finally, all their shredded belongings were thrown over. Flynn wasn't surprised to find there was nothing that identified either of them in their gear. They had two bundles of ten thousand euros between them, which he kept.

He hoped they would stay deep down in the locker but wasn't too concerned they would eventually be found, maybe dragged up in a trawl net, but by that time there would be very little remaining of them once the fish had had their fill.

He sat back naked in the fighting chair, having also removed his own blood-soaked clothing, shredded it and then dumped it overboard. He had a few reflective moments, wondering how he felt. Usually revenge was a dull sensation, but this wasn't. It was good.

Then he looked at the state of the deck.

The next hour was spent returning it to its pristine condition with hard scrubbing and many buckets of sea water, which he knew was good at getting rid of blood. After this he doused himself with buckets of the same, standing naked on the deck.

By this time he had reached the southern tip of Majorca and the uninhabited island of Cabrera where he found anchorage in a quiet cove. Here he had a freshwater shower, sluicing all the salt out of his skin, then hosed the deck down again. It now bore no trace of the terrible fight, unless of course a very skilled and dedicated crime-scene investigator ever got to work on it, in which case he was sure its secrets would be unearthed.

That was never going to happen.

In the morning he ate breakfast off the island, just muesli and black coffee and a couple of paracetamols for his leg wound. It was sore again but it had stayed together during the fight.

Next he put a call through to his friend Paul in Ibiza, telling him the charter party, Mr and Mrs Jackson, had decided that boating wasn't for them and had left him at Cala de Sant Vicente, electing to make their own way back to their accommodation. Flynn told him he himself had decided to make his way back to Gran Canaria and thanked him for the summer work he had provided.

In fact, he was travelling in the complete opposite direction. Flynn then called Karl Donaldson.

EIGHTEEN

The Mediterranean weather stayed mostly kind for Flynn over the next few days, for which he was grateful. It allowed him time to reconnect with the boat and also himself.

He found that *Maria* was probably the best sportfishing boat he had ever skippered or owned. There were many much better, bigger, more expensive boats out there, but *Maria* was exactly suited to him, handled well and loved being pushed against the sea. Over the course of his journey east he became as one with her, fell in love with her all over again.

He spent a long time contemplating himself, too.

He wasn't particularly great at introspection but by the end of the journey he knew exactly what he wanted and it wasn't vastly different to anything he had wanted before – just with a few more roots.

He wanted to be back in Puerto Rico. Years ago, on leaving the cops under that dark cloud, he had scuttled off to Gran Canaria with his tail between his legs and started a new life as a sportfishing skipper. It had become his home. He had friends there, occasional lovers but no permanent home. He wanted that last aspect to change when he eventually returned and intended to look at renting somewhere long term instead of crashing out and depending on the goodwill of others who usually accommodated him.

Then he wanted to rebuild the business. He had no aspirations to make any great profit from sportfishing – indeed, there was no real money to be made, it was all about the lifestyle. All he wanted was to break even, make enough to live on and keep his boat afloat, go to sea six days a week and eat paella and drink lager on the seventh, tan himself the colour of teak and grow as ancient as the old man and the sea. He would keep fishing until he was physically or mentally incapable of doing so.

In terms of companionship, he was undecided.

Women who tagged themselves along with him seemed to come to tragic ends. That alone made him wary of relationships. Not that he really wanted anyone else at the moment. He still had to grieve properly for Maria and he knew it would be a long process, although he was well on the way now that her killers had been brought to justice. As it were.

He didn't want to rush anything in the love department, although he did think a lot about Molly Cartwright.

So that was it: Gran Canaria, his boat, an apartment, work and maybe some fun.

His journey across from Ibiza was a series of hops: firstly to Cabrera, where he spent the night before nipping to Palma on Majorca to refuel and take on supplies. From there was a longish haul to Sardinia, where he again refuelled and resupplied in Cagliari, spending a night in the harbour. An early departure saw him sail across the Tyrrhenian Sea and into Palermo in Sicily for another refuelling stop, all paid for by Mr and Mrs Jackson. He then crossed to the pretty island of Pantelleria, where he anchored offshore for a day and night before setting off on the short skip across to Malta, the very famous George Cross Island.

He chugged between Dragut Point and Tigné Point and entered Marsamxett Harbour, the natural harbour located to the north of the much larger Grand Harbour, and found the berth he had pre-booked by phone in Lazzaretto Creek by Manoel Island.

It was eight p.m., the fifth day of his journey, as he manoeuvred the boat into the tight berth, connected to the electricity and fresh water supply and slid the gangplank across from the deck to shore.

He was met by Karl Donaldson.

Two other figures lurked behind the American: Rik Dean and Molly Cartwright.

'All customs, health and immigration procedures catered for,' Donaldson announced, 'courtesy of Homeland Security.'

They had rented two spacious but nondescript three-bedroom apartments on Tigné Street, Sliema. Flynn, Donaldson, Rik and Molly were taken there from the quayside in a people carrier driven by one of the guys who had previously driven Flynn from Blackpool to Blackburn a few days earlier. He was now wearing a baseball cap, cool shades, a tight-fitting T-shirt and shorts for the change of climate. He still did not speak.

Flynn was shown to one of the bedrooms which had its own en suite, and although he had managed to get some sleep at sea and keep clean, he found himself in need of a proper shower and a proper bed. The first, he was told, he could have; the latter would have to wait.

With hardly any conversation, he closed the door of his room and stripped off.

The shower was good, the shave great.

When he stepped out, a clean set of clothes had been laid out for him on the double bed and a tray of cold food and hot soup on the dressing table. He had also eaten well on his journey, but the sight of fresh chicken sandwiches and the smell of minestrone soup made him ravenous. He ate heartily, sitting by the open window at the Juliet balcony overlooking the narrow street below.

Only then did he show his face in the living room where Donaldson, Rik and Molly sat chatting softly. Flynn had worked out that these three, plus him, were in this apartment. Donaldson's assistants occupied the apartment across the hall. He didn't know how many there were, but he had spotted and nodded at one of the other guys who had abducted him in Blackpool, so there was at least two of them in non-speaking roles.

Not that he was remotely bothered.

Donaldson, Rik and Molly clamped their mouths shut when he entered.

Rik was in the process of pouring whisky and he shook the bottle at Flynn, who nodded a yes and joined them, sitting alongside Molly on the large sofa, taking the half-filled glass that Rik offered.

'Didn't expect to see you here,' Flynn said to Rik. Then, 'Or you,' to Molly.

'You don't ditch me that easily,' she said.

Flynn looked at Donaldson. 'Where are we up to?'

'*Halcyon* is due to arrive at midday tomorrow by all accounts. We've kept an eye on her progress and all indications are to that effect.'

Flynn nodded.

Donaldson said, 'We – you and me, that is – need to have a conversation. Maybe not now but certainly first thing in the morning.'

'OK.' Flynn knew what that meant: a debrief and maybe a briefing.

'For now, though, we chill.'

Flynn took a mouthful of his whisky. It tasted orangey and smoky at the same time.

Twenty minutes later, he needed to hit the sack.

Thirty minutes after that there was a light tap on his door.

He had been sitting up sipping more whisky by the Juliet balcony. A very big part of him had wanted to hear the knock – he was pretty sure it wouldn't be Donaldson or Rik – but the thirty-minute wait was testing his nerves and his capacity to stay awake. He crossed to the door and opened it.

He was right. Gently, he pulled Molly into the room.

'The other two are sharing a bedroom. I can hear them bickering like a couple of old queens,' Molly laughed.

Flynn smiled nervously.

He and Molly were now sitting on chairs either side of the open window, drinks in hand. Conversation had been stilted but not unpleasant. Flynn had been in two minds about her. He had desperately wanted her to be the one knocking, yet at the same time he was conflicted over Maria and did not want to be unfaithful to her memory, especially at this stage in the game when hope-fully the winning post was in sight. He could tell Molly was also unsettled.

'I think possibly they are a couple of queens,' Flynn said.

'Wouldn't that be fantastic?'

They lapsed into silence, listening to the street.

Molly eventually broke it. 'Karl told me about what happened on the boat. That must have been horrific.'

'Bit like dealing with a nasty road traffic accident,' he said. 'You just do it.' He raised his chin so Molly could properly see the nasty red wheal across his Adam's apple made by Matt's garrotte.

'Hell!' she said. 'How did you . . .? No, no, I don't want to know.' She closed her eyes. 'What a mess. What's going to happen, Steve?'

'A lot depends on Karl, I think. I get the impression he's running the show now. Just have to suck it and see.'

Molly got it.

'He's obviously got the firepower and manpower and the inside track . . . I just don't know how it will pan out. I might get sidelined.'

'If I'm honest, that's what I'd hope.'

They looked at each other over their whisky glasses.

Flynn tried to form the words as best he could. 'Look, Molly, I want to be with you. You've been on my mind all the time, and to be honest I never really thought I'd see you again, so you being here is great.' He paused. She watched him. 'I'm only making assumptions here and I could be well off the mark. You might not feel the same – but my problem is I really haven't dealt with Maria's death properly yet and I've kinda learned that revenge is only part of the process . . . Ugh, crikey,' he said. 'I've run out of words. Making a cock of this, methinks. Sorry.' He closed his eyes tightly.

He heard Molly move. When he opened his eyes she was kneeling upright in front of him between his legs. She had put her glass down. She embraced him and his arms slid around her body, pulling her tenderly up to him. Her face rested on his chest.

They held each other like that for a long time before separating.

Molly's bright, sparkling eyes looked into his.

Flynn could actually feel his heart pounding like mad.

She placed the tip of her forefinger on his lips. 'Your assumptions are correct, Steve Flynn, but let's just do this one step at a time.' She kissed his cheek, then rose stiffly to her feet, still with the whiplash injury giving her grief, out of his embrace. She walked to the door and, with one last glance at him, she was gone.

Flynn shook his head, and as he tossed the remains of his whisky down his throat he rebuked himself with the old adage, *You wanker, mate, you should never, ever waste an erection.*

*   *   *

They met for a light continental breakfast at the French Affaire coffee room on the corner of The Point, Malta's newest shopping mall overlooking Tigné Point. There was not much talk and Flynn noticed Donaldson's and Rik's tetchy exchanges with each other as clearly they had not slept well. He also noticed their occasional knowing looks at himself and Molly.

Flynn couldn't have cared less.

After breakfast they walked back to the apartment where Donaldson's *three* FBI assistants were waiting, all dressed in T-shirts and cargo shorts and wearing dark glasses even indoors. Even their shaved-head haircuts were all the same.

Donaldson talked to one of them out of earshot in the hallway, then both men came into the lounge to join the others. Donaldson looked uncomfortable.

'At this juncture, I think I need to speak privately to Steve,' he announced. 'Only because you two guys . . .' he indicated Molly and Rik, '. . . won't be able to unhear things. I know you've come out here to help but I think it would be better for you both to sit this out now.'

Rik and Molly looked stunned.

'I don't think so,' Rik said solidly. 'I haven't just come here as an observer.'

'And I'm not here as totty,' Molly stated.

Donaldson's look paused on Molly and he frowned.

'Look, guys,' he said, recovering himself, 'this is a black operation now and I'm not even sure which way it's going to go, but I do know that things might happen you won't want to know anything about.'

'Things have already happened I don't want to know about,' Molly pointed out. 'So why are we here?'

Donaldson went tight-lipped for a moment. Then he shrugged. 'It wasn't a great idea in retrospect. It's not like I'm going to issue you with guns and body armour, is it? This is my trade, it's what I do, what these guys do.' He indicated his colleagues.

'And what about Flynn?' Molly asked.

Donaldson looked at him. 'I'm not as bothered about him hearing.'

Flynn gave a 'whatever' shrug.

'We have to be involved,' Rik said. 'Even if we don't pull

triggers, don't treat us like kids. Our chief constable has author-
ized me and Molly to be here, fully aware of the implications.
The truth of the matter is we are as deeply involved as anyone
else here. You lost an agent to the Bashkims. I lost a good firearms officer in Mike Guthrie, and don't forget Jerry Tope and
all those other people who took bullets in the head, all part of
the constabulary brotherhood.' He turned to Molly. 'And Molly
was a victim of the hit on the police escort and had to defend
herself from the Bashkims, plus Alan Hardiker, for all his faults,
did not deserve to be knifed to death.' He then looked at Flynn
and jerked a thumb at him. 'And this guy got involved through
no fault of his own and has had to react all the way. Now we all
have the chance to be proactive for once. If taking old man
Bashkim out by any means possible is the answer, then so be it,
because I know that simply arresting him and putting him before
a court is not the answer. I'm a cop, I believe in justice . . . and
I think this is justice. Yeah, OK, you're not going to give us guns
and the final decision on how this all pans out is yours, Karl,
but we should be allowed to be in at the kill even if it's only
metaphorically speaking. Molly and I can live with that.'

Rik's keynote speech hung in the air until Flynn said, 'I want
a gun, though.'

The lounge in the apartment was set up with a laptop computer
HD wired to the large-screen TV already in the room.

The chairs and sofa were arranged so everyone could see the
screen.

The three FBI agents sat on dining chairs at the back of
the room.

Donaldson had the laptop on his knee.

He had put up a photo of Viktor Bashkim's boat, *Halcyon* on
the screen followed by scanned documents from a sales brochure
for the boat, which also gave details of the boat's layout – useful
information for any team who had to board her.

'Since we last talked, we found out that Viktor paid thirty-five
million euros for this boat from a dealer in Istanbul in 2010. It
wasn't called *Halcyon* then but was renamed by Viktor.'

'It is a nice boat,' Rik said.

Donaldson nodded. 'We hardly knew that Viktor existed until

fairly recently, but I have found out that he has been at sea for the last four years since his wife died, a pretty lonely existence surrounded by his crew and the one remaining grandson, Niko.'

'What do we know about Niko?' Flynn asked, watching Donaldson carefully.

'Er, not much, really. Likes his women. Likes his money.' He sounded cagey to Flynn, who asked, 'When are you going to tell us who the source is, Karl? Presumably someone on board?'

Blank-faced, Donaldson said, 'Like I said, that isn't for sharing, not at this stage. It's all very delicate, as you can imagine, and his or her safety has to be ensured.' He went on, 'So our intel is that *Halcyon* is currently en route to Malta, confirmed by a booking with the port authority and a snippet from our source. We think Viktor is coming here to collect his dues for all the migrants now mustering in Libya, number confirmed by satellite. The boat is booked in for four days, after which she will sail back across to Greece. Our intention, at this moment – and things might change – is to take Viktor out while he's here in an operation sanctioned by no one, and should it go wrong then a lot of questions will be asked and a lot of egg will be flying in faces – which is why I did not want you guys to be involved.'

He looked hard at Rik and Molly, who scowled back at him.

'Anyway, I have a specialist black ops team arriving from the US tonight and when they arrive we'll start talking dirty.' He looked around the room. 'That's basically it for the moment . . . any questions?'

'When is the boat actually due to arrive?' Molly asked.

'Sometime after two today.'

'So we're kicking our heels for a while,' Flynn said, looking through narrowed, suspicious eyes at Donaldson.

'It all seems so surreal,' Molly said to Flynn. 'A bit like prepping for D-Day.'

'It is,' he agreed. 'But it gets more and more real once you start putting body armour on. You know that feeling now, don't you?'

'Yeah, guess I do . . . But the thing is, it still feels like a bizarre dream even when the bullets start flying, like you're in a film or something.'

'Until one hits you.'

They were sitting on a bench on the harbour front in Sliema looking across to Grand Harbour in Valetta. Directly in front of them, two boats taking tourists on trips around the magnificent harbour were filling up nicely and Flynn thought that might be quite a nice job. He had been to Malta on a couple of occasions as a lad, brought on holiday by his grandfather, who had passed through the island on his way to serve in Egypt during the Second World War. The old man had got a bit of a bug for the place on his brief wartime visit and had returned many times since. He had infected Flynn with his love of the island's history and its role in many conflicts over the centuries, not least the siege of 1565 when the Turks were repelled and 1942 when the Germans were unsuccessful in taking the spunky little island.

Flynn didn't bother boring Molly with the details, although he could probably have answered questions on *Mastermind* about them.

'What do you think about all this?' she asked him.

'Not much, to be honest. There's something I can't quite get a grip of. Now I'm beginning to wish I'd taken all this on alone and cut out Donaldson, because there's something not quite right that he isn't telling us about. I get the FBI want to take Viktor out – sometimes it's the only way – but I know I'm losing my chance of wringing the old bastard's neck.' Flynn couldn't weigh it up. He'd come to Malta thinking he would be let loose but that clearly wasn't going to happen. 'I mean, a black ops team, for God's sake.'

Molly chuckled but said seriously, 'At least there's less chance of you dying.'

'Maybe so.'

'That's a good thing.'

'Is it?'

'Yes . . . I don't want to see you die, Steve.'

'I'll try not to. Whatever happens now, I think it's out of our hands, and if I do get a look in it'll be from the back of an assault team. They won't want me anywhere near the front. They'll be well drilled and I'll just be a hindrance, which I understand and I suppose you do, too. Could you imagine someone on your firearms team who didn't know the drill?'

'Yeah, you're right.'

'Donaldson still does worry me slightly, though.'

'How do you mean?'

Flynn tapped his nose. 'This need to know stuff . . . I don't know. Anyway,' he checked his watch. 'Fifteen hundred hours. By my reckoning, the good ship *Halcyon* should be in port by now.'

They jumped on a very crowded bus on the harbour side which chugged them around the waterfront and deposited them on the 720-berth Msida Creek marina situated in Grand Harbour, one of the world's deepest and largest natural harbours.

'Is this a good idea?' Molly asked uncertainly.

'Probably not, but the marina is a tourist attraction. People like seeing boats of all types and sizes, so it's not as though we'll stand out from a crowd, especially if we link arms like a real couple. Then we can saunter past and have a nosy at the boat and, if the opportunity presents itself, I'll slip on board and kill Viktor . . . Just kidding,' he added quickly on seeing Molly's shocked face. Although he did mean it. 'We'll mingle, see if we can spot any celebrities, and I'll pull my hat down over my eyes because I'm a master of disguise.'

They walked along the quayside and made their way to the magnificent anchorage. The larger, more expensive boats were moored separately to smaller vessels and they were able to meander along with other holidaymakers rubbernecking the expensive craft. There were a lot of beautiful boats, many valued in the tens of millions, but the standout was *Halcyon* docked at the far end of one of the jetties. The entrance gate was locked, preventing them from walking up the jetty to the boat itself.

Even from a distance, she looked magnificent.

'Nice boat,' Molly said grudgingly.

'Paid for on the back of other people's suffering. Drugs, prostitution, you name it . . . probably shoplifting, too. Not an honest day's work in it,' Flynn said, a dirty sneer on his face.

'Horrible.' Molly shuddered – and Flynn felt that shudder through his arm and liked it, just as he liked having Molly's arm linked through his.

The roar of engines made Flynn look back over his shoulder

down the quayside. Three Range Rovers with greyed-out windows were hurtling along the road in a convoy. They had a look, a presence that made Flynn draw Molly to one side across the road to an open air café, where they sat down and watched as the Range Rovers stopped at the head of the jetty. The drivers, all wearing dark glasses, stayed put behind the wheels, but the front-seat passenger of all three dropped on to the roadside with the awareness of leopards. There were two men and one woman but Flynn recognized them all to be of the same ilk – professional, ex-military individuals trained to live their lives by a code of violence. None openly displayed firearms but Flynn could see the bulges under the T-shirts at the waistbands at the small of their backs – pistols, Flynn guessed – and they were all connected by some kind of fairly sophisticated radio system; he could just about make out earpieces and flesh-coloured microphones running from their ears to their mouths.

'Well, well, well,' said Flynn. A waiter appeared at the table but Flynn waved him away saying, 'Two minutes, please.'

'They're here, Grandad,' Niko said, opening Viktor's cabin door and poking his head through.

The old man stood up from the dressing table. To Niko, he looked even older today.

'Have you heard anything from them yet?' he asked.

'No, Grandad, not yet.'

'So what does that mean? It's been almost a week.'

'It may simply mean they haven't completed their task yet for some reason,' Niko said. 'They will be in contact, I assure you.'

'Or has this Flynn killed them?'

'I very much doubt it,' Niko said. He winced, clutched his stomach and gasped, then belched and farted at the same time.

'You still ill?'

'I have the shits like I've never had them in my life,' Niko said. 'Bad seafood, Grandad.'

'So you are not coming?'

'Not unless there's a shitter in the Range Rover. Mikel and Andrei will be with you.'

'OK.'

Viktor walked ahead to the stern of the boat. Just before

crossing the gangplank on to the quayside, Viktor stopped and said to Niko, 'You know, I will not rest until this Flynn man's head is in my lap.'

'I know, Grandad. I'll see if I can contact them for you, find out where they are up to,' Niko promised.

Viktor nodded and crossed over to the land where Mikel and Andrei were waiting for him.

Niko watched them walk along the jetty towards the three Range Rovers who were waiting to pick them up. He put his phone to his ear.

'Borrow your phone, please?' Flynn held out his hand to Molly. 'Left mine in my room, just in case someone wanted to track me.'

'Paranoid,' Molly said. 'Who'd do a thing like that?' She handed him her mobile.

Flynn sank low in the chair, pulling the peak of his baseball cap over his eyes as he watched the three men walk down the jetty towards them and the Range Rovers, the central figure being Viktor, who he had never seen in the flesh before but recognized instantly. The old man in total control, the one who gave the kill orders, the one Steve Flynn needed to kill. Viktor was dressed casually in an open-neck shirt, chinos and sandals. His infamous gold necklace hung around his scrawny neck.

Flynn's teeth ground as his breath shortened.

Molly placed a hand on his forearm, sensing the change coming over him.

'We need to be following them,' Flynn said.

They reached the gate. One of the men accompanying Viktor swiped a plastic card and the gate swung open.

The three who had been passengers in the Range Rovers were suddenly, visibly more tense and alert, and the right hand of each one sought out the handles of the pistols in their waistbands under their shirts. They were on the balls of their feet, ready to act.

Viktor Bashkim, it seemed, warranted an armed guard when he stepped away from the security of his boat.

Viktor passed through the security gate.

In his hand, Molly's phone rang before Flynn could dial out: Donaldson.

'Where the hell have you got to, Molly?' the American demanded.

'It's me, Flynn – and we're watching Viktor Bashkim about to step into a Range Rover and get whisked away somewhere like a fucking A-list celebrity.'

'You're fucking where?'

'Like I said . . .'

'I know what you said,' Donaldson interrupted. 'What the hell? Suppose he sees you?'

'Why is that a problem? He doesn't know me, does he?'

'Yes he fucking does, he's seen your picture all over fucking social media,' Donaldson blurted.

'And how would you know that?'

'I know. Just trust me, I know.'

'OK. Look, I'm going to follow him, see what he's up to. I'll keep my head down.'

'No, you stay where you are, Flynn. I'll send one of the guys to pick you up.'

'But this looks interesting. Could be a meet of some description.'

'Interesting or not, you do nothing – understand?'

Flynn ended the call there and then and looked at Molly, who had earwigged the conversation. 'Like I said, that guy knows more than he's letting on.'

'Y'think?'

'I know.'

Viktor was directed into the middle Range Rover. The small retinue from the boat split and jumped into the front and rear cars and the bodyguards got back into the passenger seats they had just vacated. The line of vehicles then set off in the direction of Sliema.

Flynn shot to his feet as a young man on a rickety moped swerved into a narrow parking space in front of the café and eased the bike on to its stand. He removed his helmet and shook out his long, golden hair. Flynn saw a second helmet resting on the pillion seat, its straps threaded through the framework of the bike. The young guy was wearing a black T-shirt bearing the logo of the café that Flynn and Molly had taken refuge in.

'Our transport has arrived,' Flynn blurted, pushing the mobile phone into his pocket. It had started to ring again. 'Come on, Molly.'

He vaulted the low wall and stopped the young guy in his tracks in a non-threatening way, he hoped. He was also trying to keep an eye on the progress of the Range Rovers.

'You speak English?' Flynn asked.

'Yeah, 'course.' He sounded almost offended.

'Rent your bike, please.' His hand went to his back pocket and extracted a thick wad of euros, maybe a thousand of them. He didn't care. He held them up to the lad's face. 'What time do you finish work?'

'Midnight.' His eyes were transfixed by the money, like a cobra on the flute.

'One thousand euros and I'll have it back by then.'

'Seriously?'

'Yes. Decision time.'

'It's not insured.'

'Nor am I. One grand in euros. Now. In your hand. The bike's only worth seventy.'

It was too good an offer to refuse, even if he never saw the bike again. 'Midnight,' the lad said and snatched the cash from Flynn's fingers. Flynn grabbed his helmet plus the ignition key.

Seconds later with Molly on the pillion, her arms wrapped tightly around Flynn's middle, the moped was accelerating along the waterfront, hopefully catching up with Viktor Bashkim. Glancing in one of the cracked mirrors, Flynn saw the young lad waving madly at him but there was no time to turn around.

In his pocket, Molly's phone continued to vibrate.

Flynn spotted the rear Range Rover a long way in front, turning left. He twisted the throttle and the small, very underpowered moped screamed and unleashed just a little more muscle.

Molly clung on, trying to keep track of the journey. Flynn kept the convoy in sight as it threaded and bullied its way through the streets of San Giljan just behind Sliema, through to the northern coast of Malta and then picking up the coast road itself, leaving the urban areas behind for a few miles before turning back inland at the small bay opposite the resort of Buggiba, passing some big salt pans on the way.

Flynn was beginning to panic a little about the amount of fuel in the moped. The needle on the gauge hovered precariously close to red and empty. Maybe that's what the owner was trying to signal to him – no fucking fuel!

'Where do you think they're going?' Molly shouted through the barriers that were hers and Flynn's full-face motorcycle helmets.

'Not a clue . . . we're heading to the top of the island this way,' he shouted back. She didn't hear a word.

Molly's phone continued to vibrate in his pocket.

That meant something. Flynn was certain. Donaldson did not like what he was doing, which in Flynn's perverse mind meant that he was doing the right thing.

Ahead, now having reached the open road, the Range Rovers had increased their speed. They were going fast, putting up a cloud of sand and grit from the road surface. Flynn would have liked to say he was hanging back but in reality he was being left behind on the moped, the distance steadily increasing between them.

Which was just as well, because that extra distance probably saved his and Molly's life, plus the fact that – frustratingly for Flynn – the moped actually did run out of fuel.

The bombs had been attached to the underside of all three Range Rovers by the man who was tasked with checking and declaring the vehicles safe. In fact, every inch of the vehicles was safe – except for the four square inches of the bombs fitted underneath the rear seats of all the cars.

That same man was sitting hidden behind a cluster of rocks overlooking the coast road, giving him a good view of the approach of the convoy from the south.

It was usually a pretty quiet road, as were most roads on the island outside the towns, and that day was no different. The man was glad about that because he never liked having the blood of innocent people on his hands, although it had happened. Many times. There was a couple on a moped well behind the Range Rovers, but he thought they should be safe enough.

The trio was moving very quickly and the man knew he had to get it right.

He had a mobile phone in his hand and a number already on the screen ready to dial and send to the three cloned SIM cards in the cheap mobile phones set in blocks of Semtex fixed under the seats which would act as part of the detonator set-up. One number, one press of the thumb, three car bombs.

Sweet.

There was a good, strong signal, five bars, on the phone in his hand.

The detonator phones were charged up and there was no reason why they would not receive the message and pass the little pulse of electricity to the actual detonators.

The Range Rovers were now almost level with his position. Glancing back, he saw that the following moped had stopped and the rider had put down a foot. Good. They were safe. Soon they would know just how lucky they were.

When the first car drew level, the man pressed send.

Then there was always that fucking delay. Maybe a second, maybe two, when all the doubts kicked in, when it felt long enough to go out, hang out the washing and come back in, the man always thought.

That horrible delay.

The middle car blew first. Then the lead, then the rear.

Perfectly judged bombs which blew upwards and outwards and threw each car up into the air as if it was being catapulted.

And killed all the occupants.

Flynn was swearing at the exact moment the middle Range Rover, the one carrying Viktor Bashkim, exploded. The sudden lack of fuel meant his little jaunt had come to an end and he was furious, swore colourfully and looked wistfully at the Range Rovers disappearing into the distance.

Until the one carrying Viktor blew up with a huge, whumping sound, quickly followed by the other two in quick succession, flames of red, orange and blue shooting out, the cars thrown in perfect arcs as their innards and occupants were ripped to shreds by the high explosive.

The heat of the three blasts rolled out in a shockwave over Flynn and Molly, taking their breath away and then showering them with harsh particles of sand and grit, the sound buffeting their ears. They cowered away instinctively, covering their faces with their arms and hands, even though both wore helmets, and then it was over and the twisted carcases of the three cars, moments ago clean and shiny, crashed back to earth and lay there, smoke billowing out of them, fires cracking.

Flynn scrubbed the grit out of his eyes.

Molly stared open-mouthed at the scene of destruction.

'Oh my God,' she said finally.

Flynn said, 'Ever felt just a bit like a mushroom, Molly?'

'Pardon?'

'Kept in the dark, fed on shit?'

She screwed her face up at him.

Flynn took Molly's phone out of his pocket. It was still vibrating, Karl Donaldson still trying desperately to contact him.

Flynn removed his helmet and answered it. 'I think you've something to tell me, Karl.'

Flynn sat on his haunches by the roadside, Molly half-perched on the moped. Two hundred metres north, the emergency services had arrived and were now, more or less, in control of the scene of devastation. The road was closed and cordoned off and screens were being erected but there was nothing to see. Flynn knew. He had been to look.

He could tell there were no survivors, and when he found the remnants of the middle Range Rover he saw there was hardly anything left of the occupants – certainly nothing to identify them visually. The bomb had been highly effective and each person had essentially been vaporized.

And he was sure that Viktor Bashkim had been in that car. At least, he thought he was sure.

Flynn was speaking to Donaldson again.

'So Niko was your source?' he said. 'Just run that by me again.'

'It was a bit like a program running in the background,' Donaldson said. 'But I wasn't sure how it would turn out. I had a plan with various options. First was just to let you loose on the old man, but I was pretty uncomfortable with that if you want me to be honest.'

'Yeah, be honest, Karl.'

'You were in a situation not of your own making and you already had too much blood on your hands. Next option was a black operation and that would have happened, but at the same time Niko was making all sorts of uncomfortable noises and eventually he bore fruit. The deal was to sacrifice Viktor and then Niko would assume complete control of the family and make certain promises.'

'Which were?'

'To dismantle the Bashkim operation from inside. All the guy wants to do is screw himself silly, shove coke up his nose and live off the money accrued. He's had no real part in the family business anyway and certainly doesn't need any more cash.'

'What about all those migrants waiting to come across from Africa?'

'He's killed it. No one will be coming across in boats provided by the Bashkims.'

'What about the money, then . . . surely that's all been collected already? What's he going to do with that – give it to charity?'

'Actually, yes. I've arranged a draft to Save the Children. They'll be three million euros richer just about now from an unknown benefactor.'

'You have been busy. Where is Niko now?'

'On *Halcyon*, just about to set sail out of Grand Harbour.'

'And your black ops team?'

'Turned around . . . on their way back to the States.'

Flynn went silent.

Donaldson said, 'It's over as far as you're concerned, Steve. Viktor's dead and Niko won't be coming for you. Go back to your life, keep your head down, grieve for Maria, accept there's nothing more for you to chase and go fishing.'

Flynn ended the call, feeling cheated but also relieved. A very heavy lead weight seemed to have suddenly been lifted from his shoulders. He looked across at Molly, who smiled at him. 'Hey, you ever been on a long sea voyage?' he called.

'Er, once went from Dover to Calais . . . Oh, wait a minute, that was on Eurostar.' She laughed. Flynn liked her laugh.

'Close enough,' Flynn said. 'Close enough.'

*   *   *

Donaldson slid his cell phone into his jacket pocket. He was standing on the quayside at the gate to the jetty leading to where *Halcyon* was berthed. He watched the beautiful boat draw slowly and elegantly away from her moorings and motor towards the mouth of Grand Harbour.

Niko, dressed in a loose-fitting linen shirt and trousers, stood at the rail on the lower rear deck, his arm hanging loosely around a very pretty woman dressed in a flowing kaftan.

He waved languidly at Donaldson, who gave him a mock half-salute back.

Then the American looked down at the cool box at his feet. He hadn't had the nerve to look at the horror inside it – Maria Santiago's severed head packed in ice – and wasn't entirely sure what he was going to do with it. One thing was for sure: he wasn't going to let Steve Flynn see it. He picked the box up and walked across to the car that was waiting to pick him up.